THE LEGACY OF
ERICH ZANN

Borgo Press Books by BRIAN STABLEFORD

Alien Abduction: The Wiltshire Revelations * *Balance of Power* (Daedalus Mission #5) * *The Best of Both Worlds and Other Ambiguous Tales* * *Beyond the Colors of Darkness and Other Exotica* * *Changelings and Other Metaphoric Tales* * *The City of the Sun* (Daedalus Mission #4) * *Complications and Other Science Fiction Stories* * *The Cosmic Perspective and Other Black Comedies Critical Threshold* (Daedalus Mission #2) * *The Cthulhu Encryption: A Romance of Piracy* * *The Cure for Love and Other Tales of the Biotech Revolution* * *The Dragon Man: A Novel of the Future* * *The Eleventh Hour* * *The Fenris Device* (Hooded Swan #5) * *Firefly: A Novel of the Far Future* * *Les Fleurs du Mal: A Tale of the Biotech Revolution* * *The Florians* (Daedalus Mission #1) * *The Gardens of Tantalus and Other Delusions* * *The Gates of Eden: A Science Fiction Novel* * *The Golden Fleece and Other Tales of the Biotech Revolution* * *The Great Chain of Being and Other Tales of the Biotech Revolution* * *Halycon Drift* (Hooded Swan #1) * *The Haunted Bookshop and Other Apparitions* * *In the Flesh and Other Tales of the Biotech Revolution* * *The Innsmouth Heritage and Other Sequels* * *Journey to the Core of Creation: A Romance of Evolution* * *Kiss the Goat: A Twenty-First-Century Ghost Story* * *The Legacy of Erich Zann and Other Tales of the Cthulhu Mythos* * *Luscinia: A Romance of Nightingales and Roses* * *The Mad Trist: A Romance of Bibliomania* * *The Mind-Riders: A Science Fiction Novel* * *The Moment of Truth: A Novel of the Future* * *Nature's Shift: A Tale of the Biotech Revolution* * *An Oasis of Horror: Decadent Tales and Contes Cruels* * *The Paradise Game* (Hooded Swan #4) * *The Paradox of the Sets* (Daedalus Mission #6) * *The Plurality of Worlds: A Sixteenth-Century Space Opera* * *Prelude to Eternity: A Romance of the First Time Machine* * *Promised Land* (Hooded Swan #3) * *The Quintessence of August: A Romance of Possession* * *The Return of the Djinn and Other Black Melodramas* * *Rhapsody in Black* (Hooded Swan #2) * *Salome and Other Decadent Fantasies* * *Streaking: A Novel of Probability* * *Swan Song* (Hooded Swan #6) * *The Tree of Life and Other Tales of the Biotech Revolution* * *The Undead: A Tale of the Biotech Revolution* * *Valdemar's Daughter: A Romance of Mesmerism* * *War Games: A Science Fiction Novel* * *Wildeblood's Empire* (Daedalus Mission #3) * *The World Beyond: A Sequel to S. Fowler Wright's The World Below* * *Writing Fantasy and Science Fiction* * *Xeno's Paradox: A Tale of the Biotech Revolution* * *Zombies Don't Cry: A Tale of the Biotech Revolution*

THE LEGACY OF ERICH ZANN

AND OTHER TALES OF THE CTHULHU MYTHOS

BRIAN STABLEFORD

THE BORGO PRESS
MMXII

THE LEGACY OF ERICH ZANN

FIRST EDITION

Published by Wildside Press LLC

www.wildsidebooks.com

THE LEGACY
OF ERICH ZANN

CONTENTS

INTRODUCTION

The idea and literary use of "cosmic horror" did not begin with the work of H. P. Lovecraft, nor can he really be said to have "popularized" it, at least in his lifetime, although there have been few other writers who have enjoyed such a rich and influential literary afterlife. When Lovecraft invited his friends to use his own literary materials—which he used himself rather sparsely, for various idiosyncratic reasons—he could not possibly have imagined that the process would continue for more than seventy years after his death, produce hundreds of volumes, and expand to include people such as me, who were not even born until long after he had passed on.

Even now, though, it is not entirely clear that the Cthulhu Mythos, as Lovecraft's key endeavor came to be known, has actually been "popularized," in spite of its overflow to such media as films, comic books and computer games. One of its chief attractions, in fact, has always been its defiant esotericism, coupled with the fact that the mere mention of it (by those whose tongues are up to the difficult task of mentioning it) can make respectable literary folk curl their lip in contempt and disdain. Like all the good stuff, the Cthulhu Mythos belongs to "unpopular culture" rather than "popular culture," and its adherents probably would not want it any other way.

The notion of cosmic horror is itself essentially esoteric. As an esthetic sensibility, or the source of a subtle frisson of dread, it is far more dependent on the imaginative capacity of the reader than tales of pursuit by serial killers, the sudden appearance of ghosts or doors bulging in response to unspecifiable forces on the other side, all of which are obvious sources of anxiety whose threat is close at hand. In its essence, cosmic horror is far more abstract, asking us to take aboard and appreciate some of the corollaries of the intellectual awareness that the horizons of our vision and our lives are extremely minuscule by comparison with the size and age of the universe.

It was not until the nineteenth century that scientific discoveries allowed awareness to grow that the true size of the universe could not be measured in mere thousands of miles, nor its real antiquity in mere thousands of years. This was significant because, by and large, the everyday imagination can cope with thousands, and perhaps, at a stretch, millions, but there is no way that it can properly encompass billons or trillions, which are simply too vast to envisage. The effect that the incapacity in question has on the psyche is indescribable, as is evidence by the fact that the most commonly-used verb invented to represent it, "boggle," is an obvious joke—one of many attempts to cope with the problem by simply refusing to recognize it. It is that denial rather than the fact itself that provides Lovecraftian fiction with its heart and soul; the fiction of cosmic horror rarely bothers to point out the mere truism of our utter insignificance in a vast and uncaring universe; what it does is to play, sometime delicately and cleverly, but always with a reserve of sheer brutality, with our inability to deal with the fact mentally, and our perverse insistence that, even if it is so, it is irrelevant.

The Mythos was important, initially within the context of Lovecraft's circle of friends and their attempts to lay siege to *Weird Tales* and a handful of other market outlets, because it provided a vocabulary of ideas that permitted certain basic aspects of an awareness of cosmic vastness to be represented. The most basic of them is perhaps Nyarlathotep, the Crawling Chaos that lurks in the cosmic background, behind the veils of matter, space and time, but there is a good reason why the honor of being its central figure was attributed to Cthulhu, who is possessed of all kinds of useful ambiguity in the shrewdly scattered details suggesting his origin, history and contemporary existence: dead but capable of eternally lying (in more ways than one); extraterrestrial but also extradimensional; associated not only with enigmatic "star-spawn" but also with the slimy mysteries of the alien world under the sea; shadowed but in no way properly documented by the cryptic pages of the *Necronomicon*....

It is because the central ideas of the Cthulhu Mythos provided the first such vocabulary that it has not only retained a unique place in literary history but continues to supply useful fuel to writers interested in working in the same territory of psychic unease. Other symbolic vocabularies have been invented since, and it can certainly be argued that some do the job more elegantly, but they can never have the primacy, and hence the "authenticity" of Lovecraft's. It can certainly be argued, too, that it is a nobler quest for writers to invent their own vocabularies and redo the work from scratch themselves, but there is a sense in which starting over robs writers of a precious asset of recognizability: the ability to help readers orientate themselves rapidly, and to draw upon what readers already know as a resource.

Writers of naturalistic fiction are, of course, always fully tooled-up with that resource, and even writers of heterocosmic fiction retain substantial provisions of it in the mimetic and naturalistic aspects of their heterocosms, but it is often useful to have extra supplies of recognition and familiarity built in even to those aspects of a world within the text that seek to differentiate it from the familiar world. There are good reasons (as well as a few bad ones) why fantastic universes invented by writers often outlive their creators and continue to expand and reproduce long after their genesis—and the Lovecraftian universe has some of the best reasons of all. If modern adventures in its expansion and reproduction—including this one—seem to some observers to be mere exercises in pastiche, so be it, but I certainly do not feel that what I am doing is copying, or even supplementation, but rather attempting to assist with a useful process of evolution.

"The Legacy of Erich Zann" first appeared in a hardcover volume published by Perilous Press, as a makeweight for a short novel entitled *The Womb of Time* (2011). I liked it so much that I wrote a series of sequels, similarly featuring Auguste Dupin as a protagonist, confronting not only elements of the Cthulhu Mythos, but other aspects of an even vaster metaphysical system of which even the apparatus of the Mythos is envisaged an exceedingly tiny fraction. The other volumes, all published by Borgo Press, are the novella double *Valdemar's Daughter/ The Mad Trist* and the novels *The Quintessence of August, The Cthulhu Encryption*, and *Journey to the Core of Creation*.

"The Truth about Pickman" and "The Holocaust of Ecstasy" were both written for anthologies of Mythos stories, the former for S. T. Joshi's *Black Wings* (P.S. Publishing, 2010) and the latter for Darrell Schweitzer's *Cthulhu's Reign* (DAW 2010). "The Seeds from the Mountains of Madness" was planned as a contribution to another such anthology, but grew far too large for such inclusion and is published here for the first time.

THE LEGACY OF
ERICH ZANN

"Infinity has a tendency to fill the mind with that sort of delightful horror, which is the most genuine effect and truest test of the sublime."

—Edmund Burke, *A Philosophical Enquiry*
into the Origin of Our Ideas of the
Sublime and the Beautiful (1756)

"The mental features discoursed of as the analytical are, in themselves, but little susceptible of analysis. We appreciate them only in their effects. We know of them, among other things, that they are always to their possessor, when inordinately possessed, a source of the liveliest enjoyment. As the strong man exults in his physical ability, delighting in such exercises as call his muscles into action, so glories the analyst in that moral activity which *disentangles*. He derives pleasure from even the most trivial occupations bringing his talent into play. He is fond of enigmas, of conundrums, hieroglyphics, exhibiting in his solutions of each a degree of *acumen* which appears to the ordinary apprehension preternatural."

—Edgar Allan Poe, "The Murders
in the Rue Morgue" (1841)

"Evidently, Erich Zann's world of beauty lay in some far cosmos of the imagination."

—H. P. Lovecraft, "The Music of Erich Zann" (1922)

1.

There were countless aspects of the enigmatic personality of Monsieur le Chevalier Auguste Dupin that puzzled me during the period when we shared the town house that I rented in the Faubourg Saint-Germain. Many such questions were eventually illuminated in the course of our long nocturnal discussions, but a few lingered long after Dupin—having eventually decided that even the close company of such a sympathetic soul as myself was too much for his reclusive temperament to bear—had elected to return to his original lodgings in the Rue Dunôt and to ration our meetings to two or three per week. Two questions, in particular, continued to intrigue me deeply.

The first of these unsolved mysteries was the question of why a man as intellectually able as Dupin—a man whose analytical powers were beyond compare—could not or would not find any sort of gainful employment suited to his eremitic tendencies. As something of an amateur in journalism myself—although I filtered my occasional works in that vein through a correspondent in my homeland, who revised them for publication there and attached his own signature to them—I suggested more than once that he might easily compensate for the exhaustion of his patrimony by means of his pen, but he only replied that his intense commitment to the truth made any such vocation unthinkable. When I suggested that there was more money to be made from fact than fiction—Alexandre Dumas and Eugène Sue had only just begun their epoch-making demonstration to the contrary at that time—he merely replied that most so-called "factual" journalism was more prone than the most fantastic fiction to the corruptions and distortions of rhetoric, and that the remainder was so trivial as to be an insult to penetrative intelligence.

The second such mystery might well have fit into the category of such trivia, but it intrigued me nevertheless, How was it, I could not help wondering, that a man of such reclusive habits and antisocial tendencies, whose very existence was unknown to all but a select few inhabitants of Paris, was able to call unannounced on a person as important as the Prefect of the Parisian Police and be sure of being received? What was even more surprising was that the Prefect in question, Lucien Groix, occasionally took the trouble to call on Dupin in person, when he was in need of particular assistance—as in the matter of which my American correspondent eventually published a brief account under the title of "The Purloined Letter". It seemed to me that the two of them must share a secret of some kind, but when I asked Dupin about it explicitly he would only confirm that it was, indeed, a confidential matter about which he was not permitted to speak.

Both of these mysteries were, however, clarified one wintry night, not long after the events recorded in "The Purloined Letter", when the Prefect came in search of Dupin yet again, this time to the old town house in the Faubourg Saint-Germain that I had then been renting for more than a year. Groix knew that Dupin and I had maintained our acquaintance to the extent that suited my elusive friend, so when he found the great logician absent from the Rue Dunôt not long before midnight, he hurried around to my residence, hoping that he would find us both there.

Dupin was, indeed, indolently accommodated in my candlelit smoking-room that night; the weather being cold enough to deter us from taking one of our nocturnal strolls, we had just spent a pleasant hour or two moving an amicable discussion through a sequence of sympathetic subjects.

I had begun the discussion by giving Dupin an enthusiastic account of a musical melodrama that I had seen two nights previously at the Délassements-Comique. Dupin never went to the theater and rarely read any dramatic criticism; since he no longer lived in my house, with all my reading-material conveniently to hand, his acquaintance with the daily newspapers was more-or-less restricted to the *Gazette des Tribuneaux*—but I thought he would be interested in the piece in question because of his long-standing interest in the phenomena of dreaming and somnambulism. The drama in question, scripted by Frédéric Soulié, with music by Maurice Bazailles, *La Cantate du Diable—The Devil's Cantata*, in English—was loosely based on the most famous recorded instance of an inspirational dream: the one that had allegedly inspired the Italian composer Giuseppe Tartini to produce his best-known work, *Il Trillo del Diavolo.*

"In Soulié's play," I told Dupin, "the violinist who makes the diabolical pact does not hand his instrument over to the Devil, as Tartini did in his dream, but plays for him instead, in order that the Devil might sing one of the hymns that he once sang in Heaven, in chorus with other angels, before his fall. At this point, by means of one of the ingenious trap-doors whose use was pioneered at the Porte-Saint-Martin in the twenties, the middle-aged actor in conventional Mephistophelean make-up who has played the role of the Devil up to that point is abruptly replaced by a blond-haired boy soprano, whose looks and voice are, indeed, perfectly angelic. For the duration of the song, the Devil reverts, as it were, to his original form—but as he sings, the notes are gradually perverted as the violin seems to go out of tune, although it retains a curious alternative melodiousness, which is matched by the boy's increasingly sinister but strangely bewitching voice."

"*Scordatura*," Dupin put in.

"I beg your pardon?"

"The use of an unorthodox tuning of a violin, to which you have just referred, is known, technically, as *scordatura*," he explained. "It is rather unusual, however, for a violinist to retune his instrument while actually playing it, in mid-piece. Is that, perhaps, one of Signor Paganini's new tricks?"

I had been to one of Paganini's concerts at the *Opéra* the

previous week, but I had not reported it to Dupin because I had not enjoyed it as much as I had hoped. That the violinist's technique was brilliant I could not doubt, but his famous *capricci* seemed to me to be far more intricate than melodious. I preferred Bach's violin sonatas. I was surprised that Dupin was even aware of the great virtuoso's existence, let alone the substance of his work, or the fact that his current European tour had recently brought him to Paris.

"I don't know," I confessed, in reply to his question. "Have you an interest in violin music, then, Dupin?"

"None whatsoever," was his paradoxical reply. "I have not touched such an instrument in twenty years, although my father saw to it that I was taught to play when I was a child and my circumstances were very different. I was once briefly acquainted with a violinist of genius, though, and met another through him who fancied himself a genius, and a memory of that circumstance caused me to listen with an attentive ear to some idle chatter related to Paganini, which I overheard during one of my nocturnal strolls. The *Opéra* is within easy walking distance of my lodgings, and although I have never been inside the institution itself, I sometimes pause for a *petit mominette* at one of the *cabarets* in which the audience tends to reassemble after performances. Their critical discussion usually washes over me unheeded, but on this occasion I listened to the comments because what was said about Paganini reminded me of my old acquaintance. Mention was made of the use of *scordatura* techniques, so I wondered whether Paganini had taken up the trick of retuning his instrument in mid-piece."

I did not care to investigate Dupin's distant memories further, because I was eager to press on with my account of the play.

"What makes the play unusual among Faustian fantasies," I told him, "in spite of the fact that the violinist is coupled with a very obvious clone of Marguerite, in the form of a pretty female soprano played by Mademoiselle Deurne, is that Soulié—who published a novel called *Le Magnetiseur* not long ago—has ingeniously recycled the research he did for that work. He makes extensive reference to the Marquis de Puységur's recent experiments in animal magnetism, in order to sustain the notion that the protagonist's Devil-induced hallucination is far more than an ordinary dream. In fact, the Devil's magnetic power combines with the protagonist's musical ambition to convert his playing into a means of access to the higher reality accessible to Mesmerized somnambulists.

"Somniloquists," Dupin said, reflexively. There was a frown on his face, as if something I had said had troubled him, and the correction he had offered seemed almost to be a means of deflecting his attention from that disquiet into a safer conversational channel.

"I beg your pardon," I said, again.

"Somnambulists, properly speaking, are individuals who walk in their sleep," Dupin informed me. "The subjects entranced by expert Mesmerists, in order that they may relate visions of dream-dimensions or operate as channels for voices from those dimensions, are more properly called somniloquists: sleep-*talkers*."

"Not according to the play's program-notes," I said, reaching for the inside pocket of my jacket—but he stopped me with a casual gesture. He did not care what the program notes might say; he was a confirmed pendant, and he was perfectly certain that he was in the right—but he still had something else on his mind. I fell silent, knowing that he would take up the thread of the discussion, in the expectation that he would explain what it was that had disturbed him.

Instead, he retreated into intellectualism, taking refuge in the produce of his esoteric scholarship. "I don't know Monsieur Soulié's work at all," he said, "but it seems to me that his choice of exemplars is somewhat misguided. The late Marquis de Puységur did, indeed, conduct some interesting experiments in animal magnetism, although he was also responsible for the lamentable popularization of the term *somnambulism* in that context, but his work in that vein has since been supplemented—some would say superseded—by that of Alexandre

Bertrand. Puységur and most of his followers are, in technical terminology, *physiologists*, primarily interested in bodily phenomena; connections between magnetism and music are far more readily drawn by the rival school of *spiritualists*, who consider what they stubbornly insist on calling the somnambulist state as fundamentally—again in a technical sense—*ecstatic*. The scene that you have just described would surely be more aptly underpinned by Bertran's theories than Puységur's. In this particular instance, of course, one ought not even to talk of somniloquism, but of *somnimusicality*—but that is a term which no one, as yet, has taken the trouble to coin, and perhaps, all things considered, we ought to be grateful for that."

I knew that I was incapable of holding my own in a discussion of that high-flown sort with Dupin, but I felt that I ought to try, if only in the hope of giving him a further opportunity to come clean about the nature of the thorn that had somehow pricked the flank of his consciousness. It happened that I had recently read Maine de Biran's *Nouvelles Considérations sur les rapports du physique et du moral de l'homme*, and I was on the point of improvising a hazardous discourse of the potential relevance of the famous physiologist's reflection on the phenomena of sleep when the bell at the house's coaching-entrance rang.

I must confess that my initial reaction to that unexpected ring was mixed; I was surprised and annoyed, as might be expected, but also perversely relieved by the suspension of a discussion that had started so well but had developed in such a way as to threaten to take me far out of my intellectual depth.

Although the town house had a lodge, I had never bothered to employ a concierge, any more than I had ever bothered to accommodate a carriage-horse in the stables or hire a groom. This rarely presented any problem, as my only regular caller was Dupin. As I got up from my armchair to answer the door myself, Dupin quipped, presumably in casual reference to the initial topic of our discussion: "Speak of the Devil and you see the tip of his tail!"

I certainly did not repeat that observation to Monsieur le

Préfet, when that worthy gentleman inquired politely whether Monsieur Dupin might perhaps be present.

Under different circumstances, the Prefect would surely have demanded to speak to Monsieur Dupin in private, but we were in my house, not Dupin's apartment in the Rue Dunôt, and Dupin was too comfortably ensconced in an armchair, sipping a glass of cognac and smoking Turkish tobacco to be easily budged. Perhaps, had he known what the Prefect was about to say, he would have decided differently, but in the event he loftily informed the august gentleman that I could be trusted with any confidence he cared to share—and once I had been admitted to the conspiracy, there could be no question of expelling me.

"Bernard Clamart has been murdered," the Prefect told Dupin, evidently believing that there was no time to beat about the bush. "He was clubbed to death in the consulting-room below his apartment in the Rue Serpente earlier this evening— two or three blows, delivered from behind to the top and back of his head. His papers were scattered in all directions; there is no way to tell whether any are missing, or, if so, which. His pocket-book was stolen from his coat pocket, but numerous heavier objects of value were left behind."

Although Dupin had been discomfited already, this news seemed to shatter his composure completely. I had never seen such a dark shadow overtake his expression and weigh upon his attitude. I had always thought his fundamental equanimity and casual indolence proof against any challenge, but this news brought him to agonized attention as if he were the leg of a dead frog stimulated by a Galvanic current. For two or three seconds, he seemed to be literally fearful. Then he mastered himself, with a visible effort, and muttered: "I must not let myself by startled by a mere coincidence! Only fools see the hand of fate in such arbitrary connections."

I could tell that Monsieur Groix was as surprised by the extent of Dupin's consternation as I was—but I could also see that he had expected his news to be more disconcerting than the announcement of any common-or-garden murder, and he too seemed to have a personal interest in this particular crime.

Dupin narrowed his eyes slightly as he strove to focus his thoughts, carefully mustering his powers of methodical concentration. "Was the murder weapon still on the scene?" he asked, in a businesslike fashion.

"Yes," said the Prefect. "It was a heavy brass candlestick taken from the mantelpiece. The Commissaire summoned to the scene found it in the fireplace, where the murderer must have dropped it after making use of it. It was lying alongside a candle that must have been displaced when he picked it up."

"Was the Commissaire able to ascertain whether the candle was lit when the murderer first picked it up?"

"It appears so. The flame had gone out, but there was wax pooled beneath the wick, and there were congealed droplets spattered around the hearth. The Commissaire concluded, from that fact and the general condition of the notary's cadaver, that the murder must have been committed after dusk, and no more than three hours before the discovery of the body. How long the murderer remained on the scene after striking the fatal blows is difficult to ascertain, but the concierge chanced to see someone she did not recognize descending the external staircase from the private entrance to Clamart's consulting-room and moving away in great haste between five and ten minutes after Saint-German-de-Près had chimed the half-hour after nine."

"Is that why she went to Clamart's consulting-room and discovered the body?"

"Principally, yes. In fact, she sent the scullery-maid up to Clamart's apartment to enquire whether he wanted supper. Clamart was in the habit of descending to the house's communal kitchens in search of sustenance when the same clock chimed nine, and the fact that he had not done so, although he was known to be at home, provided the pretext for the staff to exercise their slight concern. The concierge summoned the Commissaire immediately after the maid had found the body, and the Commissaire immediately sent word to me, in accordance with standing orders."

"Clamart was on your notification list, even after all this time?" Dupin queried.

"Yes, of course," the Prefect confirmed. There was a slight tremor in his voice. "Since the first day of my appointment, he has been on my list of persons of special interest—as you and Palaiseau have also been."

I knew Bernard Clamart by reputation, as a notary of long experience and considerable repute, but the name Palaiseau struck a very different chord in my memory. I knew that I had heard it or seen it printed within the last few days, but I could not immediately remember where, or in what context.

"Did the concierge give the Commissaire a description of the person she saw descending the staircase?"

"A very slight one—it was dark, and the street-lighting in the Rue Serpente is poor. The person was short and slender, but bundled up in a heavy overcoat, with a broad-brimmed hat pulled down over the face."

Monsieur Groix seemed to be thinking of something other than the description, in spite of its obvious importance to the investigation. Dupin had been staring into the fire while he focused his attention on the details of the crime, putting the pieces of the puzzle together, but he suddenly looked up into the face of his visitor, and doubtless read more there than I had been able to detect

"There's something else, isn't there?" Dupin asked the Prefect, frank alarm suddenly returning to his voice, even more sharply than before. "Something that complicates the affair, and increases its urgency?"

2.

Dupin had judged the Prefect's expression correctly; consummate politician as he had to be, Groix had given himself away even to me. Obviously, there *was* something else: something that seemed, at least to these two sharers of some long-held secret, to make the murder of a man with whom they were both acquainted seem even more urgent.

"Yes, alas," the official confessed. "When the notification of Monsieur Clamart's murder came through, I was mid-way through reading a routine report submitted by a *sergent de ville*, whose area of responsibility includes Père Lachaise. He had been notified of an unlicensed excavation in a wooded corner of the cemetery, which had not been registered as a violation when it was first discovered because no grave was supposed to be located there, although the *sergent de ville* found a coffin hidden nearby when he found time to investigate. The coffin had been opened, but the bodily remains were still there."

"Zann's remains?" Dupin asked, dully, obviously not expecting any contradiction.

"I'll need to see the coffin for myself in order to be sure, but I presume so."

Dupin sighed deeply. "More than coincidence, after all," he murmured. "The superstitious are wont to say that these baleful reminders always come in threes." He tried, in vain, to revert to his normal laconic manner in order to ask: "Has anyone made enquiries at the *Préfeture* recently, regarding the grave or the deposition?"

"Not exactly," the Prefect replied.

"Why not *exactly*?" Dupin wanted to know.

"No one has been to the *Préfeture* directly, Monsieur Dupin— but enquiries have been made at the *Académie* and the *Opéra* as to the fate of Monsieur Zann, and the director of the *Opéra* took the trouble to send a note to my secretary asking whether the Prefecture had any details of his death or his testament. My secretary replied, in all innocence, that there was no record in the Prefecture's files of the death or the testament, but that there was no surprise in that, if there had been no criminal circumstances involving either. He had no way of knowing about the deposition. No one at the *Académie* was able to furnish any information, of course, and as the enquirer seemed more than respectable...."

"Who was it?" Dupin demanded, curtly.

"Nicolò Paganini, the famous virtuoso," the Prefect replied. He seemed surprisingly meek under this intense interrogation, given the gap in status between the two men—which was certainly not in Dupin's favor. I immediately understood Dupin's reference to reminders coming in threes, although it was he, not I, who had introduced Paganini's name into our earlier conversation.

"I know who Paganini is," Dupin remarked, presumably to forestall the explanation that the Prefect might otherwise have felt compelled to make.

"That will save us a little time," Monsieur Groix said, dryly. "The maestro was very anxious to know the whereabouts of any unpublished music left behind by his fellow composer for the violin. He was, it seems, prepared to search high and low during his brief stay in the capital—but the momentum of his tour has now carried him away to London."

"Paganini's interest is understandable, even if all he knew of Zann were rumors picked up in his homeland," Dupin admitted, nodding his head slowly. "It was probably pure speculation on his part that Zann might have written something down during his exile in Paris...but that is one way in which rumors may be started, harmless ones and deadly ones alike."

"If that's all there is...," the Prefect murmured, plainly wishing that it was.

"Have you sent warning to Palaiseau?" was the interrogator's next question.

"Yes—and I left a man on your landing in the Rue Dunôt, and another watching the front door of the house." The Prefect finally turned the tables on his consultant by demanding: "Do you have any idea who might have done this, Dupin, or exactly what they were looking for?"

"No to the first question," said Dupin. "As for the second, to borrow your own expression, *not exactly*. As you have evidently deduced yourself, the murderer was almost certainly looking for some record or souvenir of Zann's music. Whoever he is, he does not know enough to be sure that none was buried with the corpse in Zann's coffin, but he has evidently been able to discover where the unmarked grave was. Perhaps we should have excavated it with our own hands...professional gravediggers have never been famed for their discretion, and although the two we employed were not supposed to know who they were burying, curiosity might have driven one or both of them to find out. The name would not have seemed significant at the time, but is memorable enough to have rung bells when Paganini started his enquiries during his stint at the *Opéra*."

"The murderer must know more than any tattling gravedigger could have told him" the Prefect pointed out, "if he knew that Clamart was the lawyer who had custody of Zann's testament."

"Not necessarily," Dupin replied. "Of the five of us who were present at the burial, Clamart was by far the most likely to have been recognized by one or other of the hirelings. You held a much less prominent position then, and were not well-known even in the Palais de Justice, while Fourmont was an obscure physician and Palaiseau was only a minor player in the orchestra of an obscure theater on the Boulevard du Temple."

That remark reminded me where I had seen the name Palaiseau before. It was inscribed on the program that I was still carrying in my jacket pocket. Palaiseau was the name of the violinist to whose accompaniment the Devil in angelic guise had sung his remarkable cantata, the nature of which was transformed as he played from the tacitly paradisal to the subtly diabolical. The Délassements-Comique was located at number 76, Boulevard du Temple—a suitable locale for such a drama. The Boulevard du Temple was popularly known as the Boulevard de Crime, partly because of the melodramatic productions mounted in its theaters and partly because of the rather unsavory clientèle that some of those theaters and the drinking-dens in the nearby side-streets attracted. No one had been much surprised that Fieschi's attempt to assassinate Louis-Philippe had been made by means of an infernal machine mounted in a second-floor window of the Boulevard du Temple, within a stone's throw of the Délassements-Comique. It did not seem unusual that the Prefect of Police would know the name of an old habitué of the *quartier*, but it did seem odd that Dupin knew it too, and I was inevitably driven to wonder whether Palaiseau and the mysterious Zann might be the manifest genius and the ostensible genius that Dupin had mentioned *en passant* a short while before.

"And you were as completely in the Parisian shadows as you still are, in spite of your impending American celebrity," the Prefect added to Dupin's observation, with a censorious sideways glance at me. None of my literary accounts of Dupin's exploits had yet been translated into the great man's native tongue, and only two had so far appeared in print in America, but the Prefect had obviously heard rumor of them—not unexpectedly, given that he figured as a minor character therein, although I had reduced his name to a mere initial for reasons of diplomacy. After a slight pause, Monsieur Groix continued: "Your opinion is, therefore, that the murderer is unlikely to know of our involvement, and thus unlikely to direct his attention to either of us?"

"How can we possibly make an accurate assessment of that likelihood?" Dupin riposted. "Did Clamart have any other evident injuries?"

"No," the Prefect said.

"There is no reason to suppose that any attempt was made to extract information from him by the threat or exercise of violence?"

"No readily-apparent reason. Clamart was a sturdy fellow, in spite of his years, and he had a loyal staff. Had there been any sort of confrontation, he wouldn't have been easy to subdue and the sound of a struggle would have brought his valet hurrying downstairs and his coachman bounding upstairs to his aid. That was presumably why he was hit from behind, without procrastination."

"But the murderer did not take a weapon with him for that purpose," Dupin pointed out. "The candlestick was surely picked up at hazard, in response to a hastily-made decision, unless...."

"Unless what, Monsieur Dupin?" the Prefect inquired—very politely, I thought, in the circumstances.

"Unless the candlestick was merely used to obscure the imprint of another weapon, or to deflect attention from a less obtrusive wound for which a careful search might otherwise have been revealed. Has the body been taken to the Morgue yet?"

"No—but if you wish to look at it while it is still *in situ*, we shall have to make haste."

"Then we shall make haste," Dupin decided. "The fresher the trail is, the easier it will be to pick up and follow. We could, of course, wait to see whether or not the murderer will come to us...but anything to do with Zann's memory might turn out to be darkly dangerous, and if it is possible to seize the initiative, that is what we must do."

"I thought you might say so," the Prefect said. "My carriage is waiting outside." He shot another significant glance at me, but did not saying anything to me or my guest. He simply looked back at Dupin expectantly, as if to ask for his permission to order me to stay behind.

"Too late," said Dupin. "He's heard more than enough to rouse his curiosity, and perhaps too much to guarantee his safety. If the murderer, whoever he is, does know of my involvement in the Zann affair, he will surely know that I was in residence here for some months, and that I am a frequent guest in this house. If he suspects that I might have hidden something here, my American friend could be in as much danger as I am. I would hate to think that he might be bludgeoned to death without even knowing why. He must come along, so that we can keep an eye on him."

"Very well," said the Prefect, obedient even to his interlocutor's whims.

I put on my winter coat, donned thick gloves and a felt hat, and selected a swordstick from the rack in the hallway. Dupin smiled, but retained his own perfectly ordinary cane;

he preferred brain to brawn as an instrument of competition—although I dare say that he might have developed more careful habits had he actually been forced to confront the Rue Morgue murderer, rather than identifying the brute from a safe distance.

As we went out to the Prefect's carriage, I whispered: "You will explain all this to me, won't you, Dupin?" I was genuinely worried; he had, after all, refused to talk about his relationship with the Prefect before, even though I was very well aware of the perennial delight he took in demonstrating his esoteric knowledge and powers of ratiocination.

"Of course, old man," he said. "I'll tell you the whole story, as soon as I have an opportunity. This business might simply have been promoted by Paganini's enquiries, which were surely innocent, even though their sequel has proved tragic. If so, the whole thing might fizzle out and come to nothing." He seemed far more hopeful than confident of that, but I was left in no doubt that it was his preferred alternative.

As we got into the carriage, Dupin said: "My intuition should have told me that something was amiss when you began our discussion this evening with mention of Guiseppe Tartini, and even prompted me to mention Erich Zann."

"But you didn't mention Erich Zann," I pointed out.

"Not by name, admittedly—he was the violinist of genius I mentioned in connection with *scordatura* techniques: the one who could retune his instrument mid-piece. Zann was once a pupil in Tartini's famous school, although Tartini was then very old—he died in 1770, I believe. Zann was scarcely more than a youth then, although he was not quite as old as he seemed when he perished in his turn."

"Is this the Devil's work to which you referred in jest, then?" I quipped. "I had not realized that you meant t-a-l-e rather than t-a-i-l."

"One should not be tempted to make jokes," Dupin muttered, as he settled back into a corner of the capacious carriage, as if trying to melt into the upholstery. "There are, alas, far too many true words accidentally spoken in jest."

Dupin then became stubbornly mute, though, presumably because we were not alone. The Prefect had one of his employees waiting in the carriage: a burly agent who obviously served as his bodyguard, and regarded us both with a suspicious air, signifying that he was ready to leap upon us and render us helpless if we made any suspicious movement.

3.

I took the opportunity provided by Dupin's silence to rack my memory for any information about Giuseppe Tartini that might have been stored there for future use, but I could not discover anything except the famous anecdote that had provided the inspiration for the melodrama I had been to see the night before last.

Tartini had once told the astronomer Jérôme Lalande that he had dreamed of making a pact with the Devil, who had been prepared to grant his every wish in return for his soul. In his dream, Tartini had handed over his violin, in order to investigate the Adversary's musical talents, and the Devil had played a sonata so spectacularly beautiful and original that the composer had woken up with a start and tried to play it himself. He had failed to recapture it, but the inferior piece thus inspired had nevertheless been the finest of all his works: *Il Trillo del Diavolo*, usually known in English as *The Devil's Sonata*, although the original title referred to the spectacularly difficult double-stop trills that the piece required. The rumor had been put about after his death that Tartini had had six fingers on his left hand, and could not have played the trills otherwise, but it seemed more likely to my prosaic mind that he had simply had unusually long fingers, like Signor Paganini—who made the execution of such trills, and even more esoteric notes, seem like child's play.

When the Prefect had given his coachman instructions to return to the Rue Serpente as quickly as possible, and had taken a seat beside the man who had been waiting in the carriage—

introduced to us as Inspector Lestrade of the Sûreté—I looked at Dupin, hoping that he might at least continue his discussion of the facts of Bernard Clamart's murder, but the logician continued to hold his tongue while the carriage was in progress, seemingly losing himself in memory and reflection. At that time of night, fortunately, the journey from the Faubourg Saint-Germain to the Rue Serpente did not take long, and we were soon climbing down again, in the inner courtyard of the tall house that contained Clamart's apartment and place of business.

We went upstairs to the first floor, where his consulting-room was—conveniently sandwiched between the apartment above and the principal servants' quarters beneath. The building had one other tenant on the first floor, two others on the third and another alongside further servant's quarters in the mansards, but the Commissaire had, apparently, already ruled them out as likely suspects in the murder. The mysterious individual seen running away from the external staircase was the present focus of attention and interest.

Thanks to my acquaintance with Dupin, I had seen dead bodies before, but it is a sight to which one does not become readily accustomed. This one had bled very profusely, and many of the papers that had been recklessly scattered around the corpse had become spotted and edged with absorbed blood, thus being remade—at least in my imagination—in the image of the diabolical contracts of legend.

Careless of the clotted stains, Dupin knelt down beside the body and inspected the corpse closely. He seemed disappointed when he finally proclaimed: "The appearances are not deceptive. Clamart was, indeed, taken by surprise while he was seated in the armchair, and hit from behind. The first blow certainly did not kill him, for he appears to have been able to turn his head, if not to stand up—that is why the second blow landed on the top of his head. He fell forward out of the chair then, on to his knees, and the third blow finished the job. The angle at which the blows were struck confirm that the murderer was not tall, which fits with the concierge's scant description of the person seen descending the external stairway. The blows were not particularly forceful, suggesting a relatively weak arm—again consonant with the concierge's description.

"The fact that the murderer does not appear to have been tall or strong suggests that the crime was not planned in advance. Had murder been premeditated, the assassin would surely have taken the trouble to bring a dagger with which to stab his victim quickly and cleanly. I half-expected to find that a stiletto had been thrust into his skull beneath the occiput, and that the wound thus made had been superficially disguised, but that is not the case. Perhaps the burglar did not expect to find Clamart in his study, although it is highly unlikely that he would have been in bed at the hour when the crime was committed. There is a more likely possibility." Instead of continuing immediately, he waited, rather coquettishly.

"What is the more likely possibility?" the Prefect asked, automatically responding to the cue.

"That it was only the attack that was unexpected by either party, and that the visitor was here by appointment—although any record of that appointment made by Clamart, and any notes he made in the course of it, will surely have been removed by the murderer. At any rate, Clamart and his killer might well have been engaged in a seemingly-amicable conversation—amicable enough for Clamart to have allowed his visitor to move behind him without turning his head to keep a close eye on him...or her."

"You think the murderer might have been a woman?" the Prefect asked.

"If Clamart really was sufficiently relaxed and self-confident to give his murderer the opportunity to move behind his chair and pick up the candlestick, yes, there must be a possibility that the short and slender figure seen making a hasty exit was female."

"You think she killed him in the course of an assignation? That we're dealing with a crime of passion?"

"To the first question, possibly—although, as a notary, Monsieur Clamart might well have had female clients who had reasons for maintaining strict secrecy with respect to their consultations, so there is no need to assume an assignation. To the second, it depends what you mean by a *crime of passion*. There is more than one kind of passion, and all of them may become motives for murder." He looked around the room, contemplating the scattered papers, then added: "We have no time now to sort through this welter of irrelevancy, although it will have to be done—I leave that to your agents. If the murderer left behind any documents of interest, we shall have to trust that your men will be able to identify them. What we really need to know is whether the culprit took away any other documents, in addition to Clamart's pocket-book—but we shall not be able to discover that, or figure out what they were, by inspecting those left behind. There are more urgent matters requiring my personal attention."

"Are you going to see Palaiseau?" The Prefect asked.

"That seems the best course of action. It might easily be a fruitless mission, but if he *has* developed loose lips in his old age, it will be useful to discover what he has said, and to whom. You can leave that to me if you wish—your presence might intimidate him, and you doubtless have official duties to perform. I can easily take a fiacre to the Boulevard du Temple. Is he still working at the Ambigu and living just round the corner?"

"Yes," said Monsieur Groix, but hastened to add, "although the Ambigu no longer has that name, and if you were give it to a cab-driver nowadays, he'd take you to the Ambigu-Comique in the Boulevard Saint-Martin. The old Ambigu is now called the Délassements-Comique."

Even Dupin was subject to moments of temporary fallibility. He struggled to remember where he had recently heard that name for a full three seconds before he suddenly rounded on me and said: "You reached for your pocket when you mentioned program-notes for the performance you attended two nights ago. May I see it?"

I could play the coquette too, and was harboring a certain smoldering resentment about being kept in the dark. "There's no need," I said, airily, "Monsieur Paul Palaiseau was indeed one of the performers—the lead violinist in fact."

"I had already deduced that," he told me, frostily. "What I need to know is whether he was playing a particular instrument. Is there any special mention in the notes regarding his violin?"

"Yes there is," I replied. "The theater is obviously very proud to be able to feature such an instrument, violins of that manufacture being rarely seen outside the concert hall. The notes refer to it as *the Lost Stradivarius*."

I had never heard Dupin groan before, and had not realized that his exceedingly pale face could get any paler. He looked at Monsieur Groix, to whom this news was similarly unwelcome.

"Oh, the *fool*," the Prefect murmured. "He swore that the instrument was unplayable, a mere curiosity. He said that he would never...but he did not see what you and I saw, did he? Nor did Clamart—only poor Fourmont, whose death it surely hastened, and the author of the deposition."

"Again," Dupin murmured, "it *might* simply be the influence of this Paganini fellow. I should have done my eavesdropping more assiduously, and paid more attention to the potential corollaries of what I heard." He was moving out of the room as he spoke, but his steps were slow, as if his sense of urgency had been compromised by the need to think.

"You're right," the Prefect said. "Paganini has repopularized *scordatura*, and has demonstrated new playing techniques. Palaiseau always fancied himself an undeveloped genius. He must be as envious of Paganini, albeit at a far greater distance, as he once was of Erich Zann. Paganini's celebrity, and the fact that Soulié and Bazailles have tried to cash in on it, in their own way, might well have stirred up all kinds of memories and desires that should have been as safely buried as poor Zann's corpse. But still...." He left the sentence dangling; like Dupin, he had no faith in the possibility that Paganini's interest in Erich Zann had prompted further interest of no great significance. Both men obviously felt that something more sinister was afoot—something that they both dreaded.

Dupin rounded on Clamart's valet who was waiting patiently in the corridor outside the consulting-room, holding himself available for questioning. "Tell me," he said, "has Monsieur Clamart been to the theater recently?"

The valet glanced at the Prefect, obviously wondering whether he was obliged to answer questions addressed to him by such an eccentric and slightly shabby individual. The Prefect nodded.

"Why, yes, Monsieur," the valet said. "He normally goes no further than the *Opéra*, but three days ago he went to the Boulevard du Temple to see the play that everyone is talking about—the one with the boy soprano playing the Devil."

"You don't think he actually called on Palaiseau, do you?" The Prefect asked Dupin.

"He might have done, once he read the program note about the violin," Dupin replied, tautly. "What he should have done was to notify you—or me—immediately. As you just pointed out, however, he did not see what Fourmont, you and I saw. He swore the oath along with the rest of us, but he did not understand its true significance, any more than Palaiseau did."

"Do you think that his conversation with Palaiseau might somehow have sealed his death-warrant?" the Prefect asked. "Palaiseau cannot have committed the murder, for he would have been performing in the orchestra-pit when the fatal blow was delivered."

"That's right," I put in, still relying on my memory and having no need to consult my program notes. "The play has three acts, with the customary brief intervals in between. Palaiseau plays in all three, on behalf of the actor playing the lead, and cannot possibly have left the theater between dusk and nine-thirty."

"Palaiseau is a highly unlikely murderer, in any case," Dupin opined. "If he believes that his great opportunity has come at last, though, and that he has finally succeeded, by means of assiduous and secret practice, in mastering Zann's recalcitrant instrument, he might well have sacrificed discretion in talking to the composer, his fellow players, and even the gentlemen of the press. I must find out what he has said, and to whom. If someone was willing to murder Clamart, with no particularly powerful motive that I can see—given than the worst that Clamart might have done was to send a warning to you or me, once he realized what his visitor wanted—then I, at least, might well be in danger of a similar fate."

"I have Lestrade to protect me, thank God, and the entire resources of the Sûreté to call upon, if necessary," Monsieur Groix observed, "although that's less than you might imagine, now that all the finest agents available are laboring in the political police, rooting out legitimists, Bonapartists, anarchists and God only knows how many other enemies of the State. Would you care to deliver Zann's documents into my custody, for safe keeping?"

"I can't," Dupin replied, brusquely. "In any case, it would too late to buy any immunity by that means. Palaiseau was never party to the terms of the testament, so he probably never knew of the existence of the second component of Zann's legacy, but if Clamart revealed its existence and nature, then I might be the murderer's next target. I told Clamart what I had done with the manuscript, but he might not have had the time or the inclination to mention that, and his killer probably would not have believed him if he did."

"The *Préfeture* still has the deposition," the Prefect remarked. "Palaiseau knows that *that* document exists, and that it's properly filed in the Archives."

"The murderer is welcome to consult the deposition, at this stage of the game," Dupin said, reflectively, "although it's unlikely to occasion any retreat. I need to find out exactly what Palaiseau has let slip, though, and to whom. He won't be eager to tell me, but I shall have to winkle it out of him."

"Be careful, Monsieur Dupin," the Prefect advised. "The Boulevard du Temple is not a safe place at this time of night, even if there were no further consequences of the present affair to be feared. I do have official duties to perform, as you said, but the key to this mystery probably lies with Palaiseau. I'll follow you to the Boulevard du Temple as soon as the formalities have been completed here, so that you can inform me as to what you've learned and we can discuss what steps to take next—but I repeat, you *must* be careful."

"Don't worry, Monsieur Groix," Dupin said airily, gesturing casually in my direction. "I have a bodyguard of my own—not one as accomplished, I dare say, as your faithful Lestrade, but a reliable one nevertheless. All Americans are fighting-men at heart, even bookish ones so shy that they feel compelled to employ an intermediary in order to publish anecdotes and tales in popular magazines."

4.

We walked down to the Quai in search of a fiacre, at a pace that quickly rendered us both breathless. Mercifully, we found one readily enough. It was not until Dupin had given the coach-man the address of the Délassements-Comique and settled back into a corner of the vehicle in his customary fashion that he finally condescended to begin the explanation that he had promised to give me.

"As I mentioned briefly," he said, "Erich Zann was an Austrian violinist who studied at Giuseppe Tartini's school during the famous virtuoso's latter years. Tartini had, by then, become very interested in the theory of harmony and acoustics, publishing various treatises on those subjects, and Zann shared his interest, although he approached the problem from a different direction. To borrow a metaphor from our earlier discussion, Tartini took a fundamentally physiological approach to questions of musical theory and the effects of music on the human mind, while Zann's approach was essentially spiritualistic—focused, like Alexandre Bertrand's theory of Mesmerism, on the ecstatic quality and potential of music. In spite of this difference in attitude—or perhaps because of it—Erich Zann became Tartini's favorite pupil in his later years

"The young Zann brought from his homeland a strong interest in the *scordatura* techniques employed by the Bohemian composer Heinrich von Biber in his famous Rosary Sonatas. Knowing that von Biber had drawn his inspiration from such Italian masters as Marini and Uccellini, and had had been a powerful influence in his turn on Tartini's less celebrated contemporary Pietro Locatelli, it seemed only logical to Zann that he should study in Italy. Again, this interest intrigued Tartini, whose interest in *vibrato, tremolo* and *trillo* ornamentation complemented Zann's fascination with *scordatura*. Zann was particularly fascinated by *Il Trillo del Diavolo*, and must have heard Tartini's account of its composition long before it was confided to Lalande, who did not broadcast the anecdote until the year before Tartini's death."

"In 1769, that is," I put in, to reassure him that I was keeping up.

"Exactly. Zann remained in Italy for some while after Tartini's demise, but eventually returned to his homeland to continue his research and experimentation. Unfortunately, the Empire was in turmoil long before the outbreak of the Napoleonic Wars, and Zann somehow fell foul of the remnants of the *vehmgerichte*—unofficial tribunals based in old secret societies, which were enjoying a renaissance of sorts in consequence of the upheavals—and he was forced to flee to France. The poor fellow was dumb, and such conversation as we had was therefore very limited, so I never contrived to find out exactly what it was of which the *vehmgerichte* considered him guilty, although I deduced that he was suspected of practicing witchcraft—which is to say, diabolism. Such fantasies routinely rear their ugly heads in times of social stress and strife, even in a so-called Age of Enlightenment. At any rate, he was forced to abandon his plans to play in one of the great orchestras of Europe and became a reclusive scholar laboring in obscurity.

"Zann was even more unorthodox as a composer than

Locatelli, whose work was shunned during his lifetime and remained virtually unplayed until Paganini revived it. In order to scrape a living while he continued his scholarly studies and indulged in esoteric composition, Zann found quotidian employment in the pit of a theater on the Boulevard du Temple—the Ambigu, as it was then called. It can hardly have been convenient work, for he was living in a garret in the Rue d'Auseuil, but he had no objection to long walks, and probably preferred to keep the two aspects of his life separate."

Dupin paused to glance out of the window impatiently. We had crossed the two arms of the river by the Pont Saint-Michel and the Pont du Change and were continuing northwards toward the Boulevard du Temple. The nag that was hauling us was by no means as fine a horse as the two animals tethered to the Prefect's carriage, so our progress was more stately than rapid.

"I don't know the Rue d'Auseuil," I put in. "Where is it?"

"All this happened before the July Revolution of 1830," Dupin said. "Paris had many unnamed streets in those days, and the popular names by which they were known were not always the names formally attached to them by Louis-Philippe's assiduous bureaucrats in the following decade. The Rue d'Auseuil is no longer the Rue d'Auseuil, and has never been the Rue d'Auseuil in any official sense, but that is the name by which it was known then. As to its whereabouts, it zigzagged precipitously up the slope of a butte on the bank of the Bièvre, which was sheer on the face overlooking the stream—do you know the Bièvre?"

"No," I confessed.

"It's one of the tributary rivulets of the Seine, which has been swallowed up by the city and has degenerated into an open sewer—although I don't believe that it will remain open for long. It will be roofed over, like other such tributaries, and will become a sewer in truth as well as in metaphor. The butte is close enough to the heart of Paris to have a view of the Val-de-Grâce, albeit one spoiled by intervening factory chimneys, but is far enough away for the fountain at Mulard to be within walking distance. It's a long trek from there to the Boulevard du Temple, but Erich Zann was prepared to make that journey on foot every day—much to the mystification of his immediate neighbor in the orchestra pit of the theater in which he earned his crust, Paul Palaiseau.

"As Palaiseau tells the story, he soon assessed Zann as an undeveloped genius, like himself—although Zann was, in fact, by far the cleverer of the two—and he attempted to befriend him on that account. Zann was a difficult man to befriend, though, and not only because he was unable to speak. I do not know whether he was born dumb, or became so as a result of some catastrophe, but if the condition that affected his speech also affected his hearing—as is the case with so many deaf-mutes—it did not do so in any ordinary fashion, for he had a tremendous ear for music, if not for social conversation. He had no real friends, although he was on tolerably good terms with his landlord, a cripple named Blandot, and he also became an object of fascination to one of his fellow tenants in the house in the Rue d'Auseuil—the author of the deposition to which Monsieur Groix and I made reference earlier.

"Zann did, however, confide certain documents, including a testament, to a well-known notary, Bernard Clamart, and he certainly tolerated the acquaintance of Palaiseau and the author of the deposition, even though he did not encourage it, at least to begin with. Perhaps he had a profound and earnest desire to make friends, but had learned to be very wary of other people until he felt he knew them well. It was almost unheard of for him to strike up an acquaintance on his own account, although he did make the effort to seek me out. He came to see me in search of a certain very rare book, after which he had enquired—by means of a written request—at the Bibliothéque du Senat. One of the librarians there had informed him that I possessed the only copy still known to be in Paris. I was an habitué of the library in those days, and was sometimes drawn into conversations about rare and esoteric works."

"Was it a book on violin music?" I asked, remembering that he had made a casual reference to having been taught to play the instrument during in his boyhood.

"Only indirectly. It was, in fact, the infamous *Harmonies de l'Enfer*, penned in the fourteenth century by an Averoignean heretic monk, who attached the unlikely signature of 'Abbé Apollonius' to the manuscript. A few copies were privately printed in the eighteenth century—directly from the original, it's said—allegedly at the instigation of Count Cagliostro, before the latter's expulsion from France on the trumped-up charge of involvement in the affair of the queen's necklace."

I glimpsed the suggestion of a connecting thread to Tartini's *Devil's Sonata*, and said: "Had Zann's old master read this *Harmonies of Hell* volume?"

"It's very unlikely. I doubt that Tartini had any competence in Old French, and I'm quite certain that Zann would not have been able to make head nor tail of the text, if I had been willing to lend it to him—which, of course, I was not. I was, however, sufficiently intrigued by his interest to volunteer to read him various key passages—translating them as I went into modern French, and then, to the best of my ability, into German—in exchange for private performances. At that point in my life, I did not have the marked distaste for violin music that I subsequently developed. For that reason, Zann came to the Rue Dunôt on several occasions, and we developed a friendship of sorts. Thanks to my observational and interpretative skills, I gradually acquired an unusual facility in interpreting the meanings of his improvised sign-language, and he obviously came to think of me as the one person in the world to whom he could really, as it were, *talk*.

"In spite of the relative ease with which I decoded his substitute-speech, I was rather surprised when Zann asked me to go with him to the Rue Serpente, in order to act as his interpreter while he made an alteration to his testament. Previously, Paul Palaiseau had been its sole beneficiary—unknown, I believe, to the violinist himself at that time—and Bernard Clamart its only executor. As a result of the visit on which I accompanied him, Zann added my name as a subsidiary beneficiary, and accepted the notary's suggestion that he should nominate a reserve executor, in case Clamart should predecease him. As Zann knew no one suitable, Clamart suggested the name of a young magistrate, who has since risen considerably in the world, and whom you know as the present Prefect of the Parisian police."

"But what did Zann have to leave, if he was living in a garret and playing as a hack in the Boulevard du Temple?" I asked.

"There was only one item of real significance: his violin. In his youth, Giuseppe Tartini had lived for a while in Cremona, as a neighbor of Antonio Stradivarius, who was a friend of his father. Stradivarius had given the ambitious boy two instruments that he regarded as inferior to his best work, and did not want to sell. One of them—the better of the two, which was only regarded as inferior because it did not quite measure up to Stradivarius' exceptionally high standards—Tartini passed on to one of his more prestigious pupils long before he met Erich Zann, but the other Tartini came to regard as spoiled, or at least *peculiar*. It was not defective, in any simple sense, but it was undoubtedly *strange*, and apparently unreliable in performance. Tartini tried it out and then put it away in favor of the other; apparently, he had almost forgotten its existence until he showed it to Erich Zann, who proved so skillful in the violin's use that Tartini made him a present of it.

"By that time, of course, Stradivarius was world-famous as a violin-maker beyond compare—although I understand from my eavesdropping that Paganini prefers a Guarneri—but the instrument that Tartini gave Zann was not recognizable as a Stradivarius by the ear of any connoisseur, and had no documentation of its provenance, so the Italian did not consider it a gift of any great value. Zann, however, knew what a treasure it was, and of what the instrument was capable, in the right hands. He valued it immensely, and evidently wanted to make sure that it would pass into the hands of a musician who would treasure it, once he was dead. Alas, he knew no one better than Palaiseau, who must have contrived to persuade Zann that the two of them had more in common than they really had, and that he, like Zann himself, only needed the right instrument to bring out his true genius.

"Palaiseau did, indeed, inherit the instrument—somewhat to his surprise, I think, but also to his great delight—and did appreciate its value. Unfortunately, he found the Stradivarius as difficult and as unreliable as Tartini had, and eventually abandoned his attempts to master its eccentricities—somewhat to my relief, I must confess. He continued to use his former instrument in performance, initially because he thought the Ambigu unworthy of a Stradivarius, and then because he could not imagine that the director of the orchestra would tolerate his uncertain use of the latter instrument. He kept it as a rather frustrating ornament, and might have sold it had he not been unable to convince anyone of its origin—until recently, apparently."

"I dare say that the director of the renamed theater was delighted to advertise and exploit Palaiseau's claim, even in the absence of proof of provenance, in connection with the current production." I put in.

"No doubt," Dupin agreed. "The last time I had an opportunity to ask Palaiseau about the instrument—which was, admittedly, some years ago—he claimed that he would never play it in public, because it went out of tune far too persistently and far too swiftly to be trusted with any piece but the briefest of *capricci*, and that he had even given up trying to play it in the privacy of his lodgings, for fear of annoying his neighbors. His answer was probably dishonest. He was, I suspect, moved to lie to me by a baseless anxiety."

"What anxiety?" I asked.

"Palaiseau thought—and probably still thinks—that I was jealous of him, and had wanted the Stradivarius for myself. He has long imagined that I was direly displeased with Zann's decision to leave the instrument to him, and probably thought it best when he last spoke to me about the matter to do his utmost to persuade me that the violin really was valueless and useless, even though he had not yet given up hope of mastering its difficulties."

"But if the only thing of value that Zann had to leave was the violin," I remarked, "and that went to Palaiseau, what was the subsidiary bequest that he left to you?"

At that moment, however, the weary nag finally succeeded in drawing the fiacre to a halt outside a gloomy edifice in an ill-lit side-street off the Boulevard du Temple, not far from the infamous site of Fieschi's atrocity, and Dupin was already jumping down, rooting in his pockets for a few coins with which to pay the driver. In the end I had to make up the balance of the fare, and by the time we had presented our credentials to the *sergent de ville* posted to keep watch on the door of Palaiseau's building, in order that we might be allowed to ring the bell, I had quite forgotten that the question had been asked, let alone left unanswered.

We were admitted to the building by a concierge so ancient in appearance that she put me in mind of one of Jonathan Swift's Struldbruggs. Her mind was obviously still sharp, though, for she recognized Monsieur Dupin, even though—according to his own testimony—she could not have seen him for several years. She greeted him by name, politely.

"It's good to see you again, Henriette," he replied, although I could not imagine that he was sincere. "Tell me, does Monsieur Palaiseau have many visitors now that he has found fame at last?"

"Not at this time of night, you may be sure," the crone replied. "And if, by *visitors*, you mean *ladies*, no. He knows the meaning of decency, does Monsieur Palaiseau, even if he is forever scraping away at that infernal fiddle of his. It was bad enough before he and Monsieur Bazailles started working together, and it became even worse when they began their rehearsals for the play...although I'm half-persuaded that the child who sings for them sometimes really does have the voice of an angel. Mademoiselle Deurne, alas, does not."

"Bazailles and both of the sopranos have been here more than once, then?"

"Oh yes, several times—and the director too, and Monsieur Mephistopheles the baritone, and other singers in the cast—but no visitors, if, by *visitors*, you mean *ladies*. I don't count Mademoiselle Deurne in that category, although there are rumors in the neighborhood suggesting that I should—but none coupling her name with Monsieur Palaiseau's, I'm glad to say. Those who do come always come by day, as decent folk should, and they don't come alone...except for Monsieur Bazailles and Monsieur Mephistopheles, once or twice. They never stay past dusk, except for the proprietor of the theater, who's only half a dozen strides from his own house—well, they wouldn't, would they? Not around *these* parts."

"Not if they're wise, my dear Henriette," Dupin agreed, "but the world has no shortage of fools."

Somehow, Dupin had kept a *sou* back from the sum he had given the coachman, and the concierge seemed glad to receive it. It was as if she were unused to receiving any larger sum, when anyone bothered to tip her at all.

"Would you be so kind as to consult your program notes for me, old friend," he asked, "and tell me the name of the actor who plays the Devil before—and presumably after—the boy replaces him in Monsieur Soulié's play?"

I took the notes out of my pocket, and squinted at them. There was enough candlelight filtering through the grille of Henriette's lodge to allow me to read the name.

"Monsieur Hood," I said. "An Englishman, fresh from Drury Lane. He's a fine baritone though—not many to match him on the French stage, outside the *Opéra* and the *Comédie-Française*. That's doubtless why he was imported—and it doesn't matter in the least that he has a strong English accent, even when he sings, since he's playing the Devil."

"Thank you," said Dupin.

The staircase that led from the central courtyard of the house to Palaiseau's first-floor apartment was a wooden one, external to the hull of the building, and seemed rather rickety. When Dupin knocked on the door it was opened almost immediately.

Palaiseau was obviously expecting someone to call, in spite of the fact that his usual visitors always left before dusk, and no one but a fool would be abroad in the vicinity of the Boulevard de Crime at such a late hour.

5.

I had somehow expected Palaiseau to be almost as ancient as the concierge, having vaguely envisaged him in the role of an old hand in the theater orchestra taking Erich Zann under his wing. In fact, it must have been the other way around, for the man who blinked at us from his doorway was no older than Auguste Dupin and definitely younger than Bernard Clamart. He evidently fancied himself as something of a dandy, for his hair was carefully curled and powdered, and he was still wearing his orchestral frock-coat, braided trousers and polished black shoes, although he must have had abundant time since finishing the evening's performance to change into a dressing-gown and *pantoufles*.

"Oh, it's you, Dupin," he said, although he did not seem unduly surprised, or unduly displeased. "I was half-expecting to see an inspector from the Sûreté. I've been promised protection, by no less an authority than *Monsieur le Préfet* himself. Someone might be after my violin, it seems, and the locks on my door and cabinet will not be enough to keep him at bay, since he's a reckless cut-throat. Come in, come in. Who's this?"

Dupin went in, as he was bid. As I followed him, he told the violinist my name—which, of course, Palaiseau did not recognize.

"Does he know our business?" Palaiseau asked, in a gruffly conspiratorial manner. "We swore an oath, remember?"

"I've begun to explain the situation to him on the way here," Dupin said, as he led the way into the apartment's sitting-room. "I think the oath is redundant now, don't you? The cat is, as the Americans say, out of the bag."

"If you say so, Dupin," the violinist said, agreeably, as he ushered us through the vestibule into the central corridor of his apartment. "I'm happy to take your lead in the matter. It's good of you to come to make sure that I'm all right—or are you simply making enquiries on behalf of Monsieur Groix? He must be short-handed when it comes to mere criminal activities, with so much political ferment in the air."

"Monsieur Groix knows that I'm here," Duping said, ambiguously. "He will follow when he can, though, to question you formally and perhaps to make further arrangements for your protection. In the meantime, you may talk quite freely in front of my friend, who has my complete confidence."

The sitting-room into which the violinist escorted us was almost as surprising as Palaiseau's own person. Either Palaiseau's landlady employed a first-rate housemaid, or Palaiseau was one of those fussy dandies who could not abide anything to be out of place or dusty. The room was magnificently neat; even the hearth, where a log fire was blazing, seemed conspicuously free of stray ashes, and the brass fire-irons were gleaming in the reflected firelight as if they had been freshly polished.

There were only two armchairs by the fire, but Palaiseau only seemed slightly irritated as he offered them to us, as the laws of hospitality obliged him to do, while he fetched a stiff-backed dining-chair from the next room for his own use. He did not offer us wine, tea or tobacco.

"You *are* here about this Clamart business, I take it?" the violinist asked, suspiciously.

"Yes," said Dupin. "Did the Prefect's messenger tell you about the grave, too?"

"Yes, albeit rather cryptically—but the Prefect is famous throughout Paris for his economy with information. Zann's body has been unearthed and the coffin smashed—did they find anything in the coffin?"

"There was nothing in the coffin to find," Dupin said. "You know that."

"Do I?" Palaiseau countered. "If you strain your memory,

you'll remember that you, Groix and the physician were the only ones who saw the dead man's face, except for that poor fool who was with him when he died. You had already sealed the lid of the coffin by the time that Clamart and I arrived at the graveside, allegedly for fear that we might suffer the same fate as the other, although why the two of you thought that you had better resistance to the threat of madness than Clamart or I possessed, I have no idea."

Dupin closed his eyes momentarily, as if to consult the distant memory. "That's true," he agreed, eventually. "It had not occurred to me that you might not have taken our word for it that the manuscript to which the deposition referred had been lost in its entirety, and that no documents of any sort had been found in Zann's rooms. Have you, perchance, confided that doubt to anyone else?"

"Certainly not," said Palaiseau, stiffly. "The five of us swore an oath, and I'm a man of my word. Besides which, I've never even met the man who's been asking questions all over the city—Paganini, that is. He's a concert performer, too grand to hobnob with hard-working players like myself." There was a distinct note of envy in his voice; I inferred that Palaiseau was able to tolerate his own obscurity while there were no virtuoso violinists on conspicuous display in Paris, but that the occasional presence in the capital of an authentic maestro aggravated the sore spot left by the ambitions to genius he had once entertained on his own behalf.

"Excuse me, Dupin," I said, "But I'm afraid that I haven't quite contrived to *catch up* yet. What does this deposition you keep mentioning actually contain? All you've told me is that it was given by Zann's fellow tenant."

"The man in question was with Zann when he died," Dupin explained. "The experience was evidently very disturbing. Instead of summoning a physician immediately, as he should have done, or even a policeman, as he might well have done, he came to see me, because he found my name and address on a piece of paper that the librarian at the Bibliothèque du

Senat had given Zann, inscribed beneath the name of the book that the dumb man had written down to facilitate his enquiry. Having seen the word *Enfer*, Blandot's other tenant was intent on persuading me that Zann had been fending off the legions of Hell, with no other weapon than his violin, but that the Devil had come to claim his soul regardless. He wanted me to supply him with some kind of amulet to ward off the Evil Spirit, and seemed disappointed to learn that I was only a humble collector of books, not a wizard at all.

"I took him to see Clamart, who summoned the magistrate, and I left the two of them to make the formal arrangements for the official certification of Zann's death by Maître Fourmont, while I accompanied the frightened man back to the Rue d'Auseuil. Because he refused to go back into the room, I went in to examine the body and to await the arrival of Clamart and the physician. The magistrate came too, but he had no clerk with him, so he left it to Clamart to take an official deposition from the witness while he came with me to assist Fourmont in attending to the body. The tenant claimed in his sworn statement that Zann had died of sheer terror, and had continued to play his violin long after he was dead. Those of us who read the deposition concluded that the man had been driven mad by Zann's sudden demise, but that its publication might stir up an unwelcome sensation, especially if rumor were to surface about Zann's reasons for leaving Austria.

"The physician was at first inclined to confirm the opinion that Zann must have died of fright, for he really did have a terrified expression imprinted on his livid features but Groix persuaded him easily enough that it was not an appropriate official cause of death. Fourmont eventually agreed to record the cause of death as heart failure. It could not be denied, though, that the expression on the dead man's face might easily have proved distressing to anyone not used to the transformations that corpses sometimes undergo as their muscles stiffen into *rigor mortis*. When the coffin arrived, we sealed the lid, and had it transported to Père Lachaise. Palaiseau is correct in remembering that Groix and I were the only ones to see the dead man's face, apart from Fourmont and the witness, because Clamart was downstairs all the while. He is thus correct in claiming that he does not know for sure that nothing was placed in the coffin with the body before it was interred, in an umarked grave, in Père Lachaise."

"But why was the grave unmarked? And why was the burial secret—apparently without the benefit of clergy?"

"Zann was an Austrian refugee, a Protestant and a reputed Diabolist."

"Are there no Protestant cemeteries in Paris?"

"Yes—but we were enthusiastic to suppress the tenant's wild tales of diabolism, and thought it more discreet to complete the burial quickly and discreetly. The man had no living relatives, and no one to miss him except for Blandot and Palaiseau."

"It seemed wisest to be discreet about the Stradivarius, too," Palaiseau put in. "I was the only other member of the theater orchestra who knew what it was, and at that time, I was reluctant to have it noised about that I possessed such an instrument." He did not explain why he had recently changed his mind.

"All in all," Dupin added, "it seemed best to avoid publicity. Groix, in his capacity as a conscientious magistrate, had no alternative but to file the tenant's deposition, whereupon it became part of the national record, but there are few better ways to make sure that no one ever reads a document than to place it in the veritable graveyard of documents that constitute the Archives of State. One day, perhaps, it will be found—and it might then be skillfully revised by a story-teller's hand into one of the horror stories that you delight in publishing in your American magazines, in order that its substance might hide in even plainer sight. I hope that will not happen, though, at least until the present century has ended. At any rate, Palaiseau received Zann's violin, as was his legal due, and the five of us swore an oath to say no more about the affair."

It had become increasingly apparent to me that there was still a part of the secret that Dupin was deliberately keeping from me, and I became rather annoyed with him. "There's obviously something more than you've confessed behind your desire for secrecy," I said, a trifle peevishly, "If you're not going to tell me everything, I wonder why you bothered to tell me anything at all."

"I said much the same thing to him myself all those years ago," Palaiseau put in, eagerly, "but he told me that what he, Groix and Fourmont had seen in Zann's room was better passed over in silence, even within the bounds of our little conspiracy. He said that what Zann had desired of me was to cherish his beloved violin, and that I had best do that discreetly. Whether he confided any more than that to Clamart, I don't know. Now, it seems, he suspects that I have been talking—but what, in all honesty, could I say?"

"You *have* been talking," Dupin told him, flatly. "You have ceased to be discreet and have started boasting about your possession of the Stradivarius, even if you haven't explicitly identified it as Erich Zann's instrument. The question is, what else have you talked about?"

"What else *could* I talk about?" Palaiseau insisted. "I could repeat the madman's ravings, of course, but what good or harm would that do me or anyone else? If anyone has been talking recently about whatever you saw in Zann's room, it must have been you or Groix, since Fourmont is dead...unless it was the madman, or Blandot, Zann's landlord."

"Blandot and his other tenant are both dead," Dupin reported, flatly. "For some years the latter spent his time roaming the streets of Paris, claiming to be looking for the Rue d'Auseuil, but to be unable to find it—and, indeed, he seems never to have found his way back to Blandot's house, although anyone in the quarter could have directed him to it. Perhaps he *was* mad; at any rate, he died seven years ago, to the Prefect's certain knowledge."

"*Perhaps* he was mad?" Palaiseau queried. "I saw no room for doubt, when he came to see me, to implore me to destroy the violin."

"Did he do that?" Dupin asked. "I didn't know. I was never entirely convinced that he was truly mad, if there is a true sense of the word. It seemed to me that he had simply lost *his sense of direction.* There are people who think that I am mad, though, so I always feel entitled to be suspicious of judgments of that sort, given that I am the sanest man alive."

Palaiseau did not seem convinced of that, but he evidently had questions of his own that he wanted to address to Dupin. "Do you believe that whoever killed Bernard Clamart will come after me next, Monsieur Dupin?" he asked, abruptly. "Is it the Stradivarius that he is after?"

"If it were the violin," Dupin countered, "Why would he— or she—go to Clamart at all? Anyone who cared to read the program notes for your theater's current production would know that you have it in your possession."

"He was the will's executor. Perhaps the murderer wanted to see the will, in the hope that there might be some grounds for a legal challenge to its terms. We don't know for certain, after all, that Zann had no relatives—and our motives for keeping the burial quiet might have been misconstrued, if he had."

"Why kill Clamart, though, if that was the reason for his visit?" Dupin asked, posing the question of himself as much as to Palaiseau.

"Perhaps Clamart refused to show him the will, or became so suspicious of the enquirer's motives that his visitor thought it politic to silence him?"

Dupin shook his head, slowly. "Clamart was so lacking in suspicion of his visitor's motives that he allowed him—or her— to move behind him and pick up the murder weapon without so much as a backward glance."

"Why do you keep saying *or her*?" Palaiseau wanted to know. "Do you think Clamart was killed by a woman?"

"I don't know," Dupin suggested. "At any rate, it seems to have been someone of whom he had no fear—but his pocketbook was stolen, which suggests that whoever killed him knew him so slightly that the information therein was worth stealing."

"Or the money he kept in it, in the form on banknotes," Palaiseau suggested.

"Perhaps," Dupin admitted. In a slightly different tone, he added: "My address will have been in the book, of course—and yours."

"So you *do* think that he—or she, if you insist—might come after me?"

"My present judgment is that he or she is more likely to come after me. I thought it best to compare notes, though. Are you perfectly certain that you have not given anyone any information that might have set this train of events in progress?"

"Perfectly—unless I have been talking in my sleep."

I was sure that the violinist had meant this last remark purely as a joke—but Dupin had told me more than once that jokes are an unreliable means of psychological defense, and had commented earlier that evening on the frequency with which remarks uttered in jest contain significant truths. Like a flash, he retorted: "Who might have heard you, Palaiseau, *if you had talked in your sleep?*"

"Why, no one!" the other replied, slightly befuddled by the question. "I have no wife, as you know full well, nor even a housemaid of my own."

"Then there's only one thing for it!" Dupin said, rising abruptly to his feet. I did likewise, but we seemed to have been too quick off the mark for our host, who remained seated. "What's that?" Palaiseau asked. "Are you going in search of Groix to ask him for protection?"

"No," Dupin replied. "I'm going to the Rue d'Auseuil."

"The Rue d'Auseuil?" Palaiseau queried. "But you just said that Blandot is dead, and reiterated your claim that nothing was found when Zann's attic room was searched. Blandot couldn't have stolen anything from Zann's rooms—he was a cripple who couldn't climb the stairs of his own building. Or do you think that Zann might have taken advantage of Blandot's infirmity to hide something elsewhere in the house? What is it, exactly, that you're looking for?"

These questions seemed to me to be more interesting in themselves than any answers Dupin might have given, in that they revealed significant details concerning the focus and extent of Palaiseau's curiosity. Apparently, the violinist thought that there might be something to be found, apart from the violin, but did not know where or exactly what it was.

"I'm not looking for anything," Dupin replied—although he surely could not have expected Palaiseau to take his word for it—"but someone else clearly is. If he does not come in search of me tonight, or fails to find me, he will surely go to the Rue d'Auseuil. He might well have been there already; if so, I need to know about it, and to examine any traces he has left. The Prefect did not think of sending anyone to the house, since it has been boarded up for years, and there is no one there in need of protection, but it is an obvious target for a speculative treasure-hunter. Unlike your house and mine, it has no watchman posted outside, so it might seem to the thief to be the most attractive target, for the present. If you're certain that you haven't said a word to anyone, and cannot give us any clue to the identity of our adversary...."

Dupin made as if to get up and stride to the door, but I knew that it was a bluff. He knew full well that Palaiseau had more to tell, and was trying to provoke him.

The musician stood up too, as if belatedly remembering his duty as a host. "Don't go yet," he said, swiftly.

"I must," Dupin retorted. "Unless you have some information to impart that will put me on the track of the solution to the mystery, I must go elsewhere in search of clues."

"I haven't said a word to anyone," Palaiseau hastened to say, trying to sound teasing, "but that doesn't mean that I don't have my own suspicions—and there's something I need to show you."

Dupin sat down again. "In that case," he said, suddenly becoming patient again—thus making it obvious that his threat to leave had been a mere ploy—"show me."

"Very well," said the violinist, leaping to his feet. "I will."

6.

Palaiseau came back into the room less than a minute later, proudly holding a violin and a bow. He held the instrument up, as if to display it, but did not offer it to Dupin so that the great analyst could actually take it into his hands.

"Do you recognize this instrument?" the violinist said.

"It's Erich Zann's violin," Dupin said. "What does your present employer call it? The Lost Stradivarius."

"He's a fool," Palaiseau said, shortly. "You and I know that it was never lost, even though it might have been, so to speak, in hiding—but successful advertisement has its own protocols. Now listen."

Without further delay, Palaiseau put the instrument to his shoulder, and positioned the fingers of his left hand very carefully before bringing the bow into play. Dupin was watching him carefully—and I thought, rather apprehensively.

As the musician began to saw away, I reflected that the music seemed pleasant enough to me, although it hardly seemed to be the sort of threnody that the angels of Heaven might be expected to sing. As someone who fell noticeably short of a connoisseur, however, I reserved my judgment. Even if Palaiseau was simply showing off, in order to demonstrate to Auguste Dupin that he really was deserving of Erich Zann's legacy, he was entitled to make his demonstration.

When he had been playing for a few minutes, Palaiseau's instrument seemed to go slightly out of tune, although he did not pause in his playing, and did not even frown in annoyance. The effect did not seem to last long, for the melody was soon restored, albeit in a darker vein. What had formerly been a pleasurable refrain now became rather ominous, although I was not at all sure how the transition had been worked—or, indeed, whether it was a real transition rather than an artifact of the ear of an inexpert beholder. I am not unaffected by music—who is?—but I have always considered myself slightly tone-deaf, in that I seem to be immune to many of its subtler effects. I have seen people moved to tears by music, and roused to literal exultation, but I have never had such a strong reaction myself. Nor am I expert enough in the theory of music to put names to all its effects, so I am unable to offer an accurate description here of exactly what Palaiseau was doing as he played. I can say with confidence, however, that there were no trills, nor any other conspicuous ornamental effects.

I closed my eyes for a while, trying to isolate the music within my head, free from other potential distractions, and I gradually surrendered to its dark charm in spite of the hint of menace that I perceived within it. It seemed to me that the music became increasingly *voluptuous*, suggestive of strange sensuous delights, but also more plaintive, as if access to those delights were being weakened by *impuissance*, spoiled by *ennui* or undermined by *spleen*.

When I opened my eyes again, I saw that Dupin was watching Palaiseau like a hawk, as if on the lookout for some tell-tale sign—of what, I could not imagine.

Eventually, Palaiseau drew to a close. "Well?" the violinist said, placing the violin and the bow very carefully on a sideboard and looking down at them in an almost reverent fashion. "Did you hear that? Do you understand its significance?"

"To the first question, yes, I did," said Dupin. "To the second...no, not exactly. Is that the music you play while the Devil, in his guise as an angel, sings his pretended abstract from the Heavenly choir?"

"No," said Palaiseau, turning his back on the violin and returning to his dining-chair. "It's from the first act, when the protagonist of the play addresses himself to the girl he loves, and she responds in song—but the two pieces do have common themes, for reasons to do with the symbolism and aesthetic balance of the play. This is no standard Boulevard de Crime melodrama, you know; it's a piece well worthy of the Stradivarius. The point is, did you hear what the instrument did as the piece progressed?"

"I noticed that you succeeded in changing the tuning of the violin part-way through the piece, with only a moment of discordant transition—a moment that could presumably be covered up in an orchestral performance by the clever deployment of another instrument. That's not entirely new, however, although you might think that it proves your originality as well as your ability. I've heard Zann do something similar."

"No you haven't," said Palaiseau, tersely.

"I can assure you...."

The violinist cut him off. "I don't doubt that you've heard it, Dupin—what I doubt is that you heard Zann *do it*, any more than you heard me *do it*."

There was a moment's silence before Dupin said: "Ah! You're trying to persuade me that the Stradivarius is making the transition of its own accord—that all *you're* doing is, so to speak, playing along with it."

"Exactly," Palaiseau confirmed. "Not that I've let on to that fool proprietor, or even to Bazailles. He didn't compose the piece, you understand, until he'd heard the trick. He played along in his way, just as I did in mine—except that he's now convinced that I'm a genius to compare with Paganini and I certainly wouldn't care to disabuse him. Don't look at me like that—I long ago disabused myself of any such notion, when I couldn't begin to duplicate Zann's skill with the instrument. I'd never realized, while he was alive, what a fiendish instrument it is. I know now...but the Fiend, it seems, has finally learned to tolerate me, or at least to find a use for my long-idle hands."

"Are you claiming that you've made some kind of diabolical pact?" I asked.

Palaiseau turned to look at me, in a distinctly unfriendly fashion. "Do I look like a man whose every wish has been granted?" he asked.

"To be perfectly honest," I said, "I thought when you took your bow two nights ago that you looked like a man who has had *one* of his dearest wishes granted. You received a standing ovation, from the cast as well as the audience, and seemed to revel in it."

"Yes," the musician admitted, "I do enjoy the applause, the recognition, especially when I'm summoned on to the stage to take a bow, which is a rare privilege for an instrumentalist. It's not until I get home, to my lonely apartment, that the knowledge that I don't really *deserve* the applause begins to eat into me."

"I can't help feeling that you're exaggerating, Palaiseau," Dupin said, "and I'm not sure what you're trying to prove. I'm entirely willing to take your word for it that the Stradivarius alters its tuning while it is being played, presumably as a result of the stresses placed upon it by playing—but as you don't want to claim that you've made a pact with the Devil, you presumably don't believe that the retuning process is to be reckoned supernatural. If all you're trying to prove is your own cleverness, in being able to turn the violin's odd behavior to your own advantage, by having tunes composed, so to speak around the fault, then you have my sincere congratulations. If you're asserting more than that, please state what you mean, honestly and plainly."

The violinist looked at Dupin with mingled disappointment and hostility. Clearly, he had hoped for a different response—presumably a more credulous one.

"The retuning doesn't happen all the time," Palaiseau said, dully.

"In that case, you've evidently mastered both sides of the problem. You've helped to develop pieces that use the transition, when the note-structure induces it, but you've also helped to develop tunes that don't induce it."

"Is that really all that you believe that Zann was doing in his own compositions?" Palaiseau asked.

"I said nothing about Zann's compositions," Dupin countered. "We're only concerned, for the present, with your own performances, are we not? Or are you really trying to persuade me to believe that the Stradivarius is performing, employing your hands as its obedient instrument?"

"I don't know!" Palaiseau complained, his voice rising in

pitch as he squirmed in his chair, glancing sideways at the violin lying quietly on the sideboard. "I honestly don't know!"

The artistic temperament is a strange thing, I thought. *Perhaps Giuseppe Tartini actually managed to convince himself that* Il Trillo del Diavolo *was a pastiche of the Devil's own work, rather than a product of his own excited mind.*

"Does it really matter?" Dupin asked—a trifle cruelly, I thought. "After all, it's only supportive music, though, is it not? If my friend's report of the plot of your play is accurate, it's the boy soprano who takes on the real burden of persuading the audience that the climactic song is Heavenly—and Mademoiselle Deurne must surely play a similar role with respect to the piece you've just played."

"I don't just play for those two pieces," Palaiseau replied, a trifle stiffly. "I play *all* the protagonist's pieces. The actor merely pretends to play. There are nine violin pieces in all, three in each act. The boy only sings one, and Marilla—Mademoiselle Deurne, that is—only sings one to the accompaniment of the solo violin. She sings one other with the full orchestra, and one without any instrumental accompaniment at all."

"But how many of the nine pieces you play on the protagonist's behalf take advantage of the instrument's tendency to retune itself?"

"Just the two," Palaiseau admitted. "I'm deeply grateful that it no longer shows any such determination to do so at other times, although I'm quite at a loss to explain its docility."

Dupin sniffed, evidently feeling that he had already explained that irregularity, at least to his own satisfaction. "How does all this help us determine the identity of the treasure-seeker who violated Erich Zann's grave and murdered Bernard Clamart?" I asked, thinking that I ought to make an attempt to defuse the accumulating tension.

"I'm not sure that it does," Palaiseau replied, defiantly, "but I wanted Monsieur Dupin to hear it anyway."

"I'm glad that you did, my old friend," Dupin said, apparently agreeing with me that some mollification was necessary.

"It might well be a significant piece of the puzzle. Can you think of anything else that might help me?"

"I doubt it—but you might conceivably be interested to know that Monsieur Bazailles only appears on stage at the end, to take his bow along with Monsieur Soulié—and he did not arrive at the theater last night, or the previous night, until it was time for him to take that bow."

I almost broke into laughter. It did not seem at all strange to me that a composer should eventually tire of hearing his work played night after night, or that he should eventually learn to trust the instrumentalists to repeat their performances flaw-lessly. Why should the composer become a suspect merely because he was not present at the Délassements-Comique the time of the murder? Was Palaiseau, I wondered, deliberately trying to steer Dupin on to a false trail? If so, he had no chance of success, for Dupin was too clever to be manipulated in such a matter.

"Why do you suspect one of your colleagues at the theater of being the guilty party, if you have said nothing to anyone?" Dupin asked, casually.

"Because I cannot suspect myself," Palaiseau retorted, "and Bazailles is as completely under the instrument's spell as I am. I merely help it to play—he helped it to determine *what* it should play. Erich Zann once played both roles, but neither I nor Bazailles is quite as versatile as he was."

"Are you suggesting that the *violin* is the true author of this heinous crime?" I asked, incredulously.

"I am merely giving Monsieur Dupin information that might be relevant," Palaiseau said—disingenuously, I thought. "The violin obviously could not be responsible, in the sense that it had a mind of its own, capable of entertaining a motive for murder and carrying out such a deed—but in the sense that it can and does cast a spell, I do believe that it might be implicated, in a deeper sense than merely being an object of the criminal's desire."

"But it has not *cast a spell* for the last fifteen years," Dupin pointed out. "Or, if it has, it has done so rather ineffectively. Would you like to come with us to the Rue d'Auseuil, and to bring the violin? Would you like to play it—or to help it play, if you prefer—in Erich Zann's old room?"

The expression on Palaiseau's face was impossible to read by candlelight—impossible for me, at any rate, but I suspected that it must be ugly. "No," he said, "I wouldn't. Not that I believe the madman's assertion that it was something that Zann was trying to hold at bay with his playing that struck him dead, let alone he continued to play long after he was dead. My superstition, if that's what it is, doesn't extend quite as far as *that*."

"You'd prefer to be left alone here, then, with the violin—and no one to protect you, until Groix and Lestrade arrive, but a *sergent de ville* posted in the street?" Dupin still seemed to be testing the water, to see whether Palaiseau was really prepared to let him leave.

"I'd certainly prefer that to carrying the Stradivarius through the streets of this *quartier* at dead of night," Palaiseau countered, "or the *quartier* where Zann lived, for that matter. Robbers love winter, for the long hours of darkness, and there'll be hundreds on the prowl in rise tonight, if not thousands. You'd be better advised to stay the night here, and not set off to the Rue d'Auseuil until after dawn." He hesitated, then added: "Do you, perchance, have the all-important envelope about your person?"

"What envelope?" Dupin parried.

"The envelope that Clamart gave you—the one that Zann left you in his will. Oh, don't look at me like that—I didn't get the information hot off the press from Clamart's killer. Fourmont told me years ago, just as he told me what you and he saw through Zann's window—the reason why the Rue d'Auseuil acquired its name. Why should he not, given that we were both parties to the oath? The poor fellow needed to talk to someone. Groix became effectively inaccessible once he was appointed Prefect, and Fourmont considered you to be dangerously eccentric—which is why, when Clamart tried to fob him off by telling him that you were the one who received the secondary legacy, and thus the only one privy to the real facts of the case, he came to see me instead."

Dupin came to his feet, abruptly. "*That*'s what I wanted to know!" he exclaimed. "Thank you, Palaiseau, for clearing that up. And thank you for keeping your word, for I know now that you gave nothing away...unless you talked in your sleep, in answer to the wrong questions." He saw my puzzled expression then, and immediately clarified his deductive process: "Whoever violated the grave and killed Clamart presumably had no idea that I had the envelope containing Zann's scores, until Clamart told him—or her. I didn't know, until just now, that Palaiseau ever knew that I had the envelope, but now I do know that he had that information, I know that he cannot have been the person who set this monster loose—not wittingly, at any rate."

"I already told you that," Palaiseau reminded him.

"Yes, and I apologize for not quite being able to believe you— for I knew that you, like Fourmont, have always mistrusted me, and might well be wary of telling me the truth. I can see now that the reason you are not overly afraid that you might be the murderer's next victim is that you really do suspect Bazailles of Clamart's murder. You know that he has already had every opportunity to do you harm and steal your violin, but has not taken any such opportunity, so you do not fear him now. Be warned, though—if the murderer really is one of your fellow players, your immunity will only last as long as the other requires the play to be performed. And to answer your question, in case anyone asks you while you sleep, no, I do not have the *all-important envelope* about my person, or anywhere else. It no longer exists: I burned it fifteen years ago. It broke my heart to do it, but it was necessary. I let Clamart and Groix know, but I did not see the need to inform you or Fourmont."

"Why, then did Clamart tell Fourmont that you had it?" Palaiseau asked.

"He didn't," Dupin pointed out. "He merely said that I was privy to the facts of the case. He knew that I had seen and read the scores, for that was why I had decided to get rid of them."

Palaiseau looked at the Chevalier for a moment or two, and I wondered how resentful he might be that Dupin had not handed over the scores to him, if he did not want them for himself. Eventually, though, all he said was: "I believe you when you say you burned them, because I know what kind of man you are— but no one else will believe it."

"I know that," Dupin replied. "I know it only too well—and I know, too, that it might cost me my life, if this murderer comes after me."

7.

It is not as easy to find a fiacre in the Boulevard du Temple at dead of night as it is on the Quais, and when we actually took our leave of Palaiseau I believed that Dupin's intention was simply to wait for Monsieur Groix to collect us in his relatively luxurious carriage. Indeed, I half-expected him to knock on the door of Henriette's lodge and ask whether we might sit by her fire rather than standing out in the cold, but he did not even glance in that direction, and the old woman did not come out or appear at her grille, which was now dark. Instead, Dupin really did set about searching for a cab.

"Shouldn't we wait here, as we agreed, in order to bring the Prefect up to date?" I asked.

"With what?" Dupin countered. "We have deduced that Palaiseau hasn't talked, or the murderer would have come after me directly rather than going to Clamart after searching the coffin. We have obtained no other significant clue."

I was startled by that, for it seemed to me that Dupin had spent a long time in conversation with the violinist, and surely would not have done so merely to obtain a single clue. He was still holding something back—and now, it seemed, he intended to hold it back from the Prefect of Police, as well as his closest friend.

"You don't believe that Monsieur Bazailles is implicated, then?" I said, warily.

"Perhaps he is—but Palaiseau's vague suspicion is certainly not sound evidence of any such implication. I want to know whether Clamart's murderer has been to the Rue d'Auseuil—and, if so, whether he went there before or after the murder. If he has not, or has only been there this evening, then we will know that he did not know where Zann once lived until he had talked to Clamart."

"Another datum that he could not have got from a loose-lipped gravedigger," I remarked.

"Indeed. I also want to know whether, if this mysterious person *has* been to the house in the Rue d'Auseuil, he has spent time gazing out of Erich Zann's window as well as searching his mansard. With any luck, the dust will be thick enough on the floor to have preserved a detailed record of any visitor's movements."

I half-expected that we might have to walk as far as the Champs-Élysées to find a cab, but we were fortunate. The restaurants with which the theaters were interspersed had not yet disgorged the last of the post-performance diners, and there were one or two fiacres still waiting by their side-doors in the hope of picking up late fares.

Dupin had no money at all on him now, but he had such an unshakable trust in my financial stability that he did not even bother to ask me whether I would be able to pay the coachman on arrival.

"Rue d'Auseuil," he said to the driver.

"Where?" that worthy queried.

"The street on near side of the sheer butte overlooking the Bièvre," Dupin explained. I got the impression, however, that there had been more surprise than ignorance in the coachman's reaction. He looked at me, as if to confirm that Dupin was, indeed, sane—and perhaps for confirmation that I was good for the fare. I nodded, confident, at least, of the answer to the second part of the tacit enquiry.

As the horse moved off, at the same weary pace as the nag that had brought us to the Boulevard de Crime, I said: "I still feel lost in the midst of a maze that seems to be increasing in complexity all the time. Did you really burn this mysterious envelope for which the murderer appears to be searching, or did you merely tell Palaiseau that in order that he might pass the information along, now that you've freed him from the terms of his oath?"

Dupin ignored the specific question. "I apologize for keeping you in the dark," he said. "Had I taken the opportunity earlier to talk abut Erich Zann, when your description of the play triggered my memory, you would have been better equipped to understand all this—but I had my reasons for discretion, as you are now aware. The business is so tangled that I hardly know where to begin the process of disentanglement, but it is usually best to tackle such problems by beginning at the beginning, and this affair began, so far as I was concerned, when Erich Zann asked to borrow my copy of the *Harmonies de l'Enfer* and I made the counter-offer of a verbal translation, in return for private performances of his music. I was unduly curious in those days, and not yet wholly rigorous in my thinking.

"The author of the *Harmonies de l'Enfer* signed himself Apollonius in honor of Apollonius of Tyana, although he added the title of Abbé as a primitive shield against accusations of heresy. Unfortunately, almost everything the modern world knows about Apollonius of Tyana is derived from a fictitious biography written by Philostratus, who tried to promote a cult by advertising the sage as a miracle-worker, in frank imitation of the manner in which early Christians represented Jesus of Nazareth. In fact, the original Apollonius was a neo-Pythagorean philosopher, who attempted to elaborate Pythagoras' notion that a proper understanding of the nature of the universe required to be sought in terms of the hidden virtues of numbers and musical harmonies, and the parallels between them.

"In recent times, of course, the uses of mathematics in producing representations of the universe, in matters of precise measurement and the formulation of scientific laws, have proved spectacularly successful, but such endeavor has been severed from its once-intimate connection with the concept of harmony. Although musicians like Johann Sebastian Bach have continued to find mathematics useful in the understanding and composition of music, the contribution of music to the understanding of reality has been minimized, and some of the key properties of music—in particular, the ability of music to represent and communicate emotional states, appealing to aspects of mind more fundamental than consciousness itself—have long been abandoned by the majority of philosophers as unfathomable mysteries, unamenable to rational analysis.

"The Medieval Apollonius and Erich Zann were, however, among the rare exceptions to this generalization. The former took his initial inspiration from his namesake, while the latter took his from his former mentor, Giuseppe Tartini, but both men set out in search of ecstasy: a musical and spiritual path to a paradisal state of mind. Both, alas, found their initial quests betrayed and subverted as soon as they achieved their initial successes."

"Subverted by what?" I put in. I was struggling to cope with Dupin's discourse, as usual, but I knew from experience that inserting prompts and questions sometimes helped me to cling on to the thread of his arguments.

"Something that has been given many names by those who have sensed its presence," Dupin said. "The Sumerians called it Tiamat, the Persians Ahriman. Christians, inevitably, have subsumed it within the concept of the Devil, but the Christian tendency to personalize the Devil, as a caricature of Pan or, more recently, as an urbane Mephistopheles, is a distraction. Of all the various conceptualizations, the one perhaps best-suited to the description of the phenomenon as it is humanly experienced is Nyarlathotep, the Crawling Chaos."

"I don't know that name," I admitted.

"It is to be found in the *Harmonies de l'Enfer* and various other texts that are sometimes called *forbidden*, in a stronger sense than merely being placed on the Roman Church's Index. Nyarlathotep is one of the Old Ones—a company of entities that are something other than gods or demons, although they have powers and inclinations that are somewhat similar. They reside, though not completely, in the dream-dimensions: spaces that surround and are connected to the three dimensions of space experienced by humans but lie beyond the scope of the human sensorium's mundane sustenance of consciousness. Nyarlathotep's seat is sometimes called Kadath: a region of the dream-dimensions that is exceedingly difficult to reach, even by the utmost exertions of the unentranced human mind.

"In our scientific era, we tend to think of consciousness in terms of observation and recording, as if it were merely a device for collecting and collating data, organizing them into a coherent and meaningful image of the world—albeit a device whose efficient operation is troubled by the anarchic workings of emotion and appetite, and the sometimes-nightmarish absurdity of dreams. Ever since Plato, philosophers have routinely conceived of human being as something fundamentally *divided*, in which noble and orderly rationality is engaged in a constant struggle with baser animal urges and the hectic distractions of dreams—but humans are still capable of feeling whole and undivided on occasion, especially when immersed in works of art, and most especially of all when immersed in music.

"It is possible, however, to conceive of consciousness in a different way, not as a collector but as a composer, not as a dealer in atomized data building rational edifices threatened, troubled and undermined by the seismic shocks of emotion and dream, but as a seeker and synthesizer of harmonies, forever attempting to bind all experience into a whole whose nature is essentially ecstatic, or sublime, in the technical sense of either term.

"The creative process of consciousness, seen in this light, is a fundamentally hopeful one, in that it works on the assumption that ecstasy and sublimity, once fully achieved, will be blissful and paradisal: the mental and moral optimum of which the human mind is capable. Insofar as we have been able to determine the truth, however, the reality is that the final fulfillment of consciousness is not blissful or paradisal in any simple or straightforward sense, but has an emotional texture that is far more frightful and horrific.

"Within this version of spiritualist philosophy, Heaven and Hell cannot be opposites or alternatives, in such a way that one might arrive at one or the other, dependent upon the moral health of one's soul. In the holistic way of thinking, Heaven and Hell can only be co-existent, intricately inter-twined, not merely bound together but somehow *in harmony*. In this way of thinking, therefore, Nyarlathotep, the Crawling Chaos, is not some external threat menacing the human mind with dissolution into madness, although it can easily take on that semblance in the rational imagination; it is something inherent within the human mind and essential to it—just as fundamental, in its own way, as the order inherent in methodical logic and mathematics.

"However we may choose to conceive of consciousness in the broadest sense, however, one truth that remains is this: in our waking lives, we are fugitives, taking refuge in a deliberately limited consciousness that strives to master and control emotion and to deny the capriciousness of dreams. When we sleep, our defenses are eroded, but we have countered that erosion by the strategic forgetfulness that dispels our dreams. There are, however, states intermediate between waking and sleep, in which that physiological strategy is far less effective. We enter one such state when we listen to, and respond to, music; we enter another when we submit to the magnetic effects that induce a somnambulistic or somniloquistic trance. We become particularly vulnerable when the two effects operate in combination: when we surrender, as players or as listeners to somnimusicality. We are uniquely well-equipped, then, to storm the heights of ecstasy and sublimity, paradise and bliss—and, by the same token, we are uniquely vulnerable to the effects of the Crawling Chaos. As the wisest of modern aesthetic philosophers, Edmund Burke, has pointed out, the sublime always contains an element of horror, and that element of horror is its truest essence, its most fundamental note."

It was high time for another interruption. "And is that what Erich Zann achieved, by means of his spoiled Stradivarius?" I said. "He attempted to storm the heights of ecstasy and sublimity, but failed, and only opened his soul to horror: to Nyarlathotep, the Crawling Chaos."

"Sometimes, my friend," Dupin said, despairingly, "I think that you are ever-intent on misunderstanding me, by oversimplifying everything I say. The whole point of what I have been saying is that Zann's Stradivarius—Palaiseau's Stradivarius— is not *spoiled* at all. In one scheme of reckoning, at least, it is the most perfect of all the instruments made by that man of genius, although even he seems to have been blind to the fact. Erich Zann did not make a failed attempt to storm the heights of ecstasy and sublimity, opening his soul to horror because he failed; it would be more correct to say that, thanks to his unique instrument, he *succeeded* in storming the heights of ecstasy—and that he opened his soul to horror *in consequence* of his success."

"But it killed him," I pointed out.

"Yes, it did," Dupin replied. "Another fault of rational consciousness is to regard death as if it were a kind of *failure of life*. The neo-Pythagoreans, of course, saw things differently; to them life and death were not contrasted opposites, but aspects of the same whole, essentially and intricately bound together. The truth is that 'death' is not the point at which life ends, but a process that runs alongside it, acting in collaboration with it.

"As individuals, we begin to die before we are even born; anatomists furnished with microscopes have now revealed that it is the selective death of cells within an amorphously-expanding embryo that sculpts the form of the individual, and physiologists of a more empirical stripe than the Marquis de Puységur have suggested that it is the selective withering of neural connections within the brain that sculpts the thinking mind. As a race, death is the price we pay for the eternally-progressive evolution that the Chevalier de Lamarck has recently identified, continually clearing the way for improved generations. We all must die, my friend, and we are all dying as we live; the horror of our consciousness of death is something intrinsic to that consciousness.

"Yes, Erich Zann died, and he died in the grip of the ultimate horror of the Crawling Chaos. If the witness to his death can be believed—and I think, in the main, that he can—then he died trying to ward off some subsidiary chaos-spawn: one of those entities that humans call demons. As that witness concluded, however—correctly, in my opinion—*he died of fright*. He died because he tried, in the end, to undo what he had done; terrified by his own success, he tried to use his music to *drive back* the horrors he had revealed, to refuse and escape them. From one viewpoint, at least, the tragedy was not so much that he died, but that he died a coward, having repented of his own success, trying in vain to retreat to mundanity—just as my tragedy, seen from that same viewpoint, is that, from the moment that I glimpsed what Erich Zann had seen in all its horrid glory, I elected to live as a coward, taking refuge to the full extent of my mental and moral abilities in fugitive, divided *rational* consciousness.

"Palaiseau was quite wrong to believe that I craved his inheritance, for I was not so reckless or brave as that. Indeed, I wanted *him* to have the violin, precisely because I considered him too dull a fellow ever to be able to play it as it required to be played. Nor was I wrong—but I had not taken into consideration the potential effects of animal magnetism. If my guess is sound, Palaiseau has been entranced—willingly, of course, but in a fashion that he could not have achieved without assistance. He has a collaborator now, just as Erich Zann briefly had a collaborator in me, although the balance of the collaboration is very different. There is, it appears, someone in the circle of his acquaintances who wants to scale the heights of ecstasy and sublimity, at any cost, but who cannot play the violin himself... or herself...and requires Palaiseau's assistance.

"The process works both ways, I think: the player needs an audience, just as the audience needs a player. When I proved too weak a reed in terms of providing a suitable audience for his greatest endeavor, Erich Zann grasped at the only other available straw: his fellow tenant. I doubt that he could have succeeded in what he did without the presence of the witness—although the witness was probably lucky to escape with his life, let alone his injured sanity."

"What has all this to do with the murders?" I asked.

Dupin groaned. "Is it not obvious, after all that I have said?" he complained. "Palaiseau has learned to play the Stradivarius at last, but he is no genius, no Erich Zann. He cannot *improvise*, as Zann could. He cannot compose as he plays; he can only play from someone else's score. If he is to reach the heights of ecstasy and sublimity, he needs *the music of Erich Zann*. He needs the *Harmonies of Hell*. His partner in ambition thought that the scores might be found in Zann's coffin, or in his lawyer's files—but all that he, or she, was able to learn from Clamart was that I received the subsidiary fraction of Zann's inheritance, and perhaps that I had burned it. We now know that Palaiseau could have told his partner that himself, had the question only been put to him—but somniloquists are notorious for their lack of initiative. If information is not demanded of them explicitly, they do not reveal it."

"Do you think that Clamart might have been magnetized too?" I asked. "Could that be how the murderer was able to strike him from behind, while he sat meekly in his chair?"

"Of course it could," said Dupin—but there was no contempt in his tone, and he seemed quite relieved that I had made an intelligent suggestion at last. "If that is the case, though—and I certainly cannot eliminate it from consideration on this account—then we are dealing with an exceptionally cold-blooded killer. If Clamart was Mesmerized, then he could easily have been instructed not to alert me to the danger I was in, and not to identify the source of that danger, without there being more than the slightest chance that the injunction might be ineffective. The fact that the Mesmerist preferred to murder his victim marks him as a very dangerous individual."

"Or her," I supplied, as Dupin seemed to have grown tired of inserting the caveat.

"Or her," he agreed.

"Are you convinced that it is someone involved in the production of the play?" I asked, my hand moving reflexively toward the pocket that held the program notes.

"It seems likely," he admitted, carefully, "but we must not blind ourselves to other possibilities."

"If your analysis of the situation is correct," I said, after a slight pause, "the problem might be partly solved simply by giving our adversary what he, or she, wants—by simply handing over the subsidiary element of Zann's legacy. I ask you again: did you really burn the manuscript?"

"You seem to be convinced that I could not have done so," Dupin observed. "You cannot believe that any collector of arcana could do such a thing."

He was correct in his estimation, but all I said in reply was: "It is as a collector of arcana that I have known you, my friend. I did not know you fifteen years ago."

"Well, if handing over the legacy was ever a possibility, it would have been eliminated from consideration now," Dupin said, with a sigh. "Bernard Clamart is dead, and our adversary must be held accountable for that—as he or she ought to have realized, before committing the murderer and obliterating the possibility of a negotiated settlement. Perhaps the person in question did not know who and what I am when Clamart revealed my name...or perhaps he knew exactly who and what I am, and it was sheer frustration at the prospective difficulty of his task that drove him to murder...although I should not leave out of account the possibility that his plan is more convoluted than I have so far imagined."

"If it is only Clamart's murder that has eliminated the possibility from consideration," I pointed out, "then you must have been telling a strategic lie when you told Palaiseau that you burned the envelope containing your part of the inheritance."

"Must I?" he retorted, deliberately teasing me. "Well, perhaps. Have you also deduced, by means of your ever-scrupulous logic, why Zann split his legacy in two?"

"You explained it yourself a few moments ago," I pointed out. "He realized, after he began playing to you, that his endeavor was an implicitly collaborative one—that his ultimate success would require an audience of at least one. He realized that if Palaiseau was to continue his work after his wealth, then he would need a collaborator too. He was trying to bring the two of you together. Obviously, the ploy failed—if anything, it had the opposite effect, by promoting mutual suspicion and antipathy."

"Obviously," Dupin echoed, in a sarcastic tone, which I took to imply that not only was the conclusion not obvious, but that it was obviously not the case. I was nettled by his seeming contempt; I felt that if I had made a mistake, it could only be by virtue of neglecting some item of information that he had not yet revealed to me. If his intention was to suggest that the mysterious Erich Zann had intended to provoke, and somehow to exploit, the mutual suspicion and antipathy that his divided bequest had produced, I could not see any possible motive for that in what I had so far been told.

The cab drew to a halt, then, and the coachman took the trouble to shout: "Rue d'Auseuil." I got down first, as I had to pay for the ride, and fumbled for coins. As I handed the correct amount over, with an extra few centimes as a tip, the fellow murmured: "You've a hard climb still ahead of you, mind."

I frowned, but did not take him to task. It was not until I turned round and looked at the most remarkable street in the entirety of Paris that I saw what he meant.

8.

The animal drawing the fiacre had not actually set foot on the Rue d'Auseuil itself, because that insane thoroughfare became too steep for easy negotiation within the span of the horse-drawn vehicle. We had been dropped on the bank of the stream, whose sluggish waters must have been as black by day as they were by night, to judge by the stench they emitted—although the surface carried a pallid shroud at present, by courtesy of a freezing fog that had formed as the evening cooled. The Bièvre was rimmed by brick warehouses whose greasy windows must have been almost opaque in daylight, although they reflected the light of the sparse lights distributed along a narrow towpath in an eerie fashion.

The slope of the steam itself was gradual, but the initial phase of the Rue d'Auseuil climbed up the butte that loomed over it like a cliff path, consisting of sharply-inclined ramps punctuated by flights of steps, some of them stone and some of them wooden, like slanted bridges extending over gaps in the natural ledge. Then it veered inwards into the body of the hill, so that there was a short and exceedingly narrow section with houses on both sides, before it emerged again as a mere ledge protected from the precipice by a wooden rail. All the houses distributed along the street, regardless of whether they faced the empty abyss or one another, seemed to be etched into the face of the butte, or jammed into crevices—all except for the one at the very top, which loomed up from the great mound of earth and rock like a battered hat unsteadily perched on a tramp's head, its brim turned up into a high wall blocking off the edge of the abyss. Because of the broadness of the mound's base, and the fact that the higher section of the street ran through a cleft, the house at the top was the only one that stood close enough to the edge to offer an uninterrupted view of the precipice, although its uppermost gable window was the only one whose view was not blocked by the wall.

I never had the slightest doubt that the topmost house was the one to which we were headed, or that the gable window of its awkward mansard was that of Erich Zann's garret. As Dupin and I toiled up that miniature mountain, I reflected that Erich Zann had made the same climb every night for years, having already walked all the way from the old Ambigu. Surely, I thought, exhaustion would have killed him eventually, if terror had not intervened.

When we finally reached the house at the top of the hill, even though we could not yet look down upon the mist-shrouded stream, or outwards over the broader waters of the Seine and the vast city, I felt that we were already on the threshold of another world—even though, in terms of mere measurement, we were not nearly so far above the level of the river as the heights of Montmartre.

The door of the house had previously been boarded up, rather comprehensively, but the boards had been recently stripped away. The lock on the door had been broken, and the only thing securing it shut at present was a timber prop.

"Someone has clearly got here ahead of us," I remarked, exercising my gift for understatement.

Dupin did not answer, but removed the prop and made his way inside. Just inside the threshold, in a narrow vestibule, he took a candle from his pocket, and a flat tray with a small spike on which to mount it, but he had to ask me to make use of my tinder-box in order to light it. I obliged, and we went into the hallway. The foot of the staircase was directly ahead of us, no more than a few feet away. There was a single door to our left, which apparently gave access to all the ground floor rooms.

The footprints in the dust suggested that I had been correct to use the singular. Some*one* had got here ahead of us. I watched Dupin compare the size of his own footprint with that of our recent predecessor. His feet were unusually small, for a man's, but they were still larger than those of our adversary. Dupin's careful *or she* echoed in my consciousness once more...but I could not remember, having only seen them briefly during a curtain-call, whether Monsieur Bazailles or Monsieur Soulié might have had unusually small feet for a man. I was confident that the actor playing the Mephistophelean manifestation of the Devil in *La Cantate du Diable* could not have made those foot-prints, but that was the only elimination of which I felt certain.

"Can you tell when the footprints were made?" I asked.

"Not exactly," he said, "but not tonight, I think—which means that the treasure-seeker *did* know where Zann lived before going to see Clamart, and presumably searched the whole of this building before searching the coffin. He is undoubtedly methodical."

So saying, he went through the door to investigate the ground-floor rooms. The stranger had been there before us, apparently going back and forth several times.

"The stove has not been lit recently," Dupin observed, as we peered into the kitchen, "but there is fire-wood in the bunker that certainly has not been lying there for years."

"The person with the small feet intends to come back, then?" I suggested.

"Almost certainly," Dupin agreed, "and perhaps to stay for some little while. The Prefect will need to post spies to watch the house."

After consulting the footsteps in the corridor again, Dupin went up the stairs. He did not pause, however, on any of the three intermediate floors, going straight up to the topmost one. In doing that, he ignored all the side-tracks that our predecessor had followed, so he was evidently impatient to investigate the room in which Erich Zann had died.

Once he had opened the door to Zann's apartment, Dupin went straight to the window overlooking the precipice, the stream, the warehouse roofs, the Seine and the city. Then he knelt down to examine the footprints there, lowering his candle so as to shine the light on every speck of dust and cobweb.

"No," he said, ruminatively. "There's no evidence that the seeker spent an unusually long time here, staring out of the window. Does that imply that he did not know the significance of the window, or merely that he did not feel any need to stand in contemplation?"

In the meantime, I looked around the room carefully. There was no longer a bed there—presumably it had been sturdy enough to be sold, although it must have had a bolted iron frame in order to be transported downstairs. There was, however, a battered wooden writing-desk still in place against one wall, together with a stool hewn from similarly well-seasoned wood. There was also a small side-table, badly marked on the surface, set against the opposite wall, and a moth-eaten armchair beside the fireplace. Abandoned in a corner was a folding music-stand, now straitened into a clumsy, rusty javelin, devoid of any proper functionality.

The mantelpiece bore an ill-assorted collection of candle-trays and candlesticks, together with—surely the most significant items of all—a dozen new wax candles and a tinder-box. They had not been there very long; when our predecessor returned, he—or she—evidently intended to use this garret for some purpose, if not as a bedroom.

Dupin took the time to do what the earlier visitor had apparently not bothered to do. He stood before the window-sill for an unusually long interval, staring out. The ill-glazed window had been closed and shuttered, but our predecessor had thrown back the shutters and opened the leaded casement, perhaps to let light into the room rather than to expose the view. While Dupin stood stock still, I moved forward to join him, letting the door swing to behind me, borne by its own weight, until it stood ajar.

I could hardly help remembering what Dupin and Palaiseau had said, in the course of their conversation, about there being something that he, the physician Fourmont and Monsieur Groix had seen, but that their co-conspirators had not. At first, I had assumed that the reference in question was to Erich Zann's terror-stricken face, but had relaxed that assumption as time went by. Now I felt confirmed in the hypothesis that they had actually seen something through the window.

"What is it that you're looking for?" I asked Dupin.

"Nothing," he replied. "Mercifully, that is what I see—in the conventional sense of *nothing significant*. The barrier that separates our world from the dimensions that impinge upon it must be thin here—perhaps that is why the house was originally built in such a precarious situation, although I have to admit that it has withstood the ravages of wind, rain and lightning with surprising sternness, and has amply justified the faith of its builders—but the boundary remains in place, when there is no vibratory force to breach it."

"What boundary do you mean?" I asked.

"The three dimensions of perceived space are a trifle illusory in their regularity," Dupin told me. "The dream-dimensions have a physical presence of their own, which sometimes allows them to intrude through the walls of geometrical order almost as easily as they break the papery walls of sleep. Sometimes, the Crawling Chaos can be seen as well as felt. Here, as mapmakers were once wont to say, be dragons—but not tonight."

"Did you expect to see dragons?" I asked him.

"No," he replied. "Not at present."

"But you do remember seeing dragons—or monsters, or demons—once before: on the night when Erich Zann died?"

"Yes," he said, "I did see dragons, monsters, or demons. They were ghostly by then, for the substance lent to them temporarily by Zann's playing had evaporated—but they were still lurking at the periphery of vision, and the echoes of their own ecstatic singing were still faintly audible, in my mind if not my ears."

"Were they sirens rather than dragons, then?" I asked.

"No," he replied. "Their voices had nothing seductive about them, and their singing was more akin to a series of long, slow notes sounded by a stringed instrument—not a violin, but something even lower in pitch than a bass cello—than it was to the livelier and more colorful notes produced by human vocal cords."

"What did these monsters look like?" I asked. "Had they wings? Were they serpentine? Were they the really dragons of legend, or something more akin to the Lernean Hydra, or the demons of Dante's Inferno?"

"Perhaps, had they still had material substance, they would have assumed some such form," he told me, "but I can't be sure. The witness who made the deposition did not describe them in those terms, but he saw them when they had barely begun to emerge, just as I saw them on the brink of disappearance, when they were similarly phantasmal. In his description, they had no shape at all; although the music Zann played, in combination with his own particular anxieties, had prompted him to imagine dancing satyrs engaged in a furious bacchanal, all that he actually *saw* was the blackness of infinite space itself, animated by, in his words, 'chaos and pandemonium'. What he saw, I believe, was Nyarlathotep, not crawling, as is its habit, but roused to a state of uncommon excitement, stretching the very fabric of reality in its fervor, mightier by far than any organizing divinity, insuppressible and indestructible. It seemed plural, of course, because it is the one thing in the universe that cannot be envisaged as a whole. It is the unwhole within the whole, which complements the whole by its negation of wholeness, and which is, in the purest and most absolute sense of the term, *unwholesome*."

I actually shivered in response to that bizarre description, vague as it was—but the shiver moved me to an immediate protest. "Such decadent terminology seems unnatural in your mouth," I told him. "You are the great rationalist, the master of logic. Were you not unkind to Palaiseau just now, when he hinted at a supernatural explanation for his new-bound ability to play Zann's Stradivarius?"

"I suppose I was," he admitted. "Not so much because I could not believe him, I must admit, as because I did not want to believe him, and I wanted to help him not to believe it. I have repressed the vision that I saw through this window for fifteen years, but standing on the spot brings it back to me with renewed force. Unlike the *vehmgerichte*, I cannot believe that Zann had made any literal pact with the Devil—but I heard him play, and knew by virtue of what I read to him from the *Harmonies de l'Enfer* what his ambition was. He was a reckless man, and his genius was capable of breaking the bounds of our self-imposed prison of reality."

"But he is dead now," I reminded him. "Palaiseau might have learned to play the Stradivarius, but can he really play as Erich

Zann played?"

Dupin turned toward me, and smiled. "You're right," he said. "Zann is dead, and Palaiseau—even Palaiseau armed with the un-lost Stradivarius—is only a theater musician, fit for playing a caricature of Tartini's dream, but not for breaching the walls of the world. If someone else believes he can do better...well, I remain to be convinced that he is anything more than a vain fool. Musicians of the ability of Erich Zann are rare, mercifully. I must not allow myself to be carried away by a surge of superstitious anxiety. We are here to gather evidence to help us identify a murderer, and that is all. We must focus our attention on the task in hand."

"Good," I said, nodding in approval—but then I quivered again, even more profoundly than before. I had heard a noise.

Dupin heard it too: the sound of soft footsteps ascending the stairs that we had recently climbed. In spite of the fact that the climber was obviously trying to be quiet, muffling his footfalls as best he could, there was no concealing his slow and ponderous tread. He was obviously a far heavier man than me, Dupin or our mysterious predecessor.

I was rooted to the spot, but Dupin was magnificent. He simply strode to the door, candle in hand, and drew back the unfastened batten.

"*Bonsoir*, Lestrade," he said to the man on the staircase. "Should you not be guarding your master?"

"I forbade him to come up here alone, as he urgently wished to do when he glimpsed the flicker of a candle in the high window," the inspector told him, seemingly unperturbed by the fact that he had given himself away. "He guessed that it must be your light, but I persuaded him to wait in the carriage at the foot of the hill until I had made sure. The coachman is an experienced agent, armed with a brace of pistols, and he is skilled in their use, should any necessity arise. I'm glad to see that the Prefect's instincts were sound, as usual—he felt sure that we would find you here, since you were not at Palaiseau's. I assume that you were not in time to apprehend the person with the tiny feet."

"Did Palaiseau not tell you that we had come here?" Dupin asked, his voice suddenly taking on a new edge of anxiety.

"Monsieur Palaiseau was unable to tell us anything," the inspector reported, laconically. "He was dead when we arrived, with his head bashed in from behind, like Clamart's. Monsieur Groix concluded that the murderer must have been waiting while you were interviewing Palaiseau, ready to make his move as soon as you departed."

"But Palaiseau should have been safe, at least for tonight!" Dupin exclaimed, in genuine distress. "Unless I have misjudged his motive badly, the murderer needs him to play the violin!"

"The Stradivarius has been stolen," Lestrade said, still with stolid equanimity. "Monsieur Groix assumes that its theft must have been the motive for Palaiseau's murder—and presumably the other as well."

Dupin's candlelit face was utterly distraught. "Whether it was or was not," he declared, "I have made a serious error. The chain of my logic is broken; there is a complication in the scheme that I have not even glimpsed, as yet—and it has cost poor Palaiseau his life! What a dire and culpable fool I am! I expected the schemer to come after me, not even as a murderer, but as a trickster or a supplicant. Instead, he is playing with me, as a cat plays with a mouse. He is *taunting* me."

"Or she," I said, automatically.

"Oh, don't be more of a fool than you can help!" Dupin exclaimed, intemperately. "This is not a woman's work—I have been wrong about everything, including my estimate of possibilities, and I must make up the lost ground before any further tragedy occurs. Come on!" He set off down the stairs at a rapid pace.

Lestrade and I followed him, but struggled to keep up. For once, Dupin was carried away, leaving all his native tranquility and indolence behind.

"Is Palaiseau's murder not a crime that a woman could have committed?" I asked him, when I eventually caught up—

by which time we were outside the house. I was still some-what aggrieved. "How, then, did the murderer gain access to Monsieur Palaiseau's apartment, under the noses of the *sergent de ville* and the watchful Henriette? On whom, if not a woman he knew and trusted, would Palaiseau have turned his back when he knew what had happened to Clamart?"

Dupin shook his head, as if I were merely being silly—but he did pause to ask Lestrade what Henriette had had to say for herself.

"Nothing," reported the inspector. "She's dead too—but not with a crushed skull. She was found in her armchair next to the fire, apparently having passed away peacefully in her sleep. She was very old."

"*Apparently*!" I repeated, suggestively. "And what about the *sergent de ville*? What had he to say."

"That he saw no one go in after you came out. He claimed that if the murderer really was waiting for you to leave before committing the crime, then he—or she—must have been waiting *inside* the house." We clattered down a flight of wooden steps attached to the face of the butte, which shook so tremu-lously under our combined weight that I feared it might come away from the rocky wall.

"Let us hope that it is so," Dupin said, "since it is now too late to hope for any better eventuality. Poor Henriette! Poor Palaiseau!"

"Why should we hope that the murderer was inside the house?" I wanted to know.

"Because an eavesdropper would surely have heard me say that the document has been burned—and must, therefore, heard Palaiseau say that he believed me. On the other hand, he did go on to kill Palaiseau, and probably Henriette too. The *sergent de ville* is obviously untrustworthy, though. Since he did not see the murderer make his escape, he could just as easily have failed to see him make his entrance. We do not know for sure that the murderer overheard anything at all."

We finally reached the Prefect's carriage, and Monsieur

Groix seemed very glad to see us, although we were all panting for breath. "Thank the Lord!" he said. "I feared that he might have killed you too, and left your candle burning to guide us to you. I've doubled the guard on the Rue Dunôt, although I haven't removed the sentry outside your house in the Faubourg, Monsieur—even so, I doubt that either of you will get much sleep tonight."

"On the contrary," said Dupin. "I will sleep, because I must— but I shall certainly try to do so with one eye open, with a pistol under my pillow."

"You should stay with me in the town-house," I told him.

"Quite the contrary," he said. "I should let you alone, in order not to expose you to any further danger. If the murderer wants me, I shall be pleased to deal with him man to man, in the hope that I might put an end to this madness before any more innocents are hurt. Besides which, my own apartment has but one door, and it has a good lock. The windows are inaccessible from the ground, without the assistance of wings. I shall feel much safer there than I ever could in your draughty mansion, which has a dozen easy access-points for a determined burglar."

Whether the nobler reason or the baser one was the true motive for his insistence, I felt obliged to concede the point, although I could not be grateful to him for pointing out that a single sentry could not possibly serve to keep me safe from any intrusion, although two would surely be adequate to prevent the violation of his abode. It was on the tip of my tongue to ask the Prefect for more protection, but I refrained; he would only say that I was probably irrelevant to the murderer's quest, whatever it might be, while Dupin must now be reckoned to be in greater danger than before.

When the carriage got under way again, Dupin rapidly summarized what we had learned from Palaiseau for the Prefect's benefit, and what we had deduced from the footprints in the house in the Rue d'Auseuil—but he never mentioned Nyarlathotep, the Crawling Chaos, or the Abbé Appolonius' *Harmonies de l'Enfer*, or the possibility that the music of Erich

Zann had been capable of opening the world to invasion by the ultimate horror of sublimity; nor did the Prefect mention any such possibility himself.

"Perhaps, now that he has the violin, the criminal will desist from further atrocities," Monsieur Groix suggested.

"Perhaps he will," Dupin agreed—but I could almost hear his voice adding, silently, for the sole benefit of his own calculating brain: *And perhaps the worst of his atrocities is yet to come.* I knew that he must be thinking furiously, recalculating every possibility.

"You should post a guard on the house with the high window, Monsieur," I told him. "The firewood and the candles suggest that the blackguard with the small feet intends to return."

"Yes," said Dupin. "You must do that, *Monsieur le Préfet*— but your watchers must be discreet. At all costs, they must not act intemperately—*especially if they hear music coming from that room.*"

"There will be no need for intemperate action, Monsieur," Lestrade put in. "The house has only one exit. If anyone goes in, even if they are a dozen strong, they will be caught in a trap, and we shall have all the time in the world to gather them in as we please when they come out again."

"Again, you must not act intemperately," Dupin insisted. "If anyone comes out after going in, have them followed and watched rather than arrested—don't make a move unless and until there is manifest danger."

"Very well," the Prefect conceded, with a readiness that no longer surprised me. "Let us hope, then, that the villain—or villains, if they do turn out to be a dozen strong—sticks to his plan, and returns to the scene of poor Zann's demise, bringing the Stradivarius with him."

"Yes," said Dupin, not very enthusiastically. "Let us hope that he does."

"I'll be sure to let you know of any developments, Dupin," Monsieur Groix promised. "With luck, you'll be in on the climax of the hunt."

Having made that promise—which, I had taken note, made no mention of me—the Prefect of the Paris Police, the one remaining sharer of Erich Zann's dire secret, scrupulously delivered me to my home, in advance of delivering Dupin to his—and then, presumably, went on to his own, in order to bear the brunt of his own insomnia.

9.

I suspected as soon as I had closed the door of the vestibule behind me that there was someone in the house—someone waiting patiently for my return—but I did not trust the sensation, for I thought that it was probably a product of my own overexcited imagination. I was tempted to call out to the *sergent de ville* who was stationed under the arch of the coaching-entrance, but the thought of looking foolish if he helped me to search the house and we found nothing urged me to compromise with my fear—with the result that, although I did not call for help, I did not replace my swordstick in the umbrella-stand in the hallway or take off my overcoat.

I went into the gloomy sitting-room where Dupin and I had spent the evening, and immediately went to stoke up the fire, which I had fed and bedded down before leaving, but which was on the point of going out nevertheless. There was enough life in the embers to ignite a handful of kindling, and I added two substantial logs before turning my attention to the candles. I had left three of them burning in trays on the mantelpiece, but two had burned all the way down and expired—hence the gloominess of the room. I used the sole survivor to light two fresh candles—good-quality wax candles, like those we had found on the mantelpiece of Erich Zann's old room—and then turned round to survey the illuminated room.

My hope and rational expectation was that I would find it empty, so that I might pick up one of the candle-trays by its looped handle and carry it methodically from room to room, searching the ground floor first, then the first floor, and finally the third—satisfying myself, by that process, that I really was alone in the house. Alas, the chair in which Dupin had been sitting a few hours earlier was now occupied by another man, who had been sitting so very still, shaded by the wings of the chair, that he had been virtually invisible until the renewed candlelight set the shadows to flight.

My acquaintance with Dupin had served to train my habits. The first thing I looked at, once the frisson of terror had died down sufficiently to liberate my thoughts, was his boots, which were neatly placed on the rug in front of the chair rather than extended over the rim of the fore-surround. They were larger than my own, and could not possibly have left the footprints I had recently seen in the house at the summit of the Rue d'Auseuil.

Then I looked at his face, although I took note, as my gaze shifted, of the fact that his legs were long and his torso broad. I did not recognize the face, which was that of a man in his forties, pale and clean-shaven, with odd, pencil-thin eyebrows.

I was tempted to draw the blade of my swordstick and menace him with it, although he seemed to be unarmed, and his hands were relaxed, resting in plain view on the arms of the chair. I resisted the temptation, but I kept a firm grip of the stick, ready to bring the blade into play at a moment's notice. I was almost prepared to believe that the intruder was one of Groix's multitudinous agents, commissioned to watch over me at close quarters, until he spoke—in English.

"There's no need for alarm, old chap" he said. "We have no intention of hurting you."

The significant word in that small speech was, of course, *we*—but I did not focus on it immediately, for I was too taken up by the fact that I recognized his baritone voice.

"Mr. Hood," I said. "I did not know you immediately, since you are not made up as Mephistopheles, with your widow's-peak wig, your goatee and your jet-black eyebrows."

"Actors," he said, "are required to be masters of disguise. I hope you will forgive me for taking the liberty of sitting down by your fire, but I have been waiting here for a long time, and it's a cold night. I did not want to poke the fire or relight the candles that had gone out, for fear of alarming the policeman outside."

"I could call out to him, and have you arrested," I observed. I also observed that, although he had not dared to disturb the fire or the candles, he had had no such qualms about the brandy decanter I kept on the sideboard. There was an empty glass on the little table beside the armchair, and I judged from the level of the decanter that it must have been emptied at least three times over.

"Of course you could," Mr. Hood replied, "but in that case, neither of us would learn anything—and I think that we are both willing victims of the disease of curiosity."

Only actors, I thought, *talk in such colorful terms—and they only do it because they are the puppets of fanciful writers.* Aloud, I said: "If you have been waiting here for a long time, I take it that you did not murder Paul Palaiseau?"

It was a shrewd gibe. His pathetically thin eyebrows rose, and his eyes widened. "Palaiseau is dead?" he queried. "Are you sure?"

"I have the word of the Prefect of the Parisian Police himself," I told him, loftily.

"Ah yes," he murmured. "The Prefect of Police. That is a most unwelcome complication. We do not like that at all. A dire inconvenience. If you do not intend to call for help, or attack me, perhaps you ought to sit down."

I sat down, not because he wanted me to but because I was weary, and my legs were stiff with the cold. Luxurious as the Prefect's carriage was, it was still bitterly cold in the early hours of a winter morning. When I extended my feet toward the fire the actor did likewise, as if given tacit permission. The flames were becoming more excited now that the logs had caught; the resin leaking from the heartwood was sizzling and sputtering.

"What do you want from me, Mr. Hood?" I asked.

He did not seem to be in any hurry to tell me—or, indeed, to do anything at all. His attitude was odd. There was nothing of the automaton or marionette about his speech or posture, but I had never seen a man so utterly devoid of self-alertness. The normal state of human consciousness has a certain ineffable anxiety about it; while we are awake, we are always slightly on our guard, watchful of our surroundings and ourselves, intent on making a good impression even when we are not manifestly under scrutiny. Mr. Hood was not. I wondered briefly whether it might be a simple effect of over-relaxation from playing a role on stage, but I decided almost immediately that I was, in fact, confronted by a somnambulist, who was also a somniloquist. This was not the murderer, but it *was* his instrument.

"Speak of the Devil, and you see the tip of his tail," I murmured, remembering that there is many a true word spoken in jest.

"That is not how the Devil is costumed, nowadays," the actor told me. "In Medieval miracle plays, I suppose, he wore shaggy leggings with a tail sewn on to their arse, not to mention horns glued to his forehead—but fashions change. Mephistopheles is civilized now—more so, in most respects, than his victims."

"Urbanity and civilization are not the same," I replied.

He smiled wanly. "Do you believe in the Devil?" he asked, almost as if he were genuinely interested to hear the answer.

"Not the Devil represented in miracle plays," I told him, "enthroned in a fiery Hell and wielding a culinary trident. I believe in sin, though, and temptation."

The actor nodded his head. "So do I," he said. "These Frenchmen have a nice phrase: *la beauté du diable*. They use it often to refer to the glamour and seductive magnetism that pubescent girls acquire: the appeal of lust. The theater trades on it to an inordinate extent. There is a sense, though, in which *all* beauty is the Devil's beauty—that beauty itself is pure, unalloyed temptation. Especially the beauty of music."

"The Devil is reputed to have all the best tunes," I remarked.

"The point is," he told me, "that the Devil has *all* the tunes.

Music itself is the Devil's work—perhaps his finest work."

"I don't believe that," I told him. "Nor do I believe that ecstasy and sublimity are intrinsically diabolical, or even intrinsically horrific. I have never read the *Harmonies de l'Enfer*, admittedly, but I'm not the kind of person who is easily swayed by textual rhetoric. Were you really sent here to discuss theodicy, Mr. Hood? With *me*?"

He sighed. "No," he admitted, "but I have been waiting here for quite some time, and what is a man to do when sitting in dim light beside a dwindling fire but turn to philosophy?"

"Drink, apparently," I said, dryly. "Doubtless the brandy helped to turn your philosophizing in a maudlin direction. What is it that you really want?"

"Erich Zann's manuscript," he said, in a tone of voice that suggested no expectation of success. "The finest music of all—we hope."

"I don't have it," I told him. "Dupin says that he burned it, because it was too dangerous to be played, and I have no reason to doubt him. It's gone."

Hood sighed again. "That's what Clamart said."

"Were you there when Clamart was murdered?" I asked.

"Of course not," he retorted. "I was on stage, as you know full well. You saw the play, did you not? You know what my role demands."

I nodded my head, slowly—and it occurred to me that in mentioning that Monsieur Bazailles was only required to present himself on stage for the final curtain-call, Palaiseau had called attention to an important detail. Of all the members of the cast of *La Cantate du Diable*, there was only one for whom the performance did not provide an alibi for the time of Clamart's murder.

"Do you really believe Monsieur Dupin when he says that he destroyed the sheet music?" Hood asked.

It was an awkward question. "Yes," I lied.

"But he did hear it played, did he not?" the actor persisted. "And he must have read the scores before burning them, even if he really did burn them? The music is still engraved in his memory."

"A good memory is one that is adept in forgetting," I told him. "It is a careful and judicious sieve, not a lumber-room or an Archive of State. Monsieur Dupin has an excellent memory."

He smiled, and once again, I saw the Mephistophelean play of his features, of which he had made such clever use on stage. "But he suffers far worse than you or I from the disease of curiosity. You might be surprised, my American friend, to discover how careless and injudicious the sieve of human memory becomes, in response to an expert Mesmerist."

Given that I had adapted three substantial accounts of my friend for publication in American periodicals, two of which were in print, I felt free to talk about my friend to Mr. Hood. The relevant information was, so to speak, already in the public domain. "Dupin is a master analyst," I told him, "and a brilliant logician. He has studied Mesmerism himself, and I would back his knowledge of it against your master's expertise in any circumstances whatsoever. He is little-known at present, even in Paris, but he will be very famous one day, and a cardinal exemplar to all men intent on solving the important puzzles of life. You cannot defeat him. If he holds the secret of the music of Erich Zann, you will never force or persuade him to release it"

"*The important puzzles of life*," the actor echoed. "I like that. I'll be sure to mention the phrase to Monsieur Soulié—although the fellow seems to be diverting his attention away from the theater now, in order to concentrate his efforts on *feuilleton* serials. He was not always that manner of man, though, was he? Your Monsieur Dupin, that is, not Monsieur Soulié. He once had more...Romantic inclinations."

"I have not known him very long," I said. "I have only known him as he is now—but I do know him, and I trust him implicitly. He is a great man."

Mr. Hood suddenly leaned forward, tempting me to draw my blade—but he did not raise his hands or threaten me in any way. He simply looked me in the eyes with his Mephistophelean gaze—whose power seemed tangibly diminished by the absence of the fake eyebrows that he employed in performance—and said: "He betrayed the trust of Erich Zann. He did not honor his legacy."

"I can't agree with you," I said. "On the basis of what I have learned tonight—in somewhat tangled fashion, I admit—my firm opinion is that that Monsieur Dupin has taken exceedingly good care of Erich Zann's legacy, by guarding its secret very carefully. Much more carefully, it seems, than poor Paul Palaiseau."

"Palaiseau has been a great disappointment too," Hood replied, a trifle distantly, although he was still leaning forward. "Perhaps that's why he's dead."

"His murder was not part of the grand plan, then?" I queried. "Who made the plan, and who is changing it by the hour? Who killed Clamart, Palaiseau and Henriette?"

"Henriette?" the actor countered, in seemingly-authentic bewilderment. "Who on Earth is Henriette?"

"Palaiseau's concierge," I replied, impatiently.

"The old crone? Why would he kill *her*?" Hood still seemed genuinely puzzled.

"Who is *he*?" I asked again—in search of confirmation rather than revelation. It was obvious now, who *he* must be, however difficult it might be to believe.

Hood settled back into his chair, ignoring the question. "Will you tell me where Dupin hid the Zann documents?" he asked, as if he felt obliged to ask in spite of knowing the answer.

"He burned them," I repeated.

"You had best be careful about voicing that assertion," the actor muttered. "True or not, it makes him angry. He's beautiful when he's angry—and terrible."

"Did he become angry more than once tonight?" I asked. "Is that why Palaiseau is dead?"

"Your guess is as good as mine," the actor said, his baritone voice becoming oddly plaintive.

I knew that I ought to be patient, and to prolong the interview for as long as possible, in order to obtain as much information as possible, but I was very tired, and the blazing fire seemed impotent to soothe the cold that had crawled into my very bones. "I would like you to leave my house, now, Mr. Hood," I said. "If you go quietly, I will let you leave without alerting the policeman at my door. If you will not go quietly, I'm sure that the Perfect of Police would be only too happy to accommodate you in the Conciergerie until we arrest the murderer whose accomplice you are." To emphasize my threat, I separated the two halves of the swordstick and showed him the blade.

"I'm afraid that you don't quite understand the situation, old chap," Hood murmured, quite unintimidated by the sight of the long and gleaming dagger. "I'm a sportsman, so I'll give you one more chance. If you can tell me where the manuscript is, we might be able to end this without anyone else getting hurt. If you can do that, I'll be glad to leave, quietly, and you'll probably never see me again—not on the Parisian stage, at any rate."

"I have never seen the document to which you refer," I relied, stonily, "and I have no reason to doubt my friend's word regarding its fate. Now, I give *you* one more chance: either you leave immediately, or you can explain everything to the agents of the Sûreté."

I leaned a little further forward as I spoke, in order to extend the tip of my blade toward his throat—which was undoubtedly a mistake, since it not only opened up the opportunity for him to grab my wrist, but gave the person who smashed a terracotta vase over my head more room to deliver what was, in any case, an awkward and clumsy blow. Absurdly, all I could think about, as I lurched further forward, trying in vain to turn my agonized head, was that Bernard Clamart had not been knocked unconscious by the first blow either; it had taken three to finish him off.

Had I reacted more decisively, I suppose I might have been able to stab Mr. Hood through the heart. As things were, he parried my blow with the poker, which he had snatched up from the hearth in his right hand, and seized my wrist with his left, imposing an irresistibly stern grip that completed my helplessness. He forced the blade down, all the way to the carpet, and then he trapped it with his huge boot, to ensure that I could do him no harm. With slightly blurred vision, I saw blood drops appearing on the carpet and the polished blade, having dripped from my head.

Eventually, however, I contrived to look behind me at the person who had hit me.

It was a blond-haired boy: the Devil's other half, in Monsieur Soulié's play. He seemed, even at close range, to be no more than twelve years old—a mere child, not even adolescent.

In a voice that did not seem at all angelic, at least for the moment, the seeming child said to his counterpart: "I got here as soon as I could. Palaiseau's dead."

"I thought we needed him," the English actor said. "In fact, I was under the impression that we couldn't do anything further without him."

"We never needed him," the soprano said. "I know exactly what we need to do, now." He looked down at me, then, and said: "This is all Dupin's fault. No one had to die, and you didn't have to get hurt—but don't worry. You might get out of this alive, if you behave yourself. Will you release the knife and come with us quietly, or do I have to break another of your precious ornaments?" He was being sarcastic; the vase had been valueless.

I screamed for help, although I should have been able to deduce that the *sergent de ville* outside was no longer in a position to help me. Unlike the candlestick with which the monstrous child had slain Clamart, however, the vase with which he had hit me had shattered into smithereens, and he had not had time to pick up a substitute. He had no means of silencing me himself. It was the English actor's long arm that snaked around my neck and caught me in a choke-hold, strangling the appeal. The grip continued to tighten, seemingly intent on rendering me unconscious.

Hood was right; I was a hapless victim of the disease of curiosity. The only conscious effort I made, as I struggled reflexively against the murderous grip, was an attempt to formulate questions: "Who are you? Why are you doing this?"

I was unable to get the words out, but the lovely boy seemed to understand me nevertheless. As he watched me wriggling, helplessly, in his counterpart's grip, with his beautiful blue eyes gleaming in the candlelight, he said: "I'm Erich Zann. I have a voice now, and everything else I need, for *Earthly* bliss."

10.

When I eventually recovered consciousness I was lying on a bare wooden floor, still wearing my overcoat. My head was pounding, and the only ambition I could entertain, at first, was that of remaining perfectly still. I did that while I slowly collected myself, assuming control of all my faculties, and cranking up my self-alertness to the maximum.

I caressed the dust beneath my fingers, savoring its silkiness, deducing from its texture where I must be. I activated my other senses before even trying to open my eyes, but there was nothing to be heard and the only perceptive odors, from where I lay, were those of ancient dust, replete with rotten cobwebs, and coffee. I could feel the sun's weak and wintry rays on my skin, however, so I knew that it was daylight.

I was not at all surprised, when I did contrive to open my eyes, to find that my deduction was correct. I was on the top floor of the house in the Rue d'Auseuil: the one in which Erich Zann had lived and died, in his former incarnation. Not that I believed, at that moment, in any literal reincarnation. I did not even think that the boy was mad; I simply thought that he had been toying with me, as children are wont to do.

The boy was standing by the window-sill, staring out through the closed casement, obliquely lit by the sun's pale rays. It must have been early afternoon, to judge by the sun's direction, but its zenith was low by virtue of the season, and it seemed to be in a hurry to descend and set.

When I sat up, the boy turned to face me. The English actor was sitting in the armchair, as contentedly passive as he had been when I first saw him in my own armchair, some hours before dawn. His plucked eyebrows seemed even more absurd now.

"Give him a drink of water, Mr. Hood," the boy said, speaking French. To me, he said: "You'll have to sit at the writing-desk, I fear. Mr. Hood won't give up his armchair. He's annoyed with you, for giving us so much trouble."

"Well," I said, palpating my scalp gently, through hair that was stiffened by clotted blood, "at least he didn't get angry and beat me to death. He's probably not as prone to tantrums as you are."

"Your mental faculties are unimpaired, I see," the youthful actor said, now seeming not to be a child at all—or, at least, to be a much older child in thought, manner and experience than his mere appearance suggested. He was certainly no angel, in my estimation—but he certainly was possessed of *la beauté du Diable*.

My head was aching furiously, but my mental faculties were, indeed, unimpaired. I was very grateful for the glass of water that Hood handed to me, and I sipped it in a measured fashion while I stretched my limbs in turn, attempting to recover full control of my organism. Eventually, I felt able to stand, and then to walk to the writing-desk, where I sat down.

There was a sheet of blank paper laid on the desk, with a freshly-filled inkwell and a sheaf of goose-quills. There was a plate beside it, bearing a single croissant and numerous crumbs, and a tray containing a coffee-pot and four small cups, two of which had been used.

"Help yourself to breakfast," the boy said. "Hurry, though—we need you to write a letter to your friend."

"A ransom note?" I asked, hoarsely.

"Of a sort. We already have the Stradivarius, of course—but we still need the music."

"And what if Dupin really has burned it?" I asked, before

taking a bite of the croissant and pouring a cup of coffee with a reasonably steady hand.

"That won't matter," the boy said. "At first, I thought that the manuscript was all-important—but I thought at first that Palaiseau was all-important, too. It is difficult to avoid thinking with childish simplicity, when one is trapped in the body and mind of a child. Now, though, I realize that my initial mistake extended further than the division of the legacy."

"How old are you, really?" I asked.

"Almost fifteen," he said, injecting a mocking irony into his tone as he added: "How old did you think I was? Isn't my age recorded in the program notes that you have in the inside pocket of your coat?"

"I thought you were older, in spite of appearances," I told him. "If you really are Erich Zann, you must be *much* older."

"By that reckoning, I suppose I *am* older," the boy admitted, "but I'm possessed of the bloom of youth, in all its vigor, and feel that I've made a fresh start, with a clean slate. I haven't learned to play the violin, but I have learned the art of Mesmerism. Little children have a flair for that, you know: a natural ability to charm and generate affection in others. Some retain it well into adolescence, or even adulthood. I really can convince people that I'm angelic, with absurd ease."

"Until you lose your temper," I observed. "Little children have a flair for that, too, which some retain into adolescence and adulthood. Don't you think that committing three murders has blotted your clean slate somewhat?"

"Three?" he queried.

"He thinks you killed Palaiseau's concierge too," Hood supplied. He too spoke French, although he had an atrocious accent—far worse than my own.

"Oh," the soprano said. "Well. I suppose I did, in a way. I helped her to get to sleep—but it wasn't really my intention that she wouldn't wake up again. I suppose she needed sleep more than either of us realized. I don't count that as murder. I'm usually very good with concierges—although Clamart's turned out to be a little vague, and remembered a little more than she was supposed to. If you'd taken the trouble to hire a concierge yourself, you might have saved that poor *sergent de ville* from a disciplinary charge. The Prefect will be extremely annoyed with him when he finds out that you've disappeared while his sentry was sleeping on the job. That was one complication I could have done without. Who could have imagined that Clamart's young friend would end up as the Prefect of Police? I wish I'd never given in to Clamart's recommendation that I appoint a second executor, in case anything should happen to him. Notaries can be too scrupulous for their own good. Have you finished?"

That last question referred to the croissant and the coffee. The coffee, alas, had been lukewarm before I poured it, and it had gone cold very quickly in spite of the fact that a fire was flickering in the grate.

"What do you want me to write?" I asked.

"We'll keep it simple, shall we? *Monsieur Dupin, as you will know by now, I have been captured, and am in mortal danger. If you place any value on my life, come alone to the house in the Rue d'Auseuil after dark. Do not inform the Prefect, and make certain that you are not followed. Bring the manuscript, if you still have it, but come in either case.* Then sign it. He will recognize your handwriting, I presume?"

"Of course," I said. I sharpened one of the quills and began to write. When I had finished, the boy picked it up and read it through. Then he folded it twice. He did not bother with an envelope or sealing-wax. He went back to the window-sill, picked up a small hand-bell that was resting there, and rang it.

After a few moments, a young woman appeared at the door. I recognized her as Mademoiselle Deurne, who acted the part of the violinist's inamorata in the play.

The boy handed her the note. "Get it to Dupin, with the utmost discretion," he said. "Don't come back here—the Prefect probably has the place surrounded. He'll have you followed, but that doesn't matter. Go to the Délassements, and keep your ear to the ground. If there's anything I need to know, send Roch—

but only in case of dire need." Roch was the name of the actor who played the Faustian violinist.

When the young woman had closed the door behind her and the sound of her footsteps began to dwindle away as she descended the staircase, I said: "Do you have the entire cast at your beck and call?"

"Of course," he replied. "There's a particular bond that forms between actors in a successful play. They all adore me. They'd do *anything* for me."

"Bazailles and Soulié too?"

"Perhaps—but I'd be reluctant to put my trust in a composer or a writer, beyond the exercise of their particular arts. They did a remarkable job with the play, and are utterly convinced that it was all their own work."

"Whereas, in fact, it was the Devil's," I said.

The boy smiled. For a moment, he seemed angelic again, but the diabolism of the smile was lurking at the corners of his mouth. "And you have your sense of humor too," he observed. "Very good. We are only playing the Devil—just as the Devil himself is only a player. If reliable pacts are to be made, they need to be made with entities of a different kind."

"Nyarlathotep?" I suggested.

The soprano's blue eyes widened slightly. "You've read the *Harmonies*?" he queried—but he was quick to correct his brief misconception. "No, of course not—if you had, you'd know that one cannot make pacts with the Crawling Chaos, even though it sometimes consents to become incarnate. Dupin consented to tell you that much, I suppose—but not the whole of it, I'll wager. The dream-dimensions are exceedingly populous, and there are many among their population—even including Old Ones and Elder Things—which are not entirely scornful of dealings with human beings. Some, in fact, seem to take a delight in meddling. I can understand that, I think. Did Dupin tell you about the bridge that I opened...and what my unfortunate friend was able to glimpse on its other side?"

"A little," I said, warily, not wanting to spoil my chances of learning more.

"Has he ever contrived to find a copy of the other book?"

"Which one?" I parried.

"Von Junzt's *Unaussprechenlichen Kulten*—the one that set me on the road, and attracted the attention of the *vehmgerichte*. I could not bring it to Paris with me, alas—but I had educated the violin by then." He gestured negligently as he concluded the latter sentence, and I saw a cloth on the side-table, which must have been carefully draped over the Stradivarius and its bow.

"Educated?" I queried.

"What term would you prefer? Bewitched? Accursed? Ensouled? It was a wretched instrument, you know, when Tartini had it. One of Stradivarius' rare errors of judgment. In Tartini's hands, it was simply flawed—in passing it on to me, he was being negligent at best, insulting at worst—but in my hands, thanks to what I learned from von Junzt, it became more than perfect. It became attuned to the dream-dimensions. It wasn't easy to open the bridge, mind; that took a lifetime's work—and you have no idea what an ordeal a human lifetime might be, *for a man who cannot speak.*"

"But you have the voice of an angel now," I said, "and a body to match. When you're fully grown...."

His face twisted then, into a demonic mask of rage. "*Fully-grown!*" he spat. "You think I am not *fully-grown?* You have no idea how impatient I've been, how desperate...do you imagine that I could bide my time a moment longer than absolutely necessary?" The storm passed as quickly as it had blown up, though. "You have no idea," he repeated, in a far softer tone. "You have no idea what hunger is, what thirst is, what yearning is. You have no idea how agonizingly slow the process of human growth can seem, when one is eager to attain...well, not one's majority, that's for sure."

"Bliss?" I suggested. "The sublime? The ultimate ecstasy of which mind is capable, with all its innate horror and terror?"

"Dupin must have grown weary of his loneliness, to have confided as much as that," the boy observed. "That's a good sign. It would have been far better, of course, had he yielded to his true nature sooner and more completely, but at least he has weakened in his austerity to that extent. He is ready. He always was, no matter how fervently he attempted to deny it, but I think that he might accept it now, without a fight. The moment is ripe."

I had a sudden flash of inspiration. "You expect Dupin to play the violin!" I exclaimed. "That's why you felt free to kill Palaiseau. But he hasn't touched such an instrument in twenty years—he told me so."

"Don't be silly," the boy replied. "I expect the violin to play *him*. He's a better instrument by far, if I'm not mistaken, than Palaiseau could ever have been. He has the mind, the discipline, the knowledge, the *soul*. He might have convinced himself, for a while, that he might go into retreat from his own wholesome nature and purify his consciousness, but he is too honest a man to maintain that conviction in the face of brute reality. He knows what human souls are really made of, and what their capabilities are, if taken to the extreme. Yes—he was always the one, although I never quite realized it myself, poor dumb thing that I was before my rebirth. He was *always* the one. When I played and he listened, we were merely preparing the ground for the exchange of roles. Palaiseau was as much a distraction as my fellow-lodger. Weak reeds, both of them—but not Dupin. Dupin is strong. Dupin is an instrument worthy of the violin, worthy of *me*."

By this time, of course, I had revised my earlier opinion. I now believed that the boy really was the reincarnation of Erich Zann—and that he really was utterly and completely mad. I looked at Mr. Hood, slumped in his armchair. He seemed quite relaxed and comfortable, but very much alive. There was no suggestion of a marionette waiting inertly for his strings to be twitched. He was there voluntarily. He wanted to be there. He was so thoroughly Mesmerized that he would have done anything for the master he adored.

The boy followed the direction of my gaze with his own eyes. "Do you think, even if he were dead and you still had your silly swordstick," he said, "that you could possibly stop me? Do you think that there is *anything* you can any longer do, without my permission?"

I realized then why he had bothered to spend so much time talking to me, wooing me and teasing me with tidbits of information to feed my insatiable, pathological curiosity.

"No," I said, incapable even of surprise at my self-treason. "I don't think I could stop you. I don't think I can do anything, now, without your permission."

"That's right," he said. "And not because you're under any tyrannical constraint or compulsion. You're not an automaton, or a puppet. You *want* me to succeed, in everything I'm ambitious to do."

"Yes," I admitted, "I do. I want you to succeed, in everything you're ambitious to do." I did not have to say, though, that I adored him. I had his tacit permission not to do that.

"Very well," he said, as he turned away to throw more wood on the fire. "There's no reason at all why we shouldn't spend a pleasant afternoon, chatting like good friends, while we wait for nightfall, and Monsieur Dupin's arrival."

"No," I agreed—but I felt free to add: "You didn't have to kill anyone at all. You had Clamart and Palaiseau securely in your grip, ready to do your bidding. They couldn't stop you, any more than I can. You didn't have to kill *anyone*."

"Yes I did," he said, his voice becoming a trifle plaintive, finally sounding like that of the twelve-year-old child he appeared to be. "You don't understand. No one does. You have no idea."

It was the literal truth, I realized. I had no idea. This was something not only outside the range of my experience, but beyond the reach of the concepts that I had accumulated in the process. Such minuscule access as I had been granted to the dream-dimensions, in sleep or philosophy or listening to music, had not served to give me any mental equipment for dealing with the reincarnate Erich Zann.

I realized, too, that if Auguste Dupin really did surrender

himself, as my note demanded, in order to be played by the un-lost Stradivarius and to assist in breaching the barrier that Zann had breached before—in another life, when he was not morally ready or physically equipped to face the horrors that lie beyond—then I too would be part of the audience, unable to escape until the final curtain fell...and perhaps not even then.

11.

I had abundant opportunity, before Dupin arrived, to wash the blood out of my hair and clean myself up more generally. Once the boy was sure of my co-operation, he allowed Hood to leave the room occasionally, either to prepare food in the kitchen on the ground floor or to ferry firewood and kettles of hot water upstairs; the water was used to make coffee as well as to facilitate ablutions. The fire kept the room reasonably warm, and I was able to dispense with my dirty overcoat, so that I could put on a decent appearance in my jacket and black trousers. I even contrived to polish my shoes. When I went to the privy myself, however, Hood mounted guard; evidently, the reincarnate Zann did not have complete faith in his Mesmeric powers—not, at least, at a distance, on such a recent recruit to his bizarre cause.

Dupin kept him waiting.

Twilight arrived early, in accordance with the season, and sullen darkness fell thereafter. The sky was cloudy and the night profound.

We could hear no less than five clocks chiming the hours from both sides of the river, not quite in chorus and certainly not in harmony, but with sufficiently close timing to appear to be working in collaboration. Seven o'clock sounded, then eight, and then nine.

I grew impatient along with my captors, but each of us made every effort, in his own fashion, to control himself. I had less reason than the others to doubt the inevitability of his arrival, not only because I was confident that he would not abandon me, but because I knew that his own hypersensitive curiosity would drag him with irresistible force, but I could not help being anxious anyway. The one thing of which I could not be entirely certain was that he would really come alone. The Prefect, after all, had hundreds of agents at his beck and call—enough to surround not merely the house but the entire butte. If the Prefect grew overly impatient, he might order his men to storm the building, armed with pistols or even rifles. He was, as Hood and the soprano had both observed, an inconvenient complication. I knew, though, that he trusted Dupin implicitly. If Dupin commanded him to wait, he would wait.

When the Chevalier eventually appeared, however, he definitely appeared to be alone, and the cloak of darkness shrouding the butte seemed preternaturally soundless and inert.

When he came into the garret, having been admitted to the house and escorted up the stairs by the Englishman, he barely glanced at the boy before hurrying to where I sat, still perched on the stool beside the writing-desk. "Are you hurt, my friend?" he asked me.

I rubbed my sore neck reflexively, but said: "No, I'm quite well—although the vase that the boy smashed over my head was a lumpen thing with far more substance than elegance. I should have had the good taste to prefer porcelain."

"I examined the scene," Dupin told me, "and deduced what had happened. The Prefect has been busy all day at Palaiseau's apartment and the Théâtre des Délassements-Comique, for two murders amounts to a scandal, especially in view of the cancellation of the play. Mr. Hood has come under suspicion, along with other members of the cast, but the fact that the boy is missing has only caused consternation thus far. No one suspects him; indeed, everyone swears that he is above suspicion. Tomorrow, things will be different." He turned to the soprano as he pronounced the last sentence, and their gazes locked, as if embarking upon a contest of Mesmeric will-power.

"He claims to be Erich Zann reincarnated," I supplied, helpfully. "He has the violin. He wants you to play it—or, more strictly speaking, he wants *it* to play *you*—when he breaches the boundary for a second time."

Dupin took this information aboard without a flicker of surprise. "The author of the deposition was confused," he remarked. "He thought that Zann continue to play the violin long after he was dead—but it would probably be more accurate to say that the violin continued to manipulate his corpse, like a marionette. I suspect that the greater fraction of Zann's soul had migrated long before—but I would not have believed it possible for the remainder to infect a new-born babe."

"Infect?" the boy retorted. "It was not even a matter of possession, but a matter of *becoming*."

"How did you do it?" Dupin demanded.

"It was a stormy night. The air was humid and the wind blew in capricious gusts. Sound can carry a long way in such conditions, if properly guided. The infant heard my music, and responded, with the innocent delight of which only babes in arms, uncorrupted by experience, are capable."

"You did not do that entirely by your own art," Dupin said, coldly.

"No," the boy admitted. "I had help, from within the dream-dimensions. I made a pact, and was promised everything my heart desired. I have not been disappointed, thus far, although I needed time to awaken to my opportunities—and my responsibilities."

"Now the time has come for you to fulfill your part of the bargain," Dupin said, not even bothering to phrase it as a question.

"I shall have a lifetime to do that," the boy replied, "and I shall require every minute—but that will not interfere with my heart's desire. Quite the contrary."

"Heaven and Hell," Dupin observed, mildly. "Simultaneous, inextricable and in harmony. Horror and bliss. Horror *in* bliss. The ultimate dream of Apollonius, made flesh."

"You have not forgotten the lessons you read to me all those years ago," the child remarked. "That's good. Have you brought my music with you?"

"I burned it," Dupin said. "When I realized what it was, already knowing what it might do, I had no alternative but to destroy it. If you wanted it played, you should not have divided your legacy—you should have left the whole of it to Palaiseau."

"I did not want it *played*," the child said. "I wanted it *kept safe*, until I returned. I wanted it preserved—and who better to preserve it than an avid collector. I knew that I could trust Palaiseau to hoard the violin; I thought I could trust you to hoard the music with equal care. If the accounts of your present habits and condition that I have received are trustworthy, though, you burned more than my manuscript—you have burned a part of your own soul. You are only half a man now, although that half seems to have been exaggerated out of all proportion, into a grotesque caricature. You are ratiocination personified, according to your friend, a rigorous logician who has turned his back on music, on beauty and the sublime alike."

Dupin glanced at me. "My friend is too generous," he said. "I have my flaws, like all men."

"I know," the boy replied. "I'm relying on the fact. I know you too, remember. I know what you are, not merely what you pretend to be."

"But isn't that irrelevant?" Dupin asked. "Since your music has not been preserved, in spite of your best efforts, you'll now be unable to fulfill your part of the diabolical bargain, won't you?" He was teasing; he knew why he had been brought here. He had guessed long before I had told him.

"You know better than to call the bargain diabolical, my old friend," the boy replied, "and you know that I have means of compensation. My fingers are too small to collaborate effectively with the violin, but yours are not—and even if you have not touched such an instrument in twenty years, your fingers will recall the positions they need to adopt. If you are not exactly a human Stradivarius...well, neither was Palaiseau. And if Bazailles is not an Erich Zann, or even a Giuseppe Tartini, he has a pliable mind, similarly equipped with all the necessary training."

So saying, the child removed the cloth that had been laid over the violin. Beside it on the polished sideboard, the bow lay across a manuscript: the sheet music for a capriccio, a sonata or a cantata. I did not doubt that the notes had been inscribed by Bazailles' hand, and the orchestration guided by Bazailles' intelligence, but nor did I doubt that its composition had been inspired, in the truest sense of the word.

The old, rusty music stand that had lain unheeded in the corner of the room for so many years was not so corroded that it could not be unfolded and erected. Hood set it up, in response to a flick of the child's forefinger, and placed the music on it before returning to his armchair.

"Don't get up," the boy said to me. "I can turn the pages myself." Then he picked up the Stradivarius, and handed it to Dupin.

Dupin took it meekly, but not because he was entranced.

"You can remember how to read music, I take it?" the soprano said, his tone mocking as well as challenging.

"I'm sure than any hesitations and mistakes my mind might commit will be corrected," Dupin replied. "I don't doubt that the instrument knows its own art well enough."

The monster wearing the appearance of a child laughed, as if spontaneously and sincerely. It was beautiful, sparkling laughter, like the breath of Heaven, but it chilled me to the bone and made my flesh creep.

Six church clocks chimed ten, not quite simultaneously, but with just sufficient distance between the strokes to impart a strange vibrato to the frosty air. The dull cloud covering the sky had finally begun to release clustered snowflakes—the first snow of the winter—which drifted idly down to Earth, those closest to the roof of the strange high house illuminated by the candlelight in the garret.

The boy went to the window and opened the casement, drawing it into the room as far as it would go. The shutters were still thrown back to their full extent. There was no sudden blast of cold air into the room, though; the cold air outside was like a soft, still cushion supporting the bloated snowflakes.

Feathers from the angels' wings, I thought, in English, recalling an old American saw. I wondered whether Mr. Hood had ever heard it, in his own homeland.

"Play," commanded the infernal child. Evidently, he was too impatient to wait for the propitious midnight hour.

Dupin obediently raised his bow, and applied it to the strings of the Stradivarius.

I recognized the chords of the piece that Palaiseau had been playing, night after night for several weeks, in the climax of *La Cantate du Diable,* during the crucial dream-sequence. I wondered whether the Devil had been slightly out of breath on the night when he had had to race back to the theater after killing Clamart, in time to make his entrance through the vamp-trap.

Then the soprano began to sing—but I recognized, with equal ease, that these were not Frédéric Soulié's words. Indeed, I was not absolutely convinced that they were words at all. They were not French, nor Italian, nor German, and I was morally certain that they did not belong to any other Earthly language. They were unearthly in more ways than one. They were beautiful in the extreme—more beautiful than any words that I had ever heard or read.

For once, I was grateful for the flaw that left me relatively unmoved by everyday music. I could not remain unmoved by *this* music, but at least I was not moved to the extent that I might have been, had I been a more sensitive individual. I pitied the placid Mr, Hood, and the fellow-tenant of Zann's previous incarnation, who had never recovered from his ordeal.

The external cold began to creep into the room then, insinuating itself more by conduction than convection in the windless space. It reached out insidiously, like an eerie caress, to envelop me, as it was doubtless enveloping Hood, Dupin and the reincarnate genius of Erich Zann. I was already chilled to the bone, but this was a new chill, more terrifying still.

The music feinted in the direction of the pleasurably paradisal to begin with, but that did not last long; the violin, it seemed, was as impatient to retune itself as the marvelous boy was to come into his inheritance. The instrument had been waiting a long time for this moment, forced by circumstance to be patient, and it was thirsty now to reach the extremes of beauty and sublimity, where delight fused with terror, and beauty with horror, and the boundaries drawn by the heroic human mind between reality and dream began to shift and break down.

Outside the window, something stirred, although the illuminated snowflakes continue to drift with the same entrance indolence as before. It was not the molecules of the air that were stirring, impelled by any material wind, but the very fabric of the space containing that air. The snowflakes did not begin to dash and whirl about, as they would have done in a capricious wind, but they did began to tremble, flicker and sparkle. Their distribution in the sky was evidently random, but within that randomness emerged the suggestion of a form: a form outside space, which space was not contrived to accommodate.

I did not suppose that the nascent individual was Nyarlathotep itself, or even an avatar thereof, but I was morally certain that it participated in the essential nature and quality of that ultimate chaos, that ultimate defiance of everything ordered... including—and perhaps especially—the fragile and futile order of the conscious, waking human mind. It was quintessentially *unwholesome*—and yet, by the elementary nature of its contradiction, it seemed to confirm the holistic nature of reality, the identity of all the opposites that human consciousness endeavored to identify and separate, for its rational convenience.

It *seemed* to confirm that nature, together with the conclusion that even a man like Auguste Dupin could not deny or defy it—but I clung to hope, entranced as I was. Dupin's very meekness, his polite acceptance of his role, promised that he was not yet done with, that he had a trick up his slightly threadbare sleeve.

Even so, the voice and the accompanying notes of the retuned violin began to crawl into my heart and soul, filling them with ecstasy—not the false ecstasy of human hopes and loving desires, which attempted to abandon fear and pain and sorrow and horror in search of some idyllic purification, but the *true* ecstasy that embraced and embodied fear and pain and sorrow and horror, and restored the wholeness of experience and perfection, mundanity and vision, reality and dream, life and death.

For a second, or perhaps two—though they seemed to stretch far beyond the confines of Earthly time—I believed that I understood the effect that the music of Erich Zann had been reaching for, of its own accord, and in defiance, in the first climax of Zann's life, of its own composer and player. I understood how very unfortunate, and how perversely fortunate, Zann had been in having been deprived of a voice in his previous incarnation.

He was not deprived of a voice now; his music had moved beyond the confines of the Stradivarius violin, and the unfettered human imagination.

Then the monsters came in earnest, threatening to invade the human world through the window of that absurdly-perched garret, in fulfillment of the pact that Erich Zann had made. They came to bring a flood of horror into the world, with all the corollary delight implied by the fullness of the term. No human could imagine why they had to do it, but I understood that they were acting under compulsion.

At that point in a similar *séance*, fifteen years before, Erich Zann's flesh had rebelled against the enormity of his own daring, and he had tried to play the violin that had been playing him. He had entered into a contest that had killed him, but he had kept the monsters at bay. He had lost the fight, and won it. The violin had continued to play him even after he was dead, but the music had been futile, *unaccompanied*.

This time, Zann reborn had no intention of doing any such thing, and no capacity even to attempt it. This time however, Auguste Dupin was plying the bow and pressing the strings of the Stradivarius. This time, he was the one who rebelled, and set out, heroically, to seize control of the educated, bewitched, accursed, ensouled Stradivarius.

Whether he knew it or not—and I firmly believe that he had always known it, if only on some occult but not-entirely-subconscious level—the Chevalier had been preparing for this moment for fifteen years. He had been very scrupulous in letting musical instruments alone, and extremely scrupulous in retuning his own self. The running *scordatura* that he attempted now was quite unprecedented, but it was utterly logical, rational and analytical, and in that sense, he had practiced it a million times before.

Apollonius of Tyana, the self-styled Abbé Apollonius and Erich Zann might have insisted that human beings were fundamentally undivided, and that the unending battle fought between reason and emotion, will and appetite, demonstrated by its very inconclusiveness that no such division could ever truly be effected, but Auguste Dupin did not admit that and would not admit it now. *His* somnimusicality was not ecstatic at all, but purely physiological, and he brought all of his mental and moral resources to bear on the contest in which he engaged against his would-be possessor.

Dupin launched an attack, with all his inner might, against the Stradivarius. Refusing any longer to be played, he insisted on becoming the player—the determinant not only of the notes the instrument was playing, but of the uncanny song that the reincarnate, fully articulate Erich Zann was singing.

He had no music of his own to play, but he did not need any; the point was not to play a melody but to interrupt and shatter one.

Auguste Dupin was, not merely by training but by nature, a *disentangler*, a man possessed of *acumen*. He attacked the play of the violin not as an item of music, a question of aesthetics, but as a conundrum, a puzzle to be solved. He set out to fulfill the true mission of the human mind, which was not to seek the horrific fulfillment of bliss but to analyze and separate, not by way of cultivating unwholesomeness, after the fashion of the Crawling Chaos, but to contrive a neat and orderly *division*. He set out, in his attack, to undo the knot that had been contrived in the weft of fate by Erich Zann's music and Erich Zann's reincarnation: to smooth out the boundary between the real world and the unruly dimensions of dream.

For a moment, everything hung in the balance. The snowflakes drifting outside the window seemed to stop in the course of their eldritch evolution: to stop falling; to stop shimmering; to stop sparkling.

The cold was so deeply enmeshed in my soul and my bones that I was afraid that Dupin had left it too late, that he had not solved the puzzle in time. I was terrified that the monsters had got through. It was a truly beautiful fear, a truly sublime terror; I almost contrived to experience the combination as Erich Zann yearned to experience it.

Then the boy's divine and demonic soprano voice broke.

On one level, that was all that happened; his voice broke, as the voices of adolescents routinely do. The incredible note that he was sounding turned into an all-too-credible croak, and Erich Zann's magical cantata abruptly turned into a farce.

The window, of its own accord, slammed shut.

The individual who no longer even seemed to be a child clutched his throat, and collapsed.

Hood leapt to his feet, and screamed.

Dupin stopped playing. He bent down, and set the violin down on the floor, as reverently as it deserved. It was, after all, a Stradivarius.

Then he turned to me, and simply said, without any preamble or particular emphasis: "Run for your life."

I ran—or, at least, my legs ran. I bounded down five flights of stairs, taking them four at a time, without even looking round to check that Dupin was hard on my heels. He was, though; as I burst out of the door of the house, grateful that its lock had been excised and that it was incapable of offering any material resistance, I tried to stop and turn, and the Chevalier cannoned into the back of me, rendered helpless by mere momentum.

We fell into a horribly ungainly heap, with our limbs entangled, and had to scramble along the frozen ground like a pair of broken-legged crabs in order to get clear of the vast cascade of rubble that the house had suddenly become.

The edifice did not so much collapse as disintegrate. It was as if time had been carefully storing up the ravages of decay for decades, holding them in miserly suspension in order that they might be released all at once: a hundred years of corruption and corrosion crammed into a single second.

By the time the Prefect's men arrived, swarming out of the myriad hiding-places in which they had surreptitiously taken up their stations, there was nothing left for them to do but pull a single corpse out of the ruins. It was that of the English actor, Hood—the final victim of Erich Zann's posthumous orgy of murder.

No trace of the seeming child's body was ever found. It was if it had simply evaporated, or as if it had been consumed as a tasty morsel and serenely digested by Nyarlathotep, the Crawling Chaos, the essence of unwholesomeness.

"Are you hurt?" the Prefect asked us, having come in person to make sure that the story reached a fortunate conclusion—for such dramas always need a connoisseur audience if they are to prove truly satisfying, in human terms.

"Only slightly," I assured him, as I slowly came to my feet.

"I think my dignity has suffered some distress," Dupin admitted, while still sprawled on the ground, "but in myself, I feel quite well."

"Did you manage to save the Stradivarius?" asked Monsieur Groix, ever the practical man.

"I'm afraid not," I said. "It must have been smashed to matchwood."

"There is no loss to mourn," Dupin, ever the stern rationalist, assured us. "It was a wretched instrument, forever going out of tune. It proved, at the end of the day, not to be fit for purpose."

THE TRUTH
ABOUT PICKMAN

The doorbell didn't ring until fifteen minutes after the time we'd agreed on the telephone, but I hadn't even begun to get impatient. Visitors to the island—even those who've only come over the Solent from Hampshire, let alone across the Atlantic from Boston—are always taken by surprise by the slower pace of life here. It's not so much that the buses never run on time as the fact that you can't judge the time of a walk by looking at the map. The map is flat, but the terrain is anything but, especially here on the south coast, where all the chines are.

"Do come in, Professor Thurber," I said, when I opened the door. "This is quite a privilege. I don't get many visitors."

His face was a trifle blanched, and he had to make an effort to unclench his jaw. "I'm not surprised," he muttered, in an accent that was distinctly American but by no means a drawl. "Who ever thought of building a house here, and how on Earth did they get the materials down that narrow track?"

I took his coat. There were scuff-marks on the right sleeve because of the way he'd hugged the wall on the way down rather than trust the hand-rail on the left. The cast-iron struts supporting it were rusted, of course, and the wood had grown a fine crop of fungus because we'd had such a wet August, but the rail was actually quite sound, so he could have used it if he'd had the nerve.

"It is a trifle inconvenient nowadays," I admitted. "The path was wider when the house was built, and I shudder to think what the next significant landslip might do to it, but the rock face behind the house is vertical, and it's not too difficult to rig a block-and-tackle up on top. The biggest thing I've had to bring down recently is a fridge, though, and I managed that on the path with the aid of one of those two-wheeled trolleys. It's not so bad when you get used to it"

He'd pulled himself together by then and stuck out his hand. "Alastair Thurber," he said. "I'm truly glad to meet you, Mr. Eliot. My grandfather knew your...grandfather." The hesitation was perceptible, as he tried to guess my age and estimate whether I might conceivably be Silas Eliot's son rather than his grandson, but it wasn't so blatant as to seem impolite. Even so, to cover up his confusion, he added: "And they were both friends of the man I wrote to you about: Richard Upton Pickman."

"I don't have a proper sitting-room, I'm afraid," I told him. "The TV room's rather cluttered, but I expect you'd rather take tea in the library in any case."

He assured me, quite sincerely, that he didn't mind. As an academic, he was presumably a bibliophile as well as an art-lover and a molecular biologist: a man of many parts, who was probably still trying to fit them together neatly. He was, of course, younger than me—no more than forty-five, to judge by appearances.

I sat him down and immediately went into the kitchen to make the tea. I used the filtered water, and put two bags of Sainsbury's Brown Label and one of Earl Grey in the pot. I put the milk in a jug and the sugar in a bowl; it was a long time since I'd had to do *that*. On the way back to the library I had a private bet with myself as to which of the two salient objects he would comment on first, and won.

"You have one of my books," he said, before I'd even closed the door behind me. He'd taken the copy of *The Syphilis Transfer* off the shelf and opened it, as if to check that the words on the page really were his and that the book's spine hadn't been lying.

"I bought it after you sent the first letter," I admitted.

"I'm surprised you could find a copy in England, let alone the

Isle of Wight," he said.

"I didn't," I told him. "The public library at Ventnor has internet connections. I go in twice a week to do the shopping, and often pop in there. I ordered it from the US via Amazon. I may be tucked away in a chine, but I'm not entirely cut off from civilization." He seemed skeptical—but he had just walked the half a mile that separated the house from the bus stop on the so-called coast road, and knew that it wasn't exactly a stroll along Shanklin sea-front. His eyes flickered to the electric light bulb hanging from the roof, presumably wondering at the fact that it was there at all rather than the fact that it was one of the new curly energy-saving bulbs. "Yes, I said, "I even have mains electricity. No gas, though, and no mains water. I don't need it—I actually have a spring in my cellar. How many people can say that?"

"Not many, I suppose," he said, putting the book down on the small table beside the tea-tray. "You call this place a chine, then? In the US, we'd call it a gully, or maybe a ravine."

"The island is famous for its chines," I told him. "Blackgang Chine and Shanklin Chine are tourist traps nowadays—a trifle gaudy for my taste. It's said that there are half a dozen still unspoiled, but it's difficult to be sure. Private land, you see. The path isn't as dangerous as it seems at first glance. Chines are, by definition, wooded. If you were to slip, it would be more a side than a fall, and you'd probably be able to catch hold of the bushes. Even if you couldn't climb up again you could easily let yourself down. Don't try it at high tide, though."

He was already half way through his first cup of tea, even though it was still a little hot. He was probably trying to calm his nerves, although he had no idea what *real* acrophobia was. Finally, though, he pointed at the painting on the wall between the two free-standing bookcases, directly opposite the latticed window.

"Do you know who painted that, Mr. Eliot?" he asked.

"Yes," I said.

"I knew the moment I looked at it," he told me. "It's not on the list I compiled, but that's not surprising. I knew it as soon as I looked at it—Pickman's work is absolutely unmistakable." His eyes narrowed slightly. "If you knew who painted it," he said, "You might have mentioned that you had it when you replied to my first letter."

Not wanting to comment on that remark, I picked up *The Syphilis Transfer*. "It's an interesting thesis, Professor," I said. "I was quite intrigued."

"It was quite a puzzle for a long time," he said. "First the Europeans argued that syphilis had started running riot in the sixteenth century because sailors imported it from the Americas, then American scholars motivated by national pride started arguing that, in fact, European sailors had imported it to the Americas. The hypothesis that different strains of the spirochaete had evolved in each continent during the period of separation, and that each native population had built up a measure of immunity to its own strain—but not to the other—was put forward way back in the seventies, but it wasn't until the people racing to complete the Human Genome Project developed advanced sequencers that we had the equipment to prove it."

"And now you're working on other bacterial strains that might have been mutually transferred?" I said. "When you're not on vacation, investigating your grandfather's phobic obsessions that is?"

"Not just bacteria," he said ominously—but he was still on vacation, and his mind was on Richard Upton Pickman. "Does it have a title?" he asked, nodding his head toward the painting again.

"I'm afraid not. I can't offer you anything as melodramatic as *Ghoul Feeding*, or even *Subway Accident*."

He glanced at me again with slightly narrowed eyes, registering the fact that I was familiar with the titles mentioned in the account that Lovecraft had re-worked from the memoir that Edwin Baird had passed on to him. He drained his cup. While I poured him another, he stood up and went to the picture to take a closer look.

"This must be one of his earlier works," he said, eventually. "It's a straightforward portrait—not much more than a practice study. The face has all the usual characteristics, of course—no one but Pickman could paint a face to make you shudder like that. Even in the days of freak-show TV, when the victims of genetic disasters that families used to hide away get tracked through courses of plastic surgery by documentary makers' camera-crews, there's still something uniquely strange and hideous about Pickman's models...or at least his technique. The background in this one is odd, though. In his later works, he used subway-tunnels, graveyards and cellars, picking out the details quite carefully, but this background's very vague and almost bare. It's well-preserved, though, and the actual face...."

"Only a real artist knows the actual anatomy of the terrible or the physiology of fear," I quoted.

He wasn't about to surrender the intellectual high ground. "The exact sort of lines and proportions that connect up with latent instincts or hereditary memories of fright," he went on, completing the quote from the Lovecraft text, "and the proper color contrasts and lighting effects to stir the dormant sense of strangeness."

"But you're a molecular biologist," I said, as smoothly as if it really were an offhand remark. "You don't believe in latent instincts, hereditary memories of fright or a dormant sense of strangeness."

It was a mistake. He turned round and looked me straight in the eye, with a gaze whose sharpness was worth more than vague suspicion. "Actually," he said, "I do. In fact, I've become very interested of late in the molecular basis of memory and the biochemistry of phobia. I suppose my interest in my grandfather's experiences has begun to influence my professional interests, and vice versa."

"That's only natural, Professor Thurber," I told him. "We all begin life as men of many parts, but we all have a tendency to consider ourselves as jigsaw puzzles, trying to fit the parts together in a way that makes sense."

His eyes went back to the painting: to that strange distorted face, which seemed to distil the very essence of some primitive horror, more elementary than a pathological fear of spiders, or of heights."

"Since you have the painting," he said, "you obviously do have some of the things that Silas Eliot brought back to England when he left Boston in the thirties. May I see them?"

"They're not conveniently stowed away in one old trunk and stowed neatly away in the attic or the cellar," I said. "Any items that remain have been absorbed into the general clutter about the house. Anyway, you're really only interested in one thing, and that's something I don't have. There are no photographs, Professor Thurber. If Pickman really did paint the faces in his portraits from photographs, Silas Eliot never found them—at least, he didn't bring any back with him from Boston. Believe me, Mr. Thurber, I'd know if he had."

I couldn't tell whether he believed me or not. "Would you be prepared to sell me this painting, Mr. Eliot?" he asked.

"No," I said. "I'm sorry if that ruins your plan to corner the market—but who can tell what a Pickman might fetch nowadays if one ever came into the saleroom? It's not as if he's fashionable."

The red herring didn't distract him. He wasn't interested in saleroom prices, and he knew that I wasn't angling for an offer. He sat down and picked up the second cup of tea I'd poured for him. "Look, Mr. Eliot," he said. "You obviously know more about this than you let on in your letters, and you seem well enough aware that I didn't tell you everything in mine. I'll level with you, and I hope that you might then be more inclined to level with me. Did your grandfather ever mention a man named Jonas Reid?"

"Another of Pickman's acquaintances," I said. "The supposed expert in comparative pathology. The one who thought that Pickman wasn't quite human—that he was somehow akin to the creatures he painted."

"Exactly. Back in the twenties, of course, knowledge of

genetics was primitive, so it wasn't possible for Reid to entertain anything more than vague suspicions, but there was a time when colonial America was home to numerous isolated communities, who'd often imported sectarian beliefs that encouraged in-breeding. You don't expect to find that sort of thing in a big city, of course, but Pickman's people came from Salem, and had been living there at the time of the witch-panic. The people who moved into cities as the nation industrialized—especially to the poorer areas like Boston's North End and Back Bay—often retained their old habits for a generation or two. The recessive genes are all scattered now, mind, so they don't show up in combination nearly as often, but back in the twenties...."

I felt an oddly tangible, if slightly premature, wave of relief. He seemed to be on the wrong track, or, at least, not far enough along the right one. I tried hard not to smile, as I said: "Are you trying to say that what you're actually looking for is a sample of Pickman's DNA?" I asked. "You want to buy that painting because you think it might have a hair or some old saliva stain somewhere about it—or even a blood drop, if he happened to prick himself white fixing the canvas to the frame?"

"I already have samples of Pickman's DNA," he told me, in a fashion that would have wiped the smile off my face if I hadn't managed to suppress it. "I've already sequenced it and found the recessive gene. What I'm looking for now is the mutational trigger."

I'd cut him off too soon. He was a scientist, after all—not a man to cut to the bottom line without negotiating the intermediary steps. He must have mistaken my dismay for incomprehension, because he continued without waiting for me to speak.

"We all have numerous recessive genes of various sorts, Mr. Eliot," he said, "which are harmless as long as the corresponding gene on the paired chromosome is functioning normally. The ones that give us the most trouble nowadays are those that can cause cancer, if and when their healthy counterpart is disabled in a particular somatic cell, causing that cell to start dividing repeatedly, forming a tumor. Normally, such tumors are just inchoate masses of cells, but if the recessive is paired with one of the genes that's implicated in embryonic development, the disabling of the healthy counterpart can activate bizarre metamorphoses. When such accidents happen in embryo, they result in monstrous births—the sort DeVries was referring to when he first coined the word *mutation*. It's much rarer for it to occur in the mature soma, but it does happen.

"Most disabling incidents are random, caused by radiation or general toxins, but some are more specific, responding to particular chemical carcinogens: mutational triggers. That's why some specific drugs have links with specific cancers, or other mutational distortions—you probably remember the thalidomide scandal. Jonas Reid didn't know any of this, of course, but he did know enough to realize that something odd was going on with Pickman, and he made some notes about the changes he observed in Pickman's physiognomy. More importantly, he also went looking for other cases—some of the individuals that Pickman painted—and found some, before he gave up the enquiry when disgust overwhelmed his scientific curiosity.

"People were so anxious to hide the monsters away, of course, that Reid couldn't find very many, but he was able to observe a couple. His examinations were limited by available technology, of course, and he wasn't able to study the paintings *in sequence*, but I've got the DNA, and I've also pieced together as complete a list of Pickman's paintings as is still possible, along with the dates of composition of the later items. I've studied the progression from *Ghoul Feeding* to *The Lesson*, and I think I've figured out what was happening. It's not traces of Pickman's DNA for which I want to search your canvas—and any other Pickman-connected artifacts your grandfather might have left you—but traces of some other organic compound, probably a protein: the mutational trigger that activated Pickman's gradual metamorphosis, and the not-so-gradual metamorphoses of his subjects. If you won't sell me the painting, will you let me borrow it, so that I can run it through a lab? The University of Southampton might let me use their facilities, if you don't want me to take the painting all the way to America."

I was glad of his verbosity, because I needed to think, and decide what to do. First of all, I decided, I had to be obliging. I had to encourage him to think that he might get what he wanted, at least in a superficial sense.

"All right," I said. "You can take the painting to Southampton for further examination, provided that it doesn't go any further and that you don't do any perceptible injury to it. You're welcome to look around for any other objects that take your fancy, but I doubt that you'll find anything useful."

I cursed, mentally, as I saw his gaze move automatically to the bookcases on either side of the painting. He was clever enough to identify the relevant books, even though none of them had anything as ludicrously revealing as a bookplate or a name scribbled in ink on the flyleaf. The painting was almost certainly clean, but I wasn't entirely sure about the books—and if he really did decide to scour the rest of the house with minute care, including the cellars, he'd have a reasonable chance of finding what he was looking for, even if he didn't know it when he found it.

"It's odd, though," I observed, as he opened one of the glass-fronted cases that contained older books, "that you've come all the way from America to the Isle of Wight in search of this trigger molecule. I'd have thought you'd stand a much better chance of finding it in the Boston subway, or the old Copp's Hill Burying Ground—and if it's not there, your chances of finding it anywhere must be very slim."

"You might think so," he said, "but if my theory is correct, I'm far more likely to find the trigger here than there."

My sinking heart touched bottom. He really had figured it out—all but the last piece of the jigsaw, which would reveal the whole picture in all its consummate horror. He began taking the books off the shelves one by one, very methodically, opening each one to look at the title page, checking dates and places of publication as well as subject-matter.

"What theory is that?" I asked, politely, trying to sound as if

I probably wouldn't understand a word of it."

"It wasn't just the syphilis spirochaete that was subject to divergent evolution while the Old World and the New were separated," he told me. "The same thing happened to all kinds of other human parasites and commensals: bacteria, viruses, protozoans, fungi. Mostly, the divergence made no difference; where it did—with respect to such pathogens as smallpox, for instance—the effect was a simple loss of immunity. Some of the retransferred diseases ran riot briefly, but the effect was temporary, not just because immunities developed in the space of four or five human generations but because the different strains of the organisms interbred. Their subsequent generations, being much faster than ours, soon lost their differentiation. The outbreak of monstrosity that occurred in Boston in the twenties, as variously chronicled by Pickman and Reid, was a strictly temporary affair; it hardly spanned a couple of human generations. My theory is that the trigger lost its potency, because the imported organism carrying it either interbred with its local counterpart or ran into some local pathogen or predator that wiped it out. The reverse process might easily have occurred, of course—at least in big cities—but I believe that there's a better chance of finding the trigger molecule over here, where families like the Pickmans and the Eliots probably originated, than there is in Boston or Salem."

"I see," I said. While he was leafing through the books, I went to the window to look out over the chine.

To the right was the English Channel, calm at present, meekly reflecting the clear blue September sky. To the left was the narrow cleft of the chine, thickly wooded on both sheer slopes because the layers of sedimentary rock were so loosely aggregated and wont to crumble that they offered reasonable purchase to bushes, whose questing roots could burrow deep enough not only to support their crowns but to feet them gluttonously on the many tiny streams of water filtering through the porous rock. Because the cline faced due south, both walls got plenty of sunlight in summer in spite of the acute angle of the cleft.

Directly below the window, there was only a narrow ledge—almost as narrow now as the pathway leading down from the cliff-top—separating the front doorstep from the edge. When the house had been built, way back in the seventeenth century—some fifty or sixty years before Richard Upton Pickman's ancestor had been hanged as a witch in Salem—the chine had been even narrower and the ledge much broader, but it had been no fit home for acrophobes even then. If it hadn't been for the vital importance of the smuggling trade to the island's economy, the house would probably never have been built, and certainly wouldn't have been kept in such good repair for centuries on end by those Eliots who hadn't emigrated to the New World in search of a slightly more honest way of life. The bottom had dropped out of the smuggling business now, of course, thanks to the accursed European Union, but I didn't intend to let the place go—not, at least, until one landslip too many left me no choice.

By the time I turned round again, Alastair Thurber had sorted out no less than six of Pickman's old books, along with a mere four that just happened to be of similar antiquity.

"That's about it, I think," he said. "Would you care to show me around the rest of the house, pointing out anything that your grandfather might have brought back from Boston?"

"Certainly," I said. "Would you prefer to start at the top or the bottom?"

"Which is more interesting?" he asked.

"Oh, most definitely the bottom," I said. "That's where all the most interesting features are. I'll take you all the way down to the smugglers' cave, via the spring. We'll have to take an oil-lamp, though—I never have got around to running an electric cable down there."

As we went down the cellar steps, which he handled with rigid aplomb, I filled in a few details about the history of smuggling along the south coast—the usual tourist stuff—and added a few fanciful details about wreckers. He didn't pay much attention, especially when we went down through the trapdoor in the cellar into the caves. He was a little disappointed by the spring, even though he was obviously relieved to reach the bottom of the parrot-ladder. He had obviously expected something more like a gushing fountain, and probably thought that the Heath-Robinsonesque network copper and plastic tubing attached to the pumps wasn't in keeping with the original fitments. I was careful to point out the finer features of the filtration system.

"The water's as pure as any mains water by the time it gets up to the tank in the loft," I told him. "Probably purer than much mainland water, although it's pretty hard. The real problem with not being connected to the mains is sewerage; the tanker that comes once a fortnight to drain the cesspool has to carry a specially-extended vacuum tube just for this house. They have to do it, though—regulations."

He wasn't interested in sewerage, either. In fact, he lost interest in the whole underground complex as soon as he realized how empty it was of artifacts that might have been brought back to the old country from the home of the bean and the cod. The smugglers' cave left him completely cold; there obviously wasn't a lot of romance in his soul.

He didn't notice anything odd about the kitchen, but he scanned the TV room carefully, in search of anything un-modern. Then I took him upstairs. He didn't waste much time in the bedroom, but when he got to the lumber room, his eyes lit up.

"If there's anything else," I said, unnecessarily, "This is where you'll find it. It'll take time, though. Help yourself, while I fix us some lunch."

"You don't have to do that," he said, for politeness' sake.

"It's no trouble," I assured him. "You'll probably be busy here all afternoon—there's a lot of stuff, I'm afraid. Things do build up, don't they? It was a lot tidier when I last moved back in, but when you live alone...."

"You haven't always lived here, then?" he said, probably fearing that there might be some other premises he might need to search.

"Dear me, no," I said. "I was married for ten years, when we lived in East Cowes, on the other side of the island. This is no place for small children. I moved back here after the divorce—but anything that came back from the USA in the thirties will have stayed here all along. Couldn't rent the place, you see, even as a holiday cottage. It was locked up tight and nobody ever broke in. Not a lot of crime on the island."

I left him alone then in order to make the lunch: cold meat from the farmers' market and fresh salad, with buttered bread and Bakewell tarts, both locally baked, and a fresh pot of tea. This time I used two bags of Earl Grey to one of Brown Label, and I ran the water from the other tap.

"What I don't understand," I said, as he tucked in, "is where the anatomy of the terrible and the physiology of fear fit in. What do cancers and trigger molecules have to do with latent instincts and hereditary memories?"

"Nobody understands it yet," he told me. "That's why my research is important. We understand how genes function as a protein factory, and the associated pathology of most cancers, but we don't understand the heredity of structure and behavior nearly as well. The process controlling the manner in which the fertilized ovum of a whale turns into a whale, and that of a hummingbird into a hummingbird, even though they have fairly similar repertoires of proteins, is still rather arcane, as is the process by which the whale inherits a whale's instincts and the hummingbird a hummingbird's. Most of human behavior is learned, of course—including many aspects of fear and horror—but there has to be an inherited foundation on which the learning process can build. The fact that Pickman's recessive gene, once somatically activated, caused a distinctive somatic metamorphosis rather than simple undifferentiated tumors indicates that it's linked in some way to the inheritance of structure. It's a common fallacy to imagine that individual genes only do one thing—usually, they have multiple functions—and the genes linked to structural development routinely have behavioral effects too. I suspect that the effects Pickman and his relatives suffered weren't just manifest in physical deformation; I suspect that they also affected the way he perceived and reacted to things."

"You think that's why he became an artist?"

"I think it might have affected the way he painted, and his choice of subject-matter—his understanding of the anatomy of the terrible and the physiology of fear."

"That's interesting," I said. "It took your grandfather differently, of course."

Mercifully, he wasn't holding his tea-cup. It was only his fork that he dropped. "What do you mean?" he asked.

"Art isn't a one-way process," I said, mildly. "Audience responses aren't created out of nothing. Mostly, they're learned—but there has to be an inherited foundation on which the learning process can build. It's right there in the story, if you look. Other people just thought that Pickman's work was disgustingly morbid, but your grandfather saw something more. It affected him much more profoundly, on a phobic level. He knew Pickman even better than Silas Eliot—they, your grandfather and Reid were all members of the same close-knit community. It must have been much easier for you to obtain a sample of his DNA than Pickman's, and you already had your own for comparison. Are *you* carrying the recessive gene, Professor Thurber?"

A typical academic, he answered the question with a question: "Would you mind providing me with a sample of your DNA, Mr. Eliot?" he asked, reaching the bottom line at last.

"You've been trampling all over my house for the last two hours," I riposted. "I expect you probably have one by now."

He'd picked up his fork automatically, but now he laid it down again. "Exactly how much do you know, Mr. Eliot?" he asked.

"About the science," I said, "not much more than I read in your excellent book and a couple of supplementary textbooks. About the witchcraft...well, how much of that can really be described as *knowledge*? If what Jonas Reid understood was vague, what I know is...so indistinct as to be almost invisible." I emphasized the word *almost* very slightly.

"Witchcraft?" he queried, doubtless remembering the allegation in Lovecraft's story that one of Pickman's ancestors had been hanged in Salem—although I doubt that Cotton Mather was really "looking sanctimoniously on" at the time.

"In England," I said, "they used to prefer the term *cunning men*. The people themselves, that is. Witches was what other people called them when they wanted to abuse them—not that they always wanted to abuse them. More often, they turned to them for help—cures and the like. The cunning men were social outsiders, but valued after their fashion—much like smugglers, in fact."

He looked at me hard for a moment or two, and then went back to his lunch. You can always trust an American's appetite to get the better of his vaguer anxieties. I watched him drain his tea-cup and filled it up again immediately.

"Is the ultimate goal of your research to find a cure for...shall we call it *Pickman's syndrome*?" I asked, mildly.

"The disease itself seems to be virtually extinct," he said, at least in the form that it was manifest in Pickman and his models. To the extent that it's still endemic anywhere, the symptoms generally seem to be much milder. It's not the specifics I'm interested in so much as the generalities. I'm hoping to learn something useful about the fundamental psychotropics of phobia."

"And the fundamental psychotropics of art," I added, helpfully. "With luck, you might be able to find out what makes a Pickman...or a Lovecraft."

"That might be a bit ambitious," he said. "Exactly what did you mean just now about *witchcraft*? Are you suggesting that your cunning men actually knew something about phobic triggers—that the Salem panic and the Boston scare might actually have been *induced*?"

"Who can tell?" I said. "The Royal College of Physicians, jealous of their supposed monopoly, used the law to harass the cunning men for centuries. They may not have succeeded in wiping out their methods or their pharmacopeia, but they certainly didn't help in the maintenance of their traditions. A good many must have emigrated, don't you think, in search of a new start?"

He considered that for a few moments, and then demonstrated his academic intelligence by experiencing a flash of inspiration. "The transfer effect doesn't just affect diseases," he said. "Crop transplantation often produces new vigor—and the effect of medicines can be enhanced too. If the Salem panic was induced, it might not have been the result of malevolence—it might have been a medical side-effect that was unexpectedly magnified. In which case...the same might conceivably be true of the Boston incident."

"Conceivably," I agreed.

"Jonas Reid wouldn't have figured that out—he wouldn't even have thought of looking. Neither would my grandfather, let alone poor Pickman. But *your* grandfather...if he knew something about the traditions of cunning men...."

"Silas Eliot wasn't my grandfather," I told him, unable this time to repress a slight smile.

His eyes dilated slightly in vague alarm, but it wasn't the effect of the unfiltered water in his tea. That wouldn't make itself manifest for days, or even weeks—but it *would* make itself manifest. The contagion wasn't the sort of thing that could be picked up by handling a book, a damp wall or even a fungus-ridden guard-rail, and it wouldn't have the slightest effect on a local man even if he drank it...but Professor Thurber was an American, who's probably already caught a couple of local viruses to which he had no immunity. The world is a busy place nowadays, but not that many Americans get to the Isle of Wight, let alone its out-of-the-way little crevices.

I really didn't mean him any harm, but he had got too close to the truth about Pickman, and I had to stop him getting any closer—because the truth about Pickman had, unfortunately, become tangled up with the truth about me. It wasn't that I had to stop him *knowing* the truth—I just had to affect the way he looked at it. It wouldn't matter how much he actually knew, always provided that the knowledge had the right effect on him. Pickman would have understood that, and Lovecraft would have understood it better than anyone. Lovecraft understood the true tenacity and scope of the roots of horror, and knew how to savor its aesthetics.

"You're not claiming that you *are* Silas Eliot?" said Professor Thurber, refusing to believe it—for now. His common sense and scientific reason were still dominant.

"That would be absurd, Professor Thurber," I said. "After all, I can't possibly have the fountain of youth in my cellar, can I? It's just water—it isn't even polluted most of the time, but we have had a very wet August, and the woods hereabouts are famous for their fungi. Some poor woman in Newport died from eating a death-cap only last week. You really have to know what you're doing when you're dealing with specimens of that sort. The cunning men could probably have taught us a lot, but they're all gone now—fled to America, or simply dead. The Royal College of Physicians won; we—I mean *they*—lost."

The trigger hadn't had the slightest effect on him yet, but my hints had. He looked down at his empty tea-pot, and he was already trying to remember how many taps there had been in the kitchen.

"Please don't worry, Professor Thurber," I said. "As you said yourself, the disease is very nearly extinct, at least in the virulent form that Pickman had. The attenuated form that your grandfather had, on the other hand...it's possible that you might still catch that—but what would it amount to, after all? You might become phobic about subways and cellars, and your acrophobia might get worse, but people mostly cope quite well with these things. The only that might be seriously inconvenient, given your particular circumstances, is that it might affect your attitude to your hobby...and to your work. Jonas Reid had to give it up, didn't he?"

His eyes were no longer fixed on me. They were fixed on something behind me: The painting that he had mistaken, understandably enough, for a Pickman. He still thought that it *was* a Pickman, and he was wondering how the mild fear and disgust it engendered in him might increase, given the right stimulus. But biochemistry only supplies a foundation; in order to grow and mature, fears have to be nurtured and fed with doubts and provocations. Pickman had understood that, and so had Lovecraft. It doesn't actually matter much, if you have the right foundation to build on, whether you feed the fears with lies or the truth, but the truth is so much more *artistic*.

"Actually," I told him, "when I said that I knew who'd painted it, I didn't mean Pickman. I meant me."

His eyes shifted to my face, probing for tell-tale stigmata. "You painted it," he echoed, colorlessly. "In Boston? In the 1920s?"

"Oh no," I said. "I painted it right here in the chine, about twenty years ago."

"From memory?" he asked. "From a photograph? Or from life?"

"I told you that there aren't any photographs," I reminded him. I didn't bother shooting down the memory hypothesis—he hadn't meant that one seriously.

"You do carry the recessive gene, don't you?" he said, still the rational scientist, for a little while longer.

"Yes," I said. "So did my wife, unlikely as it might seem. She was Australian. If I'd known...but all I knew about then was the witchcraft, you see, and you can't really call that *knowledge*."

His jaw dropped slightly, then tightened again. He was a scientist, and he could follow the logic all the way—but he was a scientist, and he needed confirmation. Our deepest fears always need confirmation, one way or another, but once they have it, there's never any going back...or even, in any meaningful sense, going forward. Once we have the confirmation, the jigsaw puzzle is complete, and so are we.

"The chance was only one in four," I said. "My other son's body is a veritable temple to human perfection...and he can drink the water with absolute impunity."

Now, the horror had begun to dig in, commencing the long

and leisurely work of burrowing into the utmost depths of his soul.

"But I have a family of my own at home in Boston," he murmured.

"I know," I said. "They have the internet in Ventnor public library; I looked you up. It's not really that contagious, though— and even if you do pass it on, it won't be the end of the world: it'll just engender a more personal and more intimate under-standing of the anatomy of the terrible, and the physiology of fear."

THE HOLOCAUST
OF ECSTASY

It was dark when Tremeloe first opened his eyes, and he found it impossible to make out anything in a sideways or up-ward direction. When he looked down, though, in the hope of seeing where he was standing—for he had no idea where he was, and was sure that he wasn't lying down—he saw that there were holes in a floor that seemed to be a long way beneath him, and that stars were shining through the holes.

There seemed to be a conversation going on around him, but there were no English words it in; the languages that the various voices were speaking all seemed to him to be Far Eastern in origin. The voices seemed quite calm, and in spite of the impenetrable darkness and not knowing where he was, Tremeloe felt oddly calm himself.

"Does anyone here speak English?" he asked. The words came out easily enough, but sounded and felt wrong, in some way that he couldn't quite understand.

For a moment, there was a pregnant silence, as if everyone in the crowd were deciding whether to admit to speaking English. Finally, though, a voice that seemed to come from somewhere closer at hand than all the rest, said: "Yes. You're American?" There was nothing Oriental about the accent, but that didn't make it any easier to place.

Tremeloe thought that the other might be near enough to touch, and tried to reach out in the direction from which the voice had come, but he couldn't. His body felt strange, and wrong. He couldn't feel his hands, and when he tried to touch himself to reassure himself that he was still there, he couldn't touch any other part of him with his fingers. The idea struck him that the conviction that he wasn't lying down, based on the fact that he couldn't feel a surface on which he might be lying, would be unreliable if he were paralyzed from the neck down.

"Richard Tremeloe, Arkham, Massachusetts," he said, by way of introduction. "Have I been in some kind of accident?" He tried to remember where he had been before falling asleep—or unconscious—and couldn't. "I think I've got amnesia," he added.

"More than you know," said the other voice, a trifle dolefully, "but the others are a little more relevant in their concerns."

"Can you understand what they're saying?" Tremeloe asked, knowing that it was the wrong question, but reluctant to ask one whose answer might provoke the panic that he had so far been spared.

"Some of it," the other boasted. "There's an animated discussion about reincarnation going on. The Buddhists and the Hindus have different views on the subject, but none of them really believes in it—especially the ex-communists. On the other hand...."

"Who are you?" Tremeloe demanded, wondering why the anxiety that he ought to be feeling wasn't making itself felt in his flesh or his voice. "Where the hell are we?"

"If I'm not much mistaken," the other replied, "we've been reborn into the new era, beyond good and evil: the holocaust of ecstasy and freedom. I'm not at all sure about the freedom, though...or, come to that, the ecstasy. I shouldn't be here. This shouldn't be possible. The memory wipe should have made it impossible."

"Reborn?" echoed Tremeloe. "I haven't been reborn. I'm not sure of much, but I know I'm an adult. I'm fifty-six years old—maybe more, depending on the depth of the amnesia. I'm a professor of biology at Miskatonic University, married to Barbara, with two children, Stephen and Grace...." He trailed off. He was talking in order to test his memory rather than to enlighten the mysteriously-anonymous other, but it wasn't an awareness of pointlessness or a failure of remembrance that had caused him to stop. It was the realization that the stars really were shining through gaps in...something that *wasn't* the floor. "Why has up become down?" he asked. "Why aren't I aware of being *upside-down*? Why can't I feel *gravity*?"

The voice didn't try to reassure him. Instead, the other said: "Miskatonic? Have you read the *Necronomicon*?"

"Don't be ridiculous," Tremeloe snapped—or tried to, since his momentary irritation was a mere flicker, which didn't show in his voice. "It's been locked in a vault for decades. No one's allowed to see or touch any of the so-called forbidden manuscripts, since the *unpleasantness* way back in the last century. Anyway, I'm a scientist. I don't have any truck with occult rubbish like that."

"Do you know Nathaniel Wingate Peaslee?"

That question gave Tremeloe pause for thought. He blinked and squinted—and was glad to know that he could still feel his eyelids, just as he could still feel the movements of his tongue—in the hope that he might be able to make out his surroundings now that his eyes were adapting to the extremely poor light. He couldn't. Above his head—or, strictly speaking, below it, since he seemed to be hanging upside-down—the darkness was Stygian. Around him, he had vague impression of rounded objects that might have been heads, not very densely clustered, and wispier things that were vaguely reminiscent of fern leaves, but he couldn't actually *see* anything...except the fugitive stars, shining through gaps in what was presumably a dense cloud-bank. Occasionally, the stars were briefly eclipsed, as if something had moved across them: a giant bird, perhaps.

Around him, the chorus of foreign voice was still going on. If any of the others could speak English, they were content to listen to what Tremeloe and his companion were saying, without intervening.

What was remarkable about the other's question, Tremeloe

reminded himself, when he came back to it reluctantly, was that Nathaniel Wingate Peaslee had died more than a hundred years ago...or, at least, more than a hundred years before Richard Tremeloe had turned fifty-six. He was long dead, but not quite forgotten...just as the university's famous copy of the *Necronomicon* was unforgotten, even though no one had clapped eyes on it since before Tremeloe had been born. Having no idea how to answer the other's question, Tremeloe prevaricated by saying: "Do you?"

"I did, briefly—but that was in another place, and another time. I infer from your hesitation that he's long dead, and that you...died...sometime in the twenty-first or twenty-second century."

"I'm not dead," Tremeloe retorted, reflexively, although he did realize that if all the other hanged men in this dark Tarot space were earnestly discussing reincarnation, he might be in the minority in holding that opinion, and might even be wrong, in spite of *cogito ergo sum* and all his memories of Miskatonic, Barbara, Stephen, Grace, his hands, his legs, and his heart....

His heart would have sunk, if he'd had one, and if its sinking had been possible. *I can't feel gravity,* Tremeloe thought. Aloud, he said: "Are you telling me that I really have been reincarnated?"

"Yes—probably not for the first time, although it's impossible to tell how many layers of amnesia we've been afflicted with."

"How?" This time Tremeloe succeeded in snapping. "When? *By whom?*"

"If you'd read the *Necronomicon*," the other voice replied, with a leaden dullness that probably wasn't redolent with panic because it had no more capacity to hold an edge that Tremeloe's own, "you'd know."

"And you have?" Tremeloe riposted.

"No," the other came back, quick as a flash. "I wrote it—and no, I don't mean that I'm the legendary Arab with the nonsensical name who penned the *Al Azif.* I mean that I too, like Peaslee, have lived in Pnakotus...except that to me, it was a home of sorts, though not Yith itself, and I'm not supposed to be out of it any more. The human brain I inhabited for ten years was supposed to have been cleansed of every last trace of me. I shouldn't have been available for...*this*."

"Has it occurred to you," Tremeloe asked, "that you might be barking mad?"

"Yes," the other replied. "How about you?"

Good question, Tremeloe thought. *This is a nightmare—a crazy nightmare. There's no other explanation. Please can I wake up now?* Somehow, he knew that wasn't going to happen. He might well be dreaming, but he was very clearly conscious that he was living his dream, and that he was not going to be waking up to any other reality any time soon.

Even so....

"The cloud's getting lighter," he observed. "It *is* cloud, isn't it? That *is* the sky, isn't it? It only seems to be beneath us because we're hanging upside-down."

"Yes," the other answered. "It's dawn. Whether we're barking mad or not, this might be a good time to strive with all our might to lose our minds completely: to dissolve our minds into private chaos and gibbering idiocy, if we can. On balance...."

The other shut up, somewhat to Tremeloe's relief.

The dawn was slow. The shades of grey through which the bulk of the sky progressed as its patches turned blue and the stars were drowned seemed infinite in their subtlety, but Tremeloe soon stopped watching them, in order to concentrate on the tree.

The reason that he couldn't feel his body was that he didn't have one. He was just a head and a neck—except that the neck was really a stalk, and it connected him to the bough of a tree from which he hung down like a fruit, amid a hundred other heads that he could see and probably a thousand that he couldn't. The things he's intuited as leaves really were leaves, and really were divided up in a quasi-fractal pattern, a little like fern leaves but lacier. They were pale green streaked with purple.

The tree, so far as Tremeloe could estimate, was at least a hundred feet high, and its crown had to be at least a hundred and fifty in diameter, but he was positioned on the outside of the crown, about five-sixths of the way up—or, as it seemed to him, down—and he couldn't see the trunk at all. He could barely see the ground "above" his head, but the thin streaks he could see between his head-fruit-tree and the next were vivid green and suspiciously flat, as if they might be algae-clogged swamp-water rather than anything solid.

The jungle stretched as far as his eyes could see. The birds in the sky really did look like giants, but that might have been an error of perspective.

There was no disintegration into private chaos, no hectic slide into gibbering idiocy. While not exactly calm any longer, and perhaps still capable of a kind of panic, Tremeloe felt that his consciousness was clear, that his memory was sound—so far as it went—and that his intelligence was relentless. He realized that he was no longer possessed of the hormonal orchestra of old. Presumably, he still had a pituitary master gland, which was probably still sending out its chemical signals to the endocrine glands that had once been distributed through his frail human flesh, but whatever was responding to them now was a very different organism. From now on, his feelings, like his voice, would be regulated by a very different existential system. Even so, he did still have a voice, He had no lungs, but he did have vocal cords, and some kind of apparatus for pumping air into his neck-stalk. He wasn't dumb, any more than he was deaf or blind.

All in all, he thought, only slightly amazed at his capacity to think it, *things could be worse*. Then he remembered what the other English-speaker had implied about losing his mind completely, and dissolving into gibbering mindlessness, probably being the better alternative....

The head of the other English-speaker—the only Caucasian face amid a crowd of Orientals who occasionally glanced at him sideways, with apparent curiosity but no hostility, but showed no sign of understanding what he said—seemed to be that of a man in his mid-fifties, who might have been handsome before middle-aged spread had given him jowls and thinning hair had turned his hairline into a ebbing tide. The jowls seemed oddly protuberant, but that was because they were hanging the wrong way. Gravity still existed; it was just that Tremeloe no longer had any sensation of his own weight. He felt slightly insulted by that, having always thought of his intellect-laden head as a ponderous entity.

Tremeloe didn't see the bats until they actually arrived at the tree, wheeling around it in a flock that must have been thirty or thirty-five strong. This time, there was no possibility of any error of perspective; they were *huge*. Because Tremeloe was a biologist he knew that real vampire bats were tiny, and that the common habit of referring to fruit-bat as "vampire bats" was a myth-based error, but now that he was a human fruit, the difference seemed rather trivial—especially when he saw the bats begin to settle on his fellow human fruit.

Please, he prayed—although he was an atheist—*don't let it be me*. Because he was a biologist, though, he took note of the fruit-bats' eyes. The bats were obviously not nocturnal in their habits, so their eyes were adapted for day vision; these specimens were not "as blind as bats" even in their natural state—but that didn't explain why the unnaturally huge creatures had eyes that looked almost human in their fox-like heads.

After a few seconds, during which he saw one creature's needle-sharp teeth tear into the face of an Oriental man—who did not scream—Tremeloe was on the point of withdrawing the *almost*...but he never quite got there, because one of the bats suddenly descended upon him, as if out of nowhere.

He felt the monster's breath on his cheek, caught its rancid stink in his nostrils, and looked into its not-quite-almost-human eyes, and knew that it was about to pluck out his own as it groped at it with its clawed feet...but then it was suddenly gone again, snatched away as abruptly as it had arrived.

After the bats had come the huge birds...and they really

were *huge*. They were eagles, or condors, or something akin to both but not quite either. At any rate, they were raptors, and they numbered human-fruit-bats among their prey of choice. There weren't as many birds as bats, so some of the bats were enabled to start their hasty meals in peace, but the birds were even fiercer, and they could easily carry a bat in each claw, so it wasn't long before the bats fluttered away, seeking the cover of the sprawling crowns.

The raptors too, Tremeloe realized, as he watched his own avian savior fall into the sky, clutching for its next meal with its terrible talons, had unnaturally large eyes: not eyes like a hawk's, but eyes like a man's....

Tremeloe looked his white-faced neighbor in the eyes and said: "Is this hell?" He knew that it was a stupid question. He'd done much better before, when his not-quite-immediate response to the possibility that he had been reincarnated had been: *How? By whom?*

What the other said in reply, however, was: "That depends."

A phrase that the mysterious other had used while they were still enclosed by merciful darkness floated back into Tremeloe's mind: *the holocaust of ecstasy and freedom.* Except, the other had added, presumably knowing already that he was simply a head-fruit, there wasn't much freedom in their present existential state. *Nor ecstasy either, so far as I can tell,* Tremeloe added, privately. Although it might have been more exciting, now that he thought about it, to be reincarnated as a human eagle...better, at any rate, than being reincarnated as a human fruit-bat.

Are we all vampires now?

But the real questions were still *how* and *by whom?*

"I'm not who I think I am, am I?" Tremeloe said to the other, who seemed to know a lot more than he did. "I'm just some sort of replica, created from some sort of recording. This isn't the twenty-first century, is it? This is a much later era—maybe the end of time. Is this the Omega Point? Is this the Omega Point Intelligence's idea of a joke?"

"I wish it were," the other replied. "Perhaps it is...but my suspicion is that it's not as late as you think. The Coleopteran Era is a long way off as yet, alas. This is Cthulhu's Reign...what the human race were designed to be and to become. But no, we're not just replicas reproduced from some sort of recording; we're actually who we think we are, shifted forwards in time. You are, at any rate. I shouldn't be here. I don't belong here. I only borrowed a human body temporarily, and then I returned to Pnakotus. I shouldn't be here. This isn't right."

Tremeloe thought that he had just as much right to protest as the other, but his mind—which was not only refusing to dissolve into incoherent idiocy but perversely insistent on retaining an emotional state more reminiscent of complacency than abject terror—was oddly intent on trying to pick up the thread of the narrative that the other fruit-head was stubbornly not spelling out.

"Pnakotus," he said. "That's the mythical city in the Australian desert, where some of the so-called forbidden manuscripts were found. You really believe that's where you're from?" He paused momentarily before adding the key question: "When, exactly?"

"Two hundred million years before you were born," the other replied. "But I seem to have been removed from the twenty-first century, where I spent ten years doing research. That memory was supposed to have been erased—not just blocked off, like some fraction of a computer hard disk whose supposed dele-tion is merely a matter of losing its address, but actually *wiped clean*...reformatted. I'm not supposed to be here. I'm supposed to live in Pnakotus for another hundred million years or more, and then migrate to the Coleopteran Era, in order to avoid *all this*. The members of the Great Race of Yith are inhabitants of eternity. Cthulhu and the star-spawn simply aren't relevant to us...."

There was a rustling on the bough from which Tremeloe's head was hanging down, and he saw something moving behind the head that was talking to him. He couldn't see its body, so it might have been a lizard, or a snake, or neither...but he could see its head, and its suddenly-gaping mouth, and its forked tongue, and its oh-so-*human* eyes....

However its body was formed, it had to be big: bigger than an anaconda. For a moment, Tremeloe thought that he was about to lose the only entity in this bizarre world that was capable of holding a conversation with him—that the un-man from Pnakotus was about to be swallowed whole by the monster—but then the leaves moved. The leaves were clever, it seemed, and surprisingly strong, given their apparent delicacy. They flipped the stealthy predator into the air, and it fell, crashing through the branches, seemingly moving up and up but actually tumbling down and down...until it hit the boggy surface with a glutinous semi-splash.

It was invisible by then, but when Tremeloe looked at the green streaks that were visible between the crowns of his trees and its neighbors, he saw multiple movements, as if creatures akin to crocodiles were homing in on the splash, in anticipation of a feast. He could not see the crocodiles' eyes any more than he could distinguish their bodies, but he did not doubt that they would be human.

As hells go, he thought, *it's not so bad to be a human-head-fruit, given that we have such defenders to prevent our being stolen and eaten.* As a biologist, however, he knew full well that the whole purpose of a fruit is to be eaten, and thus deduced that if he really were being defended, the purpose of that defense might only be to preserve him for the preferred fructicarni-vore...except, of course, that he was not a seed-bearing entity at all, but a mind-bearing entity, which might or might not change the logic of the situation completely.

He suddenly remembered a line that everyone at Miskatonic knew, supposedly quoted—in translation, of course—from the mysterious *Necronomicon*: "In his house at R'lyeh, dead Cthulhu lies sleeping." There was a fragment of verse, too, which ended "that is not dead which can eternal lie," but the relevant point seemed to be, if the un-man from Pnakotus could be taken seri-ously—which was surely necessary in a world where madness no longer seemed to be possible—that dead Cthulhu was no longer asleep, but awake, and that his awakening had changed the world out of all recognition, maybe not overnight, but rapidly...and purposefully.

"What did you mean," Tremeloe said to his companion, "*this is what the human race was designed to be and to become*?"

"Just that," the other replied. "That was why Cthulhu and the star-spawn came to Earth: to produce and shape human-kind. The raw material was rather unpromising when they first arrived, and seemed to be headed for insect domination, but they're patient by nature, and we saw immediately what the results of their project would be, at least in the shorter term. They didn't bother us—just worked alongside us for tens of millions of years. Ours was a parallel project, after all. They create, we record—we're complementary species. They seemed to be leaving us alone, just as we left them alone...although I always had my suspicions about the flying polyps. Maybe this is what they always intended, for all of us...except that *we* already know that *we* escaped to the belated Coleopteran Era after the Polyp Armageddon. We were only ever present in spirit in the Human Era. We never interfered, except to observe and record— for our own purposes, of course. Nothing was supposed to *leak out*. Maybe that's why Cthulhu took against us, although I can't imagine how the garbled rubbish that found its way from our records into *Al Azif* and its various supposed translations could have interfered with the star-spawn's plans for shaping human intelligence."

Tremeloe had only the vaguest notion of who—or what— Cthulhu and the star-spawn were supposed to be, even though everyone at Miskatonic knew the basics of what was, in effect, the university's own native folklore. "As I remember it," he said to his companion, "this Cthulhu character was supposed to be a sort of giant invisible octopus, which came to Earth from another star, and whose eventual resurrection after a long dormancy on the ocean bed was supposed to bring about the end of the world as we knew it. You're saying that he's real, and it's actually happened?"

"It's difficult to describe Cthulhu in terms of shape and substance," the other replied, with a calmness that now seemed rather ominous. "He's primarily a dark matter entity. You know that ninety per cent of the universe's mass is non-baryonic, right? That it interacts with your sort of matter gravitationally, but not electromagnetically? Well, Cthulhu, the star-spawn, and most of the other life-forms in the universe are essentially dark matter beings, although they can transform themselves wholly or partly into baryonic matter when conditions are right and the whim takes them. Don't ask me what counts as right or wrong in that context—we Yithians can move our minds in space and time via hyperbaryonic pathways, but we're not creative. Exactly what the relationship is between Cthulhu's kind, matter and mind, we don't know—but they're certainly interested in them, simply because they *are* creative. Why they create, and how they select their creative ends, I literally can't imagine, but the simple fact is that Cthulhu spent hundreds of millions of years shaping the ancestors of human beings, partly in order to produce the kind of intelligence that my kind can borrow—but that was only a means, not an end."

"And *this* is the end?"

"Possibly. It's just as likely to be another phase in the grand plan, requiring something more than evolution by selection. The various cultists who decided, on the basis of leaked Pnakotic lore, that Cthulhu and his hyperbaryonic kindred are gods, looked forward to his return as a holocaust of ecstasy and freedom—a time when humankind would be freed from its self-imposed moral shackles and taught new ways to revel in violence and slaughter—but that was mostly wishful thinking."

Tremeloe thought about fruit with human brains, and eagles and crocodiles with human eyes, and extrapolated that imagery to the notion of an entire ecosphere in which human intelligence had been redistributed on a profligate scale, in order that human mentality might experience all of nature red in tooth and claw in all its horror and glory...and the notion of a "holocaust of ecstasy and freedom" no longer seemed so alien. As an individual, he was certainly not free, nor had he tasted anything akin to ecstasy as yet, but if one tried to see the situation from without, as a single vast pattern....

"Are humans like the one I used to be extinct now?" he asked. "Has the harvest of minds taken place, so that all individual personalities could be relocated?"

"Probably not," replied the un-man who should not, in his own estimation, ever have been reduced to a mere fruit. "So far as our explorers could tell, original-model humans, living in societies of various sorts, lasted long into the intellectual diaspora...although they soon became as opaque to our technology of possession as entities like *this*. We only have a vague idea of the interim between the era a few millennia down the line from the time that you and I recall and the advent of the Coleopteran Migration."

There really might be things, Tremeloe thought, harking back to the *Necronomicon* again, *that man was not meant to know. Would I be better off on a tree where I had no language in common with any of my fellow fruit? Would I be better off trying to account for the situation by the force of my own unaided intellect, rather than listening to this bizarre lunacy? Except that it can't be mere lunacy, unless there are spoiled fruit here as well as healthy ones, whose sanity is being eaten away from within by mindworms....*

He quite liked the idea of mindworms, although he knew that it ought to have frightened him. His "liking" was purely aesthetic, so far as he could tell. He thought that he was capable of feeling pleasure, just as he was probably *capable* of feeling panic, but his new hormonal orchestra was obviously in a quiet mood at present, tranquilizing his brain chemistry more efficiently than the intrinsically-horrific thoughts he was formulating therein were disturbing it. If that remained the case, then his situation would surely be better than bearable, and more akin to a heaven than a hell.

It would probably be painful if any bat ever got to bite into him, or any snake were to swallow him whole, but while he remained safe, successfully protected by the leaves that surrounded him—whose photosynthesis was presumable producing the blood that nourished his flesh and thoughts alike—and the eagles who fed upon the bats, he was feeling no physical pain, and no particular mental anguish. If his fate was to suffer eternal inertia, with no idle hands for with the Devil might make work, he thought that he might be able to cope—and since it was now proven that he could be reincarnated, perhaps he had an infinite and infinitely various future to look forward to, in which he would have abundant opportunity to fly and to swim, to squirm and to walk, always knowing that even if pain and death were to arrive, however hideous they might be on a temporary basis there would be other lives to come: times to rest and times to ponder, times to eat as well as to be eaten....

Or was it, he wondered, merely his reduced capacity to feel such emotions as horror and terror that made the future seem so promising? Might he, in fact, be better off as a gibbering wreck, consumed from within by mindworms, his very consciousness reduced to immaterial dust?

The invisible sun was climbing behind the cloud-sheet. Eventually, it began to rain. The drops seemed tropically large, but when they splashed on his chin and his cheeks the liquid explosions were more pleasurable than painful, and the moisture was welcome. The shower didn't last long. When it stopped the cloud was much lighter and thinner. Rapid shadows occasionally fluttered across Tremeloe's face, but no bats or birds came close to him. The eagles patrolling the sky were drifting lazily in slow circles.

"I know that you never expected to be here," Tremeloe said to his companion, "and that you'd rather be snug and warm in Pnakotus, dreaming of one day becoming a beetle, but this really isn't as bad as all that, is it?"

"I don't know," the other replied, "and *not knowing* is something that my kind aren't used to. I shouldn't be here. I've borrowed humanity in the past, for research purposes but I'm not human. I wasn't designed for this. It's not my fate. You're a prisoner of time, so you can't begin to understand how Yithians think, any more than I can begin to imagine how Cthulhu and the star-spawn might think, but believe me when I say that *this is wrong*."

Tremeloe did believe him, after a fashion, but he couldn't sympathize. If all the silly rumors about Nathaniel Wingate Peaslee were actually true, and the professor's body really had been taken over by an alien time-traveler for several years way back in the 1900s, then the alien time-travelers in question evidently didn't observe the principle of informed consent, and could hardly complain if the tables were turned on them. They had poked their noses into human affairs, and had no right to bleat that they were only reporters, not creators, as if that somehow let them off the moral hook...except, of course, that the human world had moved beyond good and evil now, into an era when morality no longer had hooks, or claws, or censorious staring eyes.

Tremeloe remembered the bat's eyes then, and the eagle's. No, they hadn't been censorious, or even judgmental—but he felt sure that they had been more than merely avid. There had been *something* in them that was more than mere sight or mere appetite, which might well have been "beyond good and evil", but held an emotion that was by no means entirely free of dread.

I'm just a head-fruit hanging on a tree, Tremeloe thought. *The birds and the crocodiles still have animal bodies and animal hormones. Perhaps I have the best of it, in this far-from-the-best of all possible worlds...but if the cycle goes on forever, I'll have it again and again and again*, ad infinitum.

Such was the comforting positive nature of that thought that he did not notice that the sky had become even bluer until the murmur of mostly-incomprehensible voices altered him to the fact that something was going on.

At first, he thought that the cloud was simply clearing, its remnants evaporated by the hot tropical sun that was ascending towards its zenith—but then he saw the bloated sun drift free of the brilliant white clouds to take possession of the sky, and saw that its flames were redder and angrier than he had ever known them before.

It really is much later than either of us thought, he said to himself, but then doubted the judgment, as he realized that the excessive blueness of the unclouded sky and the excessive redness of the sun were both optical illusions, caused by the fact that the sky was full of *creatures*; creatures that were not quite invisible, although they had to be made of something other than the kind of matter with which he was familiar: something so alien as to be almost beyond perception. The big birds were flying far away with rapid wing-beats.

Tremeloe was conscious of gravity now, although it did not seem to be tugging him in the direction of the green Earth, but in the direction of the alien sky, whose no-longer-kindly light hid all the multitudinous stars of the incredibly, unimaginably vast universe within its dazzling glory. "What are they?" he said, his voice little more than a whisper.

The other heard him. "Star-spawn," he replied. "If you could see them, the impression of shape they'd give you would be much like Cthulhu's, on a much smaller scale: vaguely cephalopodan, with a scaly tegument, and oddly tiny wings that shouldn't work but do."

Somehow, Tremeloe grasped what the other meant by "the impression of shape". The star-spawn had mass, but their matter was utterly alien, obedient to different rules of dimension and form, whose relationship with the kind of matter making up his own flesh, and that of the tree of which he was now a part, was essentially mysterious...and far, far beyond mere matters of good and evil.

The raptors were nowhere to be seen now. If their existential role was to protect the trees of human life and their heady harvest from giant bats, they had played their allotted parts and made their exit, until the next day.

But it's not yet noon, Tremeloe thought, wishing perversely that he were capable of terror, in order that he might feel a little more human, a little more himself. *Even mayflies live for a day.*

He had been biologist, though, during his larval stage, and he knew that mayflies actually lived much longer than a day, even though their imago stage was a brief airborne climax to a life spent wallowing in mud. He knew, too, that from a detached scientific viewpoint, every mayfly had a living ancestry that stretched back through their larval stages and generation after generation of evolving living creatures, all the way back to some primordial protoplasmic blob, or some not-yet-living helical carbonic thread. Only its climax was ephemeral, and by comparison with the billion years it had taken to produce the fly, there was hardly any difference at all between an hour, a day and fifty-six years.

Beyond good and evil, Tremeloe knew, human philosophers held that there ought to be a world in which good would no longer be refined by the absence of evil—of pain, of hunger, of thirst, and so on—but in positive terms, in terms of an active, experienced good whose mere absence would replace outdated redundant evil. But the good and evil that he had now moved beyond wasn't human good and evil at all, and the speculations of human philosophers were only relevant to it insofar as they had helped to shape his own consciousness, his own expectations, and his own intellectual flavor.

The good that the world embraced now was something essentially alien, and neither Tremeloe nor any of his fellow human fruit—nor even the reluctant Yithian refugee from legendary Pnatokus—had any words, or the slightest imagination, with which to describe or get to grips with it.

As the star-spawn descended to enjoy the crop that had been hundreds of millions of years in the creative shaping, and mere hours in the final ripening, Tremeloe still had time enough to realize that his new hormonal orchestra, quiet until now, was not unequipped with sensations akin to horror and terror, agony and fury...and to appreciate the irony of the fact that those sensations too, just as much as his thoughts, his memories and his knowledge and consciousness of history and progress, of space and time, of matter and light, and most especially of strangeness, were all elements of a nutritive and gustatory experience that something so very like him as to be near-identical would have to relive time and time again, from the wrong perspective, if not *ad infinitum*, then at least until the star-spawn had finally had their fill, and had abandoned Earth to the long-delayed Coleopteran Era.

The star-spawn fed, like patient gourmets, and the blazing sun moved on in its patient arc, heading for a sunset that Tremeloe would not see...this time. He ran the gamut of his new emotions, reacting with his thoughts and his imagination as best he could, even though he wished, resentfully, that he was disinclined to do anything different.

There was a long future still ahead of him, but even that would merely be an eye-blink in the history of the New Eden that Earth had become. Eventually, the multi-tentacled monsters of dark matter would pass on to pastures new, nature would reassert itself, and the primal wilderness would return.

The only thing we were ever able to deduce about the mind of the God who was in charge of Creation before Cthulhu arrived, Tremeloe reflected, with obliging but slightly piquant serenity, as the matter comprising his delectable freshness was chewed, absorbed and digested without his ever quite losing consciousness, *is that he must have an inordinate fondness of beetles. And perhaps he had good taste.*

THE SEEDS FROM THE MOUNTAINS OF MADNESS

I was on my way back from the tropical greenhouse to the house when I saw the dead man coming up the driveway. I recognized him by his gait—not that all dead men limp, of course, but I recognized that particular limp, even at a distance of a hundred yards, and I knew that the man it afflicted was dead. Indeed, he had become one of the most famous dead men in England, the very model of heroic self-sacrifice, preserved from better times.

Another reputation blown apart, I thought. *It seems that the war isn't going to leave us any intact illusions—although it does make a change to see someone coming back from the dead, when so many hundreds of thousands like him have gone the other way, with equal futility.*

Only then did I think that I might be mistaken, and that it might not be Oates after all.

I looked around—not that there could be any reassurance of the world's normality in the sight of the wolds, the farms in the valleys with their neatly-cropped post-harvest fields, the ragged sheep on the slopes, the fleecy cloud obscuring the summits, or even the house itself. Except for the glittering greenhouses, it had all been there for centuries, superficially constant and inviolable, but in exactly the same way that every single wife who had greeted a husband returned from the war had declared that he wasn't the same man that had gone away, none of it was *the same*, none of it was normal, and none of it could prove any defense against the absurdity of a dead man limping along the drive, crunching the gravel with his strangely-distended boots.

He seemed to be looking around too. Oates had visited the estate twice during the summer vacation while we were at Eton, so he would have found it familiar, if....

The closer he came, though, the more uncertain I became, not just in the negative sense of being *less* certain, but in the positive sense of being...well, I could see his face now. In a way, it was Oates' face, but in a way it wasn't. In a way, it wasn't even human, and the way in which it wasn't human wasn't just something that death might have done to it. I'd seen the faces of men in the trenches, men who'd been gassed, men who'd been blown to Kingdome Come, but I'd never seen a face like that. He was wearing a hooded jacket, as if to keep it concealed from passers by on the road, but he wasn't trying to conceal it from me. He was coming to see me, and he knew that I'd have to see him, to recognize him. He had stopped looking round and was looking directly at me.

"Titus?" I said, when he got close enough—I'd never called him Lawrence at Eton, and in Africa I'd had to call him *Captain* or *sir*. "Is that really you? You're supposed to be dead."

"Perhaps I am," he said, proving that the uncertainty cut deeper than appearances. "It's been seven years now, so the newspapers I've glimpsed inform me, but I'm still not sure. You're the first person to have recognized me, although few others have had the chance. I wasn't sure that you would."

"We were at school together," I reminded him, "and in the dragoons. Mind you, practically everyone else with whom we were at school or in the dragoons is pushing up poppies in Flanders fields, so they won't have the chance—unless, of course, you're the beginning of a trend. The Day of Resurrection didn't arrive while I was tending to my pineapples, by any chance? I'm not sure that I'm ready for Judgment yet."

He put out his hand, and I shook it. It was cold, and the fingers were swollen—frostbitten, it looked to me. I felt a couple of tears in the corners of my eyes, and couldn't stop them brimming over, although I wasn't entirely sure what had occasioned them, my emotions having been unhinged for quite some time. Conduct unbecoming an officer, of course, whatever the reason—but I'd lost track of becoming somewhere in the Ardennes, and hadn't quite caught up with it again as yet. Unready for Judgment, as I'd said.

"It's good to see you, Linny," he said. "Would you believe that you're the first halfway friendly face I've seen in seven years?"

"I'm doing my best," I told him, although I'm sure he wasn't criticizing the partiality of my welcoming expression. Nobody had called me "Linny" for ten years—the last time I'd seen Oates was in '09, and he'd been the last habitual user of the nickname. "How on Earth did you get here?"

His face shifted then, although it wasn't what you'd normally think of as an expression. It was disconcerting to look at, and seemed to give him a twinge of some sort. All he said in reply, though, was: "I walked."

That wasn't good enough. He didn't look as if he could have made it all the way along the drive, let alone all the way from Driffield or anywhere further away. "Where the Hell from?" I demanded. "Antarctica?"

The twinge recurred, worse this time, and I felt guilty for pressing him

"Yes," he said. It made no sense, but so what? I didn't have to understand—not yet, at least. He was here, at my home, and a host has obligations.

"It's good to see you, too, old man," I said, belatedly echoing his sentiment with as much sincerity as I could—genuine sincerity, in spite of the difficulty. "Come in."

* * * * * * *

We went inside, through the side door, so that the servants wouldn't see us, and I took him straight into the study, closing the door behind us. I figured that I'd introduce him to Helen and the brat later, if he didn't disappear in a puff of sulfurous smoke in the meantime.

Oates seemed very glad indeed to be able to sit down. Quite apart from the limp, his feet seemed to be giving him a lot of pain. It didn't make any sense that he'd walked far. If he'd got to Driffield by train he ought to have taken a taxi...but I only had to look at his face to know that we were beyond that kind of mundane practicality. Wherever he'd come from, and how, he was here, and he was welcome. Even if he'd stepped out of the land of the dead directly on to the drive—which actually seemed to be the likeliest possibility, such was my state of mind—he was welcome.

I had no shortage of friendly faces around me—loving faces, even—but there was some kind of strange barrier between them and me. Dead or not, Titus was from a different world, an old world, a lost world. Maybe, I thought, he was here because I needed him.

I poured us both a stiff brandy. It was the last of the Cognac I'd brought back from the other side of the pond, but far from the last physical reminder of Hell that I had around me.

"I'm glad you came through it, Linny," he said, when he'd relaxed a little and taken a long swig of the brandy. "The war, I mean."

"Somebody had to," I told him, a trifle churlishly. Like Voltaire, I couldn't see the necessity, but it was something to say when there was nothing else. I'd said it before.

He winced again, for no obvious reason. Did he think I was criticizing him for not having gone through it? Impossible to tell. His face no longer had the capacity for readable expression. Anyway, what better excuse was there for dodging the war than being dead? Pacifism? Sanity? Neither of those had worked.

"I've brought you something, Linny," he said. "I need your help. You might be the only man in England who can help—you're the only one I could think of, at any rate."

"If it's money...."

"Don't be ridiculous, Linny," he said. "I could get that elsewhere....at least, I think I could, if I could face the family...which

I'm really not up to, at present. I knew you could take it, after the things we saw in Africa back in '07, but...I don't exactly have a face that a mother could love, any more."

"But you have to let her know that you're not dead," I said, slightly shocked for the first time—which was odd, in a way. His judgment had been harsh, but possibly true—but whether she could love him or not, she was his mother.

"Perhaps I will," he said, "if I can convince myself. Otherwise...."

"What the hell happened, Titus?" I said, unable to contain myself any longer. "According to Scott's journal, you were done in. 'I'm just going out for a walk, chaps,' you're supposed to have said, or words to that effect. 'I may be gone a while!'—and then off you went into the blizzard, trying to give the other three a chance of making it to the next supply dump. You know that they *didn't* make it, I suppose?"

"I know," he said. He tried to grimace, but couldn't quite do it. "I wish I had just said that," he replied. "I was too angry with Scott, because I thought he'd killed us all with his casual reck-lessness and lousy planning. I couldn't stand the sight of him any longer. Can't blame him for leaving the rest out, mind, and I suppose I ought to be grateful to him for deleting the exple-tives—but no, what I actually said was a good deal less worthy. Typical of Scott, still thinking of appearances, to be writing his journal for posterity."

"But you did go out into the blizzard—to die?"

"Yes, I went out into the blizzard, to die. I wasn't intending to go far—hell, my toes were all frostbitten and that old gunshot wound from '06 had opened up again because of the scurvy. I didn't think I'd get a hundred yards—but it wouldn't have been fair to Birdy or Ed just to lie down and die on the doorstep, so I figured that the least I could do was take a header into the nearest crevasse. You've no idea how difficult it is to locate a crevasse in a whiteout when you're actually trying to find one. I probably did die...except that here I am, and this isn't my first trip back to the world, or even to England. As to where else I've been in the meantime...well, I know that you've been to Hell, so I obviously wasn't there, but that only means that I can't put a label on it. The Mountains of Madness might just about cover it, I guess."

"You were on the Ross Shelf, I know—do you mean that you actually reached the slopes of Erebus?"

"Maybe—the real one, that is, not the volcano named after it. I've seen mountains compared to which that one would look like a valley—and I don't mean because it has a crater."

"You're not making sense, Titus," I told him—but not resentfully. The world had stopped making sense on day one of the Somme, and it wasn't about to start again any time soon. I won't say that I'd become accustomed to it, or even that I'd learned to live with it, but whether you learned or not, you still had to live it

"I know," he said—but he had other things on his mind. "I've brought you some seeds, Linny. I need you to grow them for me, if you can. It'll need a greenhouse, mind—as hot and humid as you can make it—and some very special soil, but you've got those, haven't you? Much bigger and better than when I was here before."

"The benefits of inheritance" I observed, brusquely. "What kind of seeds? Fruit trees?" I knew that it was a silly suggestion. Mostly I grew fruit trees in the tropical house, cereals and potatoes in the temperate enclosures, but I knew that he wouldn't be bringing me pineapples or passion-fruit from the Antarctic.

"No," he said. "That is, I don't know, exactly...but I'm pretty sure they're not fruit. I'm pretty sure that they're not really plants, in fact."

"They can't really be seeds, then."

He sighed. "Maybe not. Maybe they're eggs that just need soil and blood for incubation. Maybe they're unnamable, because we have nothing like them. But I think of them as seeds."

"Seeds from the Mountains of Madness?"

"Yes."

"Vampire seeds? Seeds that need *blood* in order to grow?"

"Yes. They'll also need minerals...exactly what might take a bit of figuring out, with a little trial-and-error, once I've given you the gist. I knew there was no point trying to plant them myself, or taking them to any common-or-garden gardener. They need an expert touch, someone used to tending...what did you used to call it? A *jardin d'acclimation*?"

Being dead obviously hadn't impaired his memory. There was no point in saying that he could have gone to Kew. He didn't know anyone at Kew. He knew me—or had, once, when we were young and innocent, and again when we lost our innocence fighting the Boers and the blacks, not knowing that the sorry mess in question was all just a tune-up for the real show.

"You're lucky I went back to my hobby," I said. "Helen says that I'm not the same man that I was when I went away, but I've really been able to let my old obsessions run free now that I've got the title, the house and the money."

The title hadn't been on the cards, of course, when he'd known me before. Jack had been the heir apparent, Hal the reserve. I'd been the idle afterthought, only fit for the army or the church—or to be a dilettante dabbling in science. But the war had changed everything, and I wasn't the same man as I had been before, according to my title. Not that anybody actually addressed me as Lord Andersley. I'd only been to the House once. London was more than two hundred miles away.

"It's not luck," Oates said. "It was always a vocation. I could see that. You're the only man I know who ever joined the army in order to further his studies in botany."

"It wasn't an original idea," I told him. "There were precedents, in France. Hell, there were even Frenchmen who became missionaries in order to further their studies in botany. In Britain it used to be the navy, following the inspiration of the great Joseph Banks and poor William Bligh, and knowing how important the science might be to the project of world colonization, to growing food where native vegetation was inadequate to the human diet: the only true conquest of the world. Not that it did them any good in the long run—or any of us. All that our great ecological adventure achieved, in the end, was to spread our war worldwide."

"Ecological adventure?" he queried.

"New jargon," I told him. "The study of organisms in relation to their environment. *Acclimation*—the attempt to adapt organisms to new environments by selectively breeding new strains—is its active branch. It's not just a matter of cultivating exotic flowers any more, or of breeding crops adapted for transplantation to new continents; it's more exploratory, delving down into the...oh, damn it: *seeds? Are you serious?* You've come back from the dead to ask me to plant some *seeds* for you?"

"I'm not actually sure that I've come back," he reminded me, "but yes, that was the price of my coming back. Back from the dead, if I really am back, and back to England, if...."

"Oh, this is England, all right. Unrecognizable, in the faces and hearts of its people, but England nevertheless. What do you man, *price?*"

"I mean the price I had to pay. It was the only way I could get back for more than a flying visit. I had to bring the seeds to you."

"To me? Specifically to me?"

"I mentioned you. I might have sung your praises a little more loudly than was necessary. I was feeling nostalgic. I told them what a *jardin d'acclimation* is, and your ambition to devote your life to one."

"Them?"

"Yes," he said, nodding his head, even though a shudder ran through him as if he'd been pierced by a red hot iron. "*Them.*"

He obviously wasn't quite ready, as yet, to specify who, or what, *they* might be. It was something he couldn't talk about. I could sympathize with that.

I shrugged my shoulders. Yet again, I remembered what the enlisted men used to say, ritually, when things got too absurd: "We just have to do it; we don't have to understand it." They had left understanding to the officers. A bad move, as it turned out. We hadn't understood—and even as a lowly captain, which was as far as my battlefield promotions had extended, I couldn't dodge the responsibility of being part of that "we"— and because we hadn't understood, the poor sods who only had to go and do it had only gone and done it, and had died without understanding. At least Titus had sacrificed himself for a cause of sorts—except that he hadn't, apparently, made the ultimate sacrifice, and had even fluffed his line in Scott's edited script, and the cause had turned out to be just as futile as...I was about to think "ours," but if Judgment was just round the corner, I wasn't entitled to that sort of lie. *Theirs*: their sacrifice, the poor sods.

Am I any better off than he is, I wondered. *Am I really sure that I'm alive?*

That was self-indulgence, though. I was alive, all right. Alive, anyway.

Oates took another gulp of brandy. Even though his face was so terrible to behold, there was an unmistakable fleshiness about it, and the way he drank left no doubt as to his solidity. He wasn't a ghost. He wasn't a hallucination. That was a pity, on both accounts. Like any aristocratic manor whose founda-tions dated back at least to Tudor times, the house must have played host to its fair share of tragedies, rapes and murders, but there wasn't a single old soldier, crying child or white lady who walked the corridors at night, plaintively demanding succor or justice. I'd always thought that the poor old heap had been a trifle deprived in that respect. As for hallucination...well, how sweet it would have been to look back and think that some of the things I'd seen might only be have been hallucinations, and that I might simply be doolally.

But Oates was real. Dead or not, he was real. And whatever he'd come to ask of me, however absurd or horrible it turned out to be, was real too.

"Seeds," I said, as if the word had become the strangest in the language. "Fair enough—let's have a look."

* * * * * * *

Oates took a package out of the inside pocket of his great-coat. It was made of brown paper, completed with string and sealing-wax—almost insultingly ordinary. I cut the string with my pen-knife and unwrapped the paper.

There were seven, but I couldn't believe, even at first glance, that they were really seeds, or even tubers. They were as big as a child's fist, and just as knobbly, not hard without exactly being squishy. They were slightly slick to the touch, seemingly more oily than damp, although nothing came off on my fingers. The tegument was more reminiscent of a mollusk than a bean, or perhaps of some weird kind of pupa. Definitely not seeds—but Oates was right; there was no ready word. They were unnamable, except by improvisation. Seeds, then. Why not?

They were cold. That didn't make sense. They'd been wrapped up in Oates' pocket next to his heart. They should at least have been equal to the ambient temperature of the air—unless poor undead Titus had a very cold heart indeed. His handshake had chilled me slightly, but it hadn't turned my fingers to icicles. He seemed to be warming up again now, thanks to the fire in the grate and the brandy inside him. His face looked more human, relatively speaking, and I'd already caught on to the fact that I could help it stay that way by not asking questions whose answers turned out to be excessively paradoxical...at least for the time being.

"What do you expect me to do, exactly," I asked, "except stick them in bloody soil and hope? There are only seven—that's not nearly enough for any kind of disciplined experimentation with different environmental regimes. Hell, if I slice one up with a microtome to examine its cellular structure under a microscope I'll already be fourteen per cent down...although I'll need to do that if I'm to attempt any kind of tissue-culture."

"Do what you have to," he said. "You don't have to grow all seven to maturity. One will do, though more would be better. Nobody expects miracles."

He meant that *they* didn't expect miracles, but *they* were unnamable, even as "they." For the time being, they were "nobody."

I was going to have to know, though. I couldn't just do it and not understand. I was an officer—I'd even caught up in rank with Oates. I was a botanist too. For those reasons and others, I *had* to understand...to the extent that understanding might be possible. Unnamable was one thing, unthinkable was something else entirely.

"Do you remember those blacks in the north, back in '08," I said, "who told us tales of jungles where there were vampire flowers that drank the blood of humans? Not that they'd ever seen a jungle, mind—we'd seen more jungle than they had—but they had their fingers on the pulse of local folklore. Are these the seeds of those vampire flowers, do you think?"

"No," he said, bluntly. "They're from much further away. I don't know what they'll produce, but I don't think you have to worry about roses with narcotic scent and bloodthirsty petals, or carnivorous trees whose branches are clawed arms or snakes with avid fangs. Tentacles, maybe...probably...anyway, I don't think that's the kind of danger they'll pose, if you really can grow them to maturity."

"But they *do* pose some kind of danger?" I queried.

"Of course," he said, colorlessly.

"I have a wife and child. Not to mention three lab assistants, four ground staff and eight domestic servants—a whole bloody colony, in effect. How *much* danger?"

"I don't know," he said. If he'd said that he wished that he did I wouldn't have believed him. Instead, he added: "I'm sorry, Linny." I wasn't entirely sure that I believed that, either.

"What if I say no?" I asked.

"You'll miss out on an unprecedented experiment," he told me, coldly. "You'll miss out on a mystery. You'll miss out on the danger. If you'd found one of those vampire plants of legend in Africa, I know full well that you'd have gone to any lengths to get their seeds back to a controlled environment, where you

could grow and nurture them, study and marvel at them....
even feed them, if you had to. These are real, and any kind of
blood will probably do. They're from...I'm not entirely sure that
another world is the right expression, but somewhere or some-
when exceedingly strange. *Can* you say no?"

His face had deteriorated again briefly, but the armchair—
and everything that went with it—seemed to be doing him good.
He was adapting to his environment, soaking up its warmth,
its atmosphere, its homeliness. He was collecting himself,
becoming more Oatesy than...but I didn't have a name to put to
that, either. He now seemed more alive than dead, at any rate.

Oates, I remembered, with a conscious effort, was a hero: a
man who had at least tried to lose his life in a Quixotic gesture,
after trying and failing to go where no man had gone before.
He had walked into a whiteout, and fallen...where? Or, given
his last hint, when? In time, presumably, he would tell me—
provided that I agreed to nurse his seeds.

Could I say no? Yes. Would I? Not in this lifetime, or in a
million years.

After all, he'd come back from the dead to give me the opportunity, even if he hadn't quite made it all the way back, as yet. I
owed it to him to do what I could. He was my friend, my oldest
friend. There had been too many friends—brothers, even—for
whom I hadn't been able to do anything at all. If any one of
them had come back, dead or otherwise, to ask me for a favor,
however absurd or dangerous, I'd have been glad to do it. At
least, I'd have been glad if I'd still been capable of gladness. I'd
have been *determined* to do it. Desperate, even.

I squinted at him, trying to make out his features—or, at
least, trying to figure out why I still couldn't quite do it, even
though I knew it was him. "What if I fail?" I said. "This *price*...."

"Don't worry about it, Linny," he said. "Just try. That's all
any of us can do."

He'd finished his brandy. I was taking my pick, judiciously,
from the thousand obvious questions that temptation was
offering me, when the door to the study opened and the brat

came in.

She hadn't realized that I—we—had a visitor. She didn't know that she was interrupting. So she had burst in, taking it for granted that I'd be as pleased to see her as I could be, even if I were busy.

Whatever it was she'd intended to say died on her lips. She came to an abrupt halt, and stared. Children do that. The poor mite wasn't old enough to understand "conduct unbecoming." She was too busy just becoming. Oates looked better, but he still looked bad—not quite as dead, but still possessed of a face that even a mother would have had difficulty loving.

It seemed best to act as if everything were normal. What alternative was there?

"This is my daughter Mary," I told Oates. "We call her Mercy. She's seven. Mercy, this is an old friend of mine from the army, Captain Oates."

"Were you hurt in the war?" Mercy asked the dead man, mildly.

I realized that the mildness wasn't feigned. She honestly and truly wasn't frightened, or even shocked—much less so than I had been, at any rate.

In the latter days of the war Helen, under the compulsion to do her bit, had allowed the east wing of the house to be turned into a military sanitarium for men who'd been badly hit in more ways than one. Mercy had seen too much for a child her age, and had earned her nickname. She had seen men who had been burned and men who had been blasted. She had played ball with some of the on the lawn. She had no real notion of the possible range of human injury; she just knew that it was possible to be horribly disfigured. She simply didn't know that what had become of Oates' face was any more improbable than what had become of others she'd seen.

"I was shot in the leg in Africa," Oates told her, deliberately misunderstanding the question. "One of my legs is shorter than the other now."

It was irrelevant. He was sitting down; she hadn't seen him

limping. The answer sufficed, though. Mercy was used to not getting straight answers. She nodded, sympathetically. It was okay. Oates' being here was okay—with Mercy, at least

Helen came in then, chasing Mercy but way behind, as usual.

"Sorry, Tom," she said, automatically. Then she stopped.

For a moment, she almost stared, because she did know the difference between a war wound and what was afflicting Titus, but she was made of exceedingly stern stuff now. She wasn't the same wife that she had been before. She was familiar with the horrible, the inexpressible and the paradoxical. She was horrified, but she just looked at me for guidance, and she looked at Mercy protectively. She knew, then, how she had to conduct herself.

Oates had stood up, hoisted by an ancient reflex, an instinctive politeness that had survived even the Mountains of Madness. He bowed politely, a trifle lop-sidedly.

"I'm sorry," Helen said. "I don't know we had a visitor. I'd better tell Hollis that there'll be an extra setting for dinner." Her voice implied that it wasn't the only thing she'd have to warn him about. If she was hoping that I, or Oates, was going to tell her that he wouldn't be staying for dinner, she gave not the slightest sign of it.

"Better tell him to have a bed made up in one of the spare rooms, too," I said. "Helen, this is Captain Oates; Oates, my wife Helen. You've heard me mention Oates, Helen—I knew him at school, and in Africa, in the dragoons."

She knew perfectly well who "Captain Oates" was, and knew perfectly well that he was supposed to be dead, but she'd *done her bit*, looking after the walking wounded, the walking dead, and wounded men who'd never walk again, or ever have faces to show. She knew she wasn't looking at a ghost. In fact, Oates looked better now than he had done just before the door opened. Mercy and Helen were part of the environment too, and by far and away the best part. Their mere appearance was helping him to get a grip.

He tried to smile, and almost succeeded.

"I'm delighted to meet you, Captain Oates," Helen lied. "I've heard a lot about you."

Poor Oates had never heard a word about her, so he couldn't reply in kind. He bowed again. "I hope that it's no trouble," he said, "but I had to ask a favor of your husband."

"No trouble at all," she said, recklessly lying again, seemingly blithely unaware that the Day of Judgment must be close at hand, since the Resurrection had begun. "I hope we can help you."

Silently, I thanked for that *we*. She was a hero.

"We've had other men here with spoiled faces," Mercy put in, helpfully. "We do our best. I played ball. An American taught me baseball."

"You're very kind," Oates told her.

*   *   *   *   *   *   *

Helen wasn't quite so understanding, of course, once Oates had gone to bed. He'd retired early, because he was very tired, but not before Helen had spotted that he was in great pain and had demanded to see his feet and the wound in his thigh. He would have had to change the dressings himself if nobody else had helped, and she now prided herself on being a trained nurse who had "seen everything."

Not everything, as it turned out. Not even almost everything.

"How long have they been like this?" she had asked, helplessly.

"Seven years," he had told her. That was incredible, of course, but Helen took it in her stride. She gritted her teeth and changed the dressings, but the expression on her face when she looked at me was far too readable for comfort. Perhaps mercifully, comfort and I had been strangers for quite a while. My frostbite was metaphorical, and didn't look any where near as disgusting as Oates', but I had my twinges when people said the wrong thing, or even looked at me in certain ways.

Afterwards, Helen came to the study, where I was examining

the seeds with a magnifying-glass. "Captain Oates?" she said, incredulously. "*The* Captain Oates?"

"One and the same," I confirmed. "Insofar as any of us is the same, any more."

"He didn't die in the Antarctic?"

"If he did," I said, content to state the obvious, "he's come back."

"Why?" That was my Helen. Always cut to the heart of the matter.

It was my turn deliberately to misunderstand. "He wants me to grow some seeds for him."

She wasn't content with the evasion. She wasn't an officer, and didn't really need to understand, but she was a hero, and couldn't be content not to, except when no understanding was possible. At the very least, I had to convince her of that.

"Apparently," I went on, "he told someone that I might be able to do it—talked me up a bit, I suspect. It was the only way he could get back here for any length of time. I don't think he really believes that I can do it, but suggesting that I might be able to do it was the only way he could get a furlough from... wherever. Or whenever. I don't really understand, and it hurts him when I ask, but given time...if he can explain it to me, I'll explain it to you."

"It's impossible," she told me, flatly.

"I know." I tried to remember the last time I had been amazed by the impossible, when it happened in front of me, but I couldn't. Africa had desensitized me even before I'd been recommissioned. Now I'd brought it home...but there was a sense in I which I'd already brought everything home, because I hadn't been able to leave it behind.

Helen gave up on the Inquisition. She knew how to be patient. During the war, she'd been very nearly the only person left on the estate, except for the vicar, who could read fluently. Even before the sanitarium, she'd had to make rounds, to read letters and telegrams to women who didn't understand, didn't want to understand, and prayed every night for the impossible. They hadn't wanted the vicar, they'd wanted her, because they knew she was a mother, like them, and thought she was an angel, unlike them. She'd had to pretend to be an angel; it was a mere matter of adaptation to her environment.

"Is he going to be here long?" she asked, angelically.

"I hope so."

That was too much, even for an angel "You *hope* so? Why?"

"Because I'm pretty sure that it's a lot better that where he's been," I explained. "He needs rest, recuperation. He needs that bleeding wound in his thigh to scar over again, and those ruined toes to heal, if that's possible. He needs to warm up as much as he can. Did you notice how cold he is?"

"Those toes aren't going to heal, Tom. I don't know why they aren't gangrenous, but they're certainly necrotic. Whatever state the rest of him is in, those toes are dead. I can't do anything for his toes, except perhaps call in a surgeon to amputate them."

Her heroism was showing again. She was focusing on the toes in order not to have to cope with the rest, although she'd done a good job with that, even to the extent of drilling the servants. She thought that she couldn't do anything for Oates' toes—but the way she'd phrased that judgment implied that there might be things she thought that she could help him with. Whatever he had was likely far worse than shell-shock, but his mind obviously wasn't dead. There was something in him that could still be nursed, and might benefit from nursing. Except that it might be dangerous....

"Leave him to me," I told her, trying not to make it sound like an order, because I knew she'd resent it if she thought it was. "We'll be in the greenhouse most of the time, or the lab, or here. I'm going to put a padlock on the tropical house, by the way. Controlled environment—can't have people coming and going willy-nilly."

"Just you and the girls," she observed, tonelessly.

Helen didn't really think that I was having an affair with one of the assistants helping me in my work. She knew that the only reason they were female was that the drastic shortage of men in that kind of employment. Before the war, the notion of female ground staff would have seemed utterly alien, but now...not that my horticultural assistants were *ground staff*, strictly speaking. Anyway, Helen had no anxieties of that sort, for all that we now had separate bedrooms, whereas before the war....

"Just me and Oates," I told her. "The girls will have to look after the cereals and potatoes for a while. The tropical house will be off limits to them too. The trees don't need much in the way of care, and it'll only take me a day or two to train Oates to help with the routine data-collection. That way, I'll be able to concentrate on the new task."

I picked up one of the "seeds" and held it up, hoping that its relatively innocuous appearance, combined with my casual manner, would help to reassure Helen that everything was fundamentally okay, and that the "task" was something I could take in my stride.

She wasn't convinced. She took the object off me, and frowned at its coldness. She turned it over and over, sniffed it, sat held it up close to get a good look at it. She knew enough botany to see that it wasn't really a seed, in the strict sense of the word, or even a spore, but she couldn't put a name to it either.

She handed it back. "What are you going to do with them?" she asked. "Grow a magic beanstalk and go giant-hunting?"

Jack had actually been golden goose hunting; the giant had simply been in the way—but I didn't bother to correct her. They weren't beans, and I hadn't even had to sell the family cow to get them, so the analogy was a non-starter anyway.

"I'll slice one of them up," I said. "I'll use the microscope to examine the cellular structure—if it has a cellular structure—and I'll try to start some tissue-cultures. I'll try to develop a couple of them in the hydroponic tank, and the rest in pots, using slightly different regimes. Hopefully, I'll be able to pick up some clues along the way that will help me optimize the conditions. I'm not convinced that any of them will actually develop, and if any of them do, it's highly likely that some won't. I'll keep you up to date."

"If not a beanstalk," she said, stubbornly, "what?"

"I have no idea, yet" I said, a trifle impatiently. "The external structure suggests that it isn't just a bag of storage-protein, but I can't tell for sure until I cut it open to see whether there's a minuscule embryo tucked inside, waiting to begin consuming the bulk. Appearances suggest that it's more like a pupa than a bean—but appearances can be deceptive when you're dealing with something new. Whatever it is, I suspect that our ready-made categories of plant and animal might not be entirely appropriate to it.

Helen didn't want to give up just yet. "Where did he get them?" she demanded.

"I don't know," I replied, honestly.

"How did he get them here with his feet in that condition?"

"I don't know. I asked—but there are some questions he can't answer. Not yet, at least."

She changed tack. "Can you get them to grow?"

I didn't know that, either, but repetition is so tedious. "I'm sure as hell going to try," I assured her.

This time, she didn't ask why. She thought she knew why. She thought that growing things had become my last redoubt, my final defense, the only activity in which could really absorb myself, to find a measure of peace and solace. She would have preferred it if my last redoubt had been the house—no, more narrowly than that, the house*hold*: the family—but she knew that I couldn't help it. She didn't doubt that I loved her, and Mercy, any more than she doubted that she and Mercy loved me, but she knew that escape from the present circumstances required more than that. She forgave me for my needs, as I forgave her for hers, and we both hoped that things would get better, with Mercy's help. From her viewpoint, Oates was a complication she could do without—but she suspected, as I did, that from my point of view, he might be something of a godsend, and that even if he'd been sent by the Devil instead, he might have something I needed: the seeds of hope.

Except that, according to him, they were actually bloodthirsty seeds from the Mountains of Madness.

Madness really had become mountainous of late: dangerous and forbidding, but strangely magnificent, magnetic in spite of its murderousness.

"The servants can cope," she said, more to reassure herself than me. "They coped with the sanitarium; this is just an extension of that. No matter how creepy they find him, they'll put a brave face on it. I'll see to it. They've done it before. They have it easy, now that there's only three of us to look after. One last traumatized cripple won't change that. We can all cope."

Before the war, the house had had a domestic staff of seventeen, and the ground staff, including the stable-lads, had numbered ten. Now, the domestic staff was reduced to six and the ground staff to two—not counting the girls—the stables having been converted into garages and equipment-sheds. Everything was shrinking—the family most of all, now reduced from ten to three. Not all the missing were dead; some had simply moved on, but the effect was the same. Relatively speaking, though, the present staff did have it easy, by comparison with the numbers the pre-war staff had had to cope with, in terms of permanent residents and frequent guests. Diminished or not, they could cope

Our wealth had diminished too, although we still had enough. My grandfather, the thirteenth Earl, had been fond of saying that land was the only true wealth, but he'd been wrong; the only true wealth now was money, a mercurial phantom deprived of any real substance. The idea that land was anything but a sticky matrix for trenches, for battles, for bloodshed....

"I'm going to take these out to the greenhouse now," I told Helen, who was still waiting, although here was nothing I could tell her, as yet, that might have been worth waiting for. "I'll get busy tomorrow, with Oates' help and guidance. Once the basics are out of the way, I'll be able to start pumping him, diplomatically, for more information as to what happened down there in the Antarctic, and where he's been since then. However crazy or horrible it is, I'll tell you everything."

She knew, I supposed, that it could hardly be anything other than crazy or horrible, but she no longer fled in fear of such realities.

"We have to look after Mercy," she said, not because I needed reminding but because she wanted to make the declaration for her own psychological purposes.

"I know," I assured her, for similar reasons.

* * * * * * *

Oates only had a few further instructions about the sticky and bloody matrix in which the seeds allegedly needed to be planted. I learned less than I hoped from the dissection and microscopic analysis of the sacrificed specimen, and the tissue-cultures I tried to set up were a complete bust—probably because the damn thing didn't have tissues in the same sense that Earthly plants and animals had. It didn't have cells, in the same way that Earthly life-forms had, either. If it wasn't a single primitive entity, then it hadn't evolved in the same way that we had, by multiplying and differentiating the same basic cell-pattern all the way from monad to man. It was more like an extremely dense, extremely elaborate network.

If a spider's web were alive, and had initiated an evolutionary sequence, it probably wouldn't have done so by dividing into more webs, conserving the same pattern. It would have expanded and become more labyrinthine, evolving, as it were, *topologically* rather than arithmetically or geometrically. That, at least, was how things seemed to me...how I managed to find a way of thinking about it that seemed to make a kind of sense. The bits of the web didn't seem to be capable of "vegetative" reproduction, at least in the conditions I could provide, but they did seem to have some regenerative capacity, as long as they weren't sliced up too small.

The two seeds I tried to grow in the hydroponic apparatus did nothing, even when bathed in blood and nutrients. In the end, I transplanted them into pots, partly because I figured that

I needed every chance I could get under what seemed to be the better conditions. Of the six, only two made any progress at all in the first week—but two was better than none, and maybe better than I had any right to expect.

It was a tense week. Oates and I put in sixteen-hour days, save for meals, and even took lunch in the greenhouse, carefully picking up the tray at the door and handing it back in the same pseudo-ceremonial fashion, without Hollis or the scullery maid ever setting foot inside the glass palace. Ninety per cent of the effort we made went to waste, or produced only enigmatic returns, but that wasn't entirely the point of making it.

The tropical house wasn't what I'd call a healthy environment, but Oates didn't seem to have brought any infectious agents back from the dead, so we did better there than we ever had in Africa. I won't say we thrived, but we got a little better, gradually and each in our own way. Talking about old times helped us both to adapt to our new selves—and while we were talking about old times, everything went smoothly. It had it frustrating dimension, though, because it certainly wasn't what I wanted to talk about *all* the time, and I think that Oates was just as keen, in his way, to tell me about the impossible things that had happened to him as I was to hear them.

That wasn't easy, though, for either of us. I probed and I winkled, as delicately and deftly as I could, and he made efforts too, but there really were things he literally could not say, and not just for lack of an appropriate vocabulary. He was back, but he was under a spell of some kind.

By the end of the first week, we'd made as little progress with his story as we had with the task that *they* had allotted to him as a condition of his return, but I had become more optimistic. Just as I'd insisted on a degree of variation and gradation in the initial planting conditions of the seeds, I tried all kinds of maneuvers to figure out how to help his story grow and develop. The whole point of a *jardin d'acclimation*, after all, is to test different environmental conditions, in search of the optimum, in advance of the dogged struggle to train subsequent generations of plants to adapt to different optima. With only seven specimens, one of them sacrificed to microscopic analysis, I hadn't been able to plan a proper multivariable grid, but I had at least made sure that all the eggs weren't in one circumstantial basket. Having given me all the advice he had to give, Oates was content to yield to my expertise thereafter—that, after all, was why he was here. The cultivation of his story was an analogical process. I approached it from different directions, until I found the most suitable matrix.

The one thing a practical agriculturalist needs more than anything else is patience. Colonies aren't built in a day. It's a matter of generations, of lifetimes, of taking the long view...and hoping that catastrophe will stay away.

"I hope you didn't tell *them* that I have some kind of magical ability," I said to him, once, when things didn't see to be going too well seed-wise. "After all, you're the one with green fingers."

It was a joke, but not a good one—in rather poor taste, in fact.

"You do have a gift," he assured me. "I always knew that, even at Eton. The others ragged you about it, but they knew too."

"Nothing like a gift to encourage bullying," I observed, drily. "Except, of course, a limp. Lucky you didn't catch that bullet until you were half a world away from the old *alma mater.*"

"It wasn't that bad," he said. He was right; it hadn't been that bad. He deserved some credit for that. Isolated, I'd have been dead meat, figuratively speaking—not just at school, where everyone dies a little, but in the dragoons. No lieutenant had ever required a sympathetic captain as much as I had. I knew how much I owed to Oates, even though he didn't.

"So," I said, when all the planning had been properly carried out, the strategy measured out, and the campaign analyzed, "you were in this blizzard, hoping to fall into a crevasse, so that your mates wouldn't trip over your body when they set off again. Then what happened?"

"I fell."

"Into a crevasse?"

"Maybe."

Things went on like that for a while longer, but in the end, the two seeds that actually consented to develop began to develop, and Oates began to find a state of mind in which he could contrive a conversational flow that went far beyond Eton and far beyond Africa.

It was a slow process, but we had time.

In order to straighten the labyrinthine story out—a much more necessary process than cutting it short—I'll summarize, and try to put things in some sort of order. What remains vague remains vague because it *was* vague, in the same way that his face had been vague when I first saw it, and still was, sometimes.

He *had* fallen into a crevasse—not maybe but almost certainly. A bottomless crevasse. It should, in terms of mere Earthly topography, have taken him down into the sea, given that Scott's party was on the ice-shelf, but it didn't.

There is, it seems, another Antarctica. There's a trivial sense in which that's true, of course: there's an island, perhaps an entire continent, under the ice. Once upon a time, it was warm—really warm, not merely less cold. It was a continent with rivers, and forests, and fields, and cities; but the ice had crushed all that. It had crushed everything.

"It looks so still," Oates said, "so nearly eternal, but it's not still, let alone eternal. Even now, the ice moves, grinding and crushing."

There are rivers and lakes underneath the ice...even life, apparently. If the ice were to disappear, as the ice that once covered Yorkshire had disappeared, tens of thousands of years ago, the land would regenerate, just as Yorkshire has. Well, not *just* as Yorkshire has, because Yorkshire was only covered for a few tens or hundreds of thousands of years: a mere eye-blink of geological time, let alone cosmic time. Antarctica....well, life would come back differently there.

And that was the point, or part of it. Because as well as the trivial other Antarctica, there was a quite different and much stranger Other Antarctica

While Oates was letting this out, he often settled into a peculiar kind of reverie, letting his intelligence idle and his mouth run on. That was the only way he could talk about it, because doing so with his consciousness focused and concentrated would have activated the spell that was inhibiting his revelations. It would also have confronted him with the indescribable, the unnamable and the unthinkable, and confused him utterly. Going with the flow, on the other hand, while avoiding the worst potential obstacles, at least allowed him to skirt the truth, and thus convey some expression of it.

He did want to explain. He was an officer, and he needed to understand—and he wanted me to understand too, not just because I'd finally made it to captain but because I was his friend, and he needed me...and he wanted to warn me, to the extent that he could, about what it was that I was being required to do.

Imagine what a pickle we'd be in, here in north Yorkshire, if the ice were to come back. If there had been people here before the last Ice Age, of course—Neanderthals, I suppose—they had simply retreated ahead of the ice, but they were nomads, hunter-gatherers. They didn't have any elaborate agriculture, any cities or any concept of the ownership of land. The notion of opposing the ice, trying to fight it, would never have occurred to them. To me, though, a lord of the manor whose family has owned and farmed the land for centuries, the idea of retreat would be a very different matter. My first impulse would be to stand fast—to find a way of holding back the ice if I could, and if I couldn't, then to find some way of living underneath it. Yorkshire folk are legendary for their stubbornness. It wouldn't just be the lords of the manor who thought that way. It would be everyone. We'd tunnel. We'd find a way, if there was any way to be found. We'd dig in.

Actually, maybe *I* wouldn't have. Maybe I'd have retreated, having learned my lesson at Mons. But that's not the point I'm trying to make. I'm really talking about the Antarcticans, and why there's still an Other Antarctica, into which a hero like Captain Oates could fall, and keep on going, dead or not.

The things that once lived in Antarctica, a *very* long time ago, in one of the periods when it was warm, had the same kind of stubbornness as Yorkshire folk, and technological resources of which dalesmen and woldsmen can only dream. I don't know why they couldn't stop the ice—it's possible that the continent itself drifted, that it came to rest on the Earth's axis having previously been located in kinder climes. Certainly, the Earth itself cooled, after a hot phase. Once, in a past remoter still, it had been completely covered in ice; in one not quite so remote it had been entirely ice-free, but in the era Oates told me a little bit about—*billions* of years ago, long before the life we know had even emerged from the sea to cover the land left vacant by yet another catastrophe—the ice was on the attack. Not just the ice, either; the Earth was a busy place in those days, apparently, with more than one kind of life—more than one kind of being—fighting for its possession. Things are quiet now, but we've only been here for an eye-blink of geological time, so we can't really tell, and if we could....

Anyhow, the Antarcticans dug in. When they couldn't stop the ice, or decided not to stop it—because they might have decided not to, figuring that the ice might make a useful defensive wall against some other enemy—they tried to live underneath it, in lacunae and under the ground. Humans couldn't do that, obviously, because life of our kind is parasitic on sunlight: no light, no plants, no food. *They* were different. *They* had other needs, other ways; they were no longer parasitic on sunlight...not, at any rate, to the same extent as us. They were highly intelligent, and Oates doubted that they thought they could establish any kind of stable situation that might endure for millions of years; they knew they'd have to keep on adapting, keep on changing... but that was their thing anyway. They were much more long-lived than we are, and they didn't think so highly of stability.

"We're mayflies," Oates said, drowsily, "and we dream of

prolongation, of settlement, of consistency. They didn't see survival in those terms; they weren't utopians."

The Antarcticans, Oates hinted—because he had no way to explain—had strange and various resources, and they had strange and various methods too. They couldn't keep things going forever, maybe because of their other enemies, but when they settled for dormancy—not death but dormancy—in order to wait for more favorable circumstances to come around again, they left a great deal behind. The ice crushed a lot of it, over the course of hundreds of millions of years, but the residue had been designed to withstand that. Oates thought that their enemies might have destroyed more, or else that the ones who were dug in might have suffered from some dire catastrophe of another sort—but still, the residue remained...and it still remains, much diminished, but still able, after a strange and distant fashion, to *cope*.

The ice melted again—more than once, Oates thought—but if that was what the sleepers were waiting for, it didn't trigger any mass awakening. Oates had no idea what would...but he did know, for sure, that among the things they left behind were *traps*. Perhaps the traps had actually been disguised as crevasses, way back when, but that was definitely the way that some of them appeared now. Oates fell into one. It was bottomless. He didn't smash his head on ice or rock, like poor Edgar Evans, and he didn't fall into the sea to be eaten by a leopard-seal. He just fell.

Maybe he died and maybe he didn't die, but either way, he came out of it again. *They* brought him out. *They* looked after him, as best they could, in ways that we can't understand. *They* communicated with him. They even kept him up to date, as best they could, with what was happening in the world. Eventually, he was released...at a price....

* * * * * * *

I'm getting ahead of myself slightly here, but things had become tangled; too many things were going on at once. The seeds were developing. Oates was telling his story in confused dribs and drabs. I was telling Helen what I'd learned, trying to sort it out as I went. She was looking after his leg, his toes and his fingers. And Mercy was being merciful, even volunteering to play ball on the lawn—an offer he always refused. Not to mentions the servants. Things became confused.

I think I lost track of time, but that wasn't a bad thing. I'd been trying to lose track of time for some while, or maybe just trying to give the time that was tracking me the slip. The tropical house became a refuge, for a while, where I dug in. I came out for dinner, of course, to keep contact with Mercy and the world, and I talked to Helen late at night, but I *was* dug in, while the seeds and the story grew and slowly took shape, and began—only *began*—to make a vestige of sense, not only of themselves, but somehow of everything.

It wasn't easy. Sometimes, Oates' face became unhuman again, and I was so close to him by then that when it happened, I became unhuman too, and it wasn't a pleasant sensation at all— but the task was doable. It wasn't quite understandable, as yet, but it as doable, and we did it. We all did it. And we all did our bit, just as everybody has to, in extreme circumstances. Paradox or not, it's only the unreal horrors that continue to horrify us. The real ones soon go beyond mere horror, and become life. They remain traumatic, still capable of turning the human unhuman, of contriving fates worse than death, but they cease to horrify us consciously.

Sometimes, when he was trying to let something out— presumably a truth that he wasn't supposed to reveal—Oates would pause, temporarily unable to continue, as if his tongue had swollen in his mouth and stuck to his palate. Sometimes, while I was listening, I felt strange frissons crawling through my flesh. Invariably, we were both was sweating profusely, because it was hot and humid in the greenhouse; the green leaves around us were dripping so profusely that it almost seemed to be raining indoors, but the fruit-trees didn't mind; they could bear it.

Sometimes, though, Oates didn't sweat. Sometimes, he was

cold. In spite of everything, he was sometimes still cold, not only to the touch but within himself. On such occasions, I gave him a cordial to drink, to replenish his energy supplies as well as his liquid balance—something Helen and I had cooked up together. It seemed to help.

The fact that Oates had made contact with the billion-year-old Antarcticans—*them!*—and made some kind of pact with them, seemed to me to imply that they were no longer dormant, but that wasn't the way that Oates saw it. They way he put it was that they *were* still dormant, or perhaps even dead—but that they were *very* good at dreaming.

We're not, it seems. We're mere infants by comparison, mere random finger-painters, dream-wise. *They* can dream while dormant, perhaps even while dead...and their dreams aren't confined to their physical bodies.

They do have physical bodies, apparently. Oates was vague, but from what I could gather they're rather like barrels, with more complex organs at the top and the bottom. They have five...well, call them tentacles for want of a better term, at one end. Oates didn't know what to call the things at the other end, and didn't seem impressed when I suggested "the scrapers at the bottom of the barrel," because he thought of the tentacles as being at the bottom end. I dare say—although Oates didn't, quite—that they include sense-organs, and maybe a mouth...or maybe not.

The "barrel-boys," as I came to think of them were the...not people, not rulers, but...well, let's just say "dreamers" and leave it at that.

There were other beings in the Other Antarctica, though: servants, slaves or maybe domestic animals....big, horrid things, swarming with tentacles and shapeshifting like amoebae. Oates had got the impression that they had got out of hand at one point—that they had revolted on their own account or had been co-opted by some enemy. The matter was too vague for him to be sure, though, let alone for him to give me the whole story.

The way Oates put it, he hadn't actually met *them*—the

Antarcticans—in the sense that he'd met me or Helen...but he had entered into their dreams. That was what had sustained him, dead or alive. *They* were dreaming...and still are, of course. That was the trap, the pitfall, the cage....

Trying to pull the threads together, Oates fell into a bottomless pit, into the collective dream of life-forms unlike ours, who'd been asleep, or maybe dead, for billions of years. Where or when he was it was impossible to say, perhaps because he was no longer anywhere or anywhen, but merely in between. He'd been outside the flow of material events, but not so far outside that he couldn't look into it occasionally. He could see the Other Antarctica, and he could see fragments of our world too, and occasionally walk therein. The Other Antarctica wasn't confined to our Antarctica, although it was rooted there. The mystery of how he's walked to the entrance to the driveway wasn't really a mystery, even though it was a paradox. He really had walked from Antarctica—directly, in the ultimate instance. He'd been back before, more than once: to London, even to Eton. "Constitutionals," he called them, although I had a sneaking suspicion that the Antarcticans had elected to carry out reconnaissance and experiments of their own before entrusting him with the seeds and the mission to grow them.

He could walk back just as easily, of course, if and when *they* summoned him. They were still watching. They were probably keeping as close a watch on my progress as I was, presumably willing the project to succeed.

Stranger things happen at sea, they say, but...well, I was about to say that I doubted it, but who am I to doubt, any longer? Who knows what might by lying at the bottom of the sea, dormant but dreaming...waiting...?

Helen didn't take kindly to that part of the story.

"You mean," she said, "that they could reach out to us at any moment...start dreaming us they way they're dreaming Oates?"

"Probably not," I said, trying to look on the bright side. "If they could do that, they wouldn't need Oates—and they needed him for something more than mere guidance to our gate. He fell into their trap, remember. I think we'd have to fall into a trap too before they could start dreaming us. And I don't think there are any traps in Yorkshire. Only in Antarctica."

"So if Oates weren't here, and you weren't growing his blessed magic beans we'd be safe?"

Safe? I wanted to say, or rather to scream. *Safe! From world war? From the Spanish flu? From everything that the world has in store from us. What the fuck is safe now, for us or for Mercy? How will we ever know safety again, even if we were to find it?* But I didn't. Conduct unbecoming.

"There's no evidence that we're under any kind of threat," I told her. "They saved Oates' life. His heart is beating, and he isn't cold any more, except for the occasional shiver. His leg-wound is scarring over, and his toes haven't dropped off. Maybe they didn't bring him back from the dead all at once, but he's alive *now*. Sure, they might be giants—probably are—but they might be gentle giants, or at least grateful ones...and Jack got the golden goose anyway, remember?"

"That was a fairy tale—and a sanitized version."

"Nevertheless," I insisted, "we have no cause for despair, or even dire anxiety. We have no idea what's going to happen—and that's a good situation, isn't it, after so many years of knowing *exactly* what was going to happen, sooner or later."

She conceded that point, as she had to.

I gave her a hug, for which she was duly grateful, although she wasn't sure, as yet, that I had come all the way back to life.

* * * * * * *

So, the Earth has been inhabited before: before our kind of life—the entire ancestral tree connecting monad to man—emerged from the sea. Perhaps there was an earlier emergence, but Oates' impression was that the Antarcticans and their enemies hadn't evolved here. They'd come from elsewhere, as colonists, and once they'd arrived and started up their plantations, as colonists do, they'd become involved in fighting colonial wars, as colonists do. Maybe the entire universe is a battlefield, and Earth is just a remote island, claimed by three or four different powers.

At any rate, our kind of life is probably the only kind *native* to the Earth—or maybe not. Oates had no idea, but I couldn't help philosophizing on the basis of what he told me. I'm a practical agriculturalist, after all; I understand colonialism far better than the poor sods who only had to do it.

Perhaps the monads that eventually gave rise of humans did emerge by some strange process of chemical evolution from the oceanic slime...it's possible. But if the Earth had been colonized, a long time ago, isn't it more likely that the oceans were seeded, like a vast *jardin d'acclimation*? The essence of the colonial project is feeding the colonists, providing them with an adequate ecological basis.

The fact that the Antarcticans seemed to be a very different kind of life argued against that, I suppose, but they weren't the only ones attempting to colonize. Some of *their* enemies, Oates thought, had been even more different from the monad/man sequence that they were—but some might have been far more like us....and the Antarcticans might, in any case, have had nutritional requirements very different from ours. Hadn't our chemists, before the war, begun exploring the possibility of "chemical nutrition" that might free us from dependency on our fellow species? Who could tell whether the Antarcticans might not have evolved in a very different way from us....

Anyway, the basics were clear enough, in principle: the transplantation of crops, the conquest of new environments, the science of assertive botany. Perhaps we—by which I mean every life-form known to us and related to us—are just the end-product of some cosmic *jardin d'acclimation*, sown in the seas of Earth with a view to...well, to begin with, to a few billon years of adaptive evolution, so that one day the Earth would be ready...that *we*'d be ready....

I put it to Oates, in a purely hypothetical manner, that being the best way not to hurt him.

He agreed that it was possible, hypothetically—even plausible, given what he knew.

"*They* aren't mayflies, Linny," he said, pensively. "They don't work on our kind of timescale. I'd say that they don't think like us if I thought that there were any other way of thinking but simply thinking, but....well, however they think, and however they dream, they do it in the long term. If Earth is a colony—and it certainly was, even if there's some doubt as to whether or not it still is—then we could well be part of its crop. Maybe not an intended part, and maybe more pest than product, but part of a *scheme*. Maybe a useful part, at least for *something*...and they've always known that we're here, Linny, even though they were only dreaming...."

I had to take up the story then, as he was treading on thin ice again.

"Not just the barrel-boys," I conjectured, "but their competitors, the rival powers. They know we're here too, and they're probably capable of dreaming us, in the right circumstances. They could keep us and use us, even when we ought to be dead... even, perhaps, when we *are* dead...if they could trap us in one of their dream-catchers. Thin pickings in the Antarctic, I suppose, if they need something brainier than penguins—but if there's an Other Arctic, the creatures hiding there might have had a better harvest, human-wise, with Sir John Franklin and all the people who went to look for him and disappeared in his wake. Is there an Other Arctic?"

"I don't know" Oates said. "I never got a glimpse, if there is. You're right about the Antarctic, though—thank God there's no reason for glory-hunters like Scott to go back, now than Amundsen's reached the Pole."

"Thank God," I echoed, automatically

"I suppose it's a horrible thought, in a way, that we might just be weeds in an alien plantation that's run wild while the owners are temporary indisposed," he said, pensively. "Certainly a blow to human esteem. You always used to say, as I recall, that we could be a good deal prouder of having evolved from a humble monad, by virtue of the marvelous progress we'd made, than we could ever have been of having sprung arbitrarily from the hand of a Creator."

"I did," I confirmed, glad to be reminded of something old and true. "I suppose that your average God-botherer probably wouldn't be delighted to learn that God is just a barrel with five tentacular feet and a mess of sense-organs at the other end, but... sorry, I'm rambling."

"That's all right," he assured me. "I do nothing but."

Having said that, and having taken a stiff drink, he rambled a bit more.

"Even if the Other Antarctica isn't horrible, which it probably is, it's passing strange. In a way, it's the old Antarctica—the Antarctica of billions of years ago—but it hasn't remained unchanged. The Antarctica that they're dreaming now isn't the Antarctica of their heyday, even though there are aspects of it that are old and decayed, but not entirely dead."

More frustrating vagueness. He couldn't say that it was really there and he wouldn't say that it wasn't *not really* there, but he knew that it was accessible. It could be dreamed—or you or I could be dreamed within it. All you'd have to do is fall into a bottomless pit.

"You could do it, I think," he mused, speaking purely hypothetically, for safety's sake, "without even knowing you'd done it, if you weren't on the point of death, expecting the lights to go out any second and forced to be astonished when they stayed on. I don't think it's just Antarctica, either, even if there isn't an Other Arctic. I think there might be Other Africas, Other Australias...."

"Other Yorkshires?"

"Perhaps."

That was a bit too close for comfort. He shivered; I shivered; we both had a stiff drink.

As to what the Other Antarctica *was* like, the one solid adjective I could get out of him was "mountainous." Except that the mountains weren't really mountains, any more than they were really cities. They were vast, and strange. The Mountains of Dreams, obviously, but the Mountains of Madness too. That wasn't by any means implausible. If you'd been dreaming for a billion years, especially if you might have died in the meantime, don't you think you might have gone a little crazy?

In my own case, it hadn't taken nearly as long as that.

Philosophizing suggested that the business with the seeds, even if it really was a plan, and even if it was a plan by means of which the waddling barrels somehow intended to take over the world, it might be a crazy plan. It might be the result of twisted monomania, or alien schizophrenia, or just plain old derangement. It was a plan of some sort, but that didn't mean that it was a *sane* plan, for world conquest or any other purpose. Seeds from the Mountains of Madness. It might be anything, or nothing, maybe even more dangerous for being insane, but maybe far less.

If we—if I—didn't try, though, or couldn't produce anything of interest, Oates would be in deep trouble. Helen and I might be unreachable from beneath the ice, but poor Oates, even though his heart was beating and his wounds were healing, was still stuck in a dream, or a nightmare, and probably subject to arbitrary dissolution at a moment's notice.

If *they* got what they wanted, there was a chance that they might let him off in exchange, honoring the bargain they'd made...if they were honest giants....

There was a chance, of course that they weren't and wouldn't, but there was nothing I could do about that possibility. I just had to play ball and hope.

I did confess to him that I was afraid, though.

"I'm afraid, given what you've told me, that the dreamers might stop dreaming you," I told him. "I'm afraid that they're keeping you suspended in a state just this side of oblivion, and that if anything goes wrong, they might simply *let go.*"

"Don't worry about that, Linny," he said. "That's a sacrifice I'm willing to make. That's not what *I'm* afraid of."

"What are *you* afraid of?" I asked, warily. I could easily

imagine that there might be an abundance of possible fears available to him beyond mere slippage into delayed oblivion.

He wouldn't say, so I had to guess. My guess was that he was afraid of what *they* might dream next. He was afraid of what he might have started, having fallen into their trap—probably the first intelligent creature to have done so for a billion years, unless penguins are a lot smarter than we imagine. He was afraid of what *they* might do, now that they not only knew that we exist, but also what we are.

It didn't matter whether the guess was right or wrong. There was nothing I could do about it. I was pretty sure, though, that it *was* a horrible thought. We couldn't hold back the ice, if the ice came again, for all the Yorkshire stubbornness in the world—and we can't hold back the kinds of dreams that *they* were dreaming.

If anything did start moving, we could easily be crushed—ground down to dust—without having any way to fight back at all. If what I was doing now, at *their* request, were to make any difference in our favor, that would be a miracle—and I didn't believe in miracles. In that respect, at least, I hadn't changed at all. I'd been at Mons, and I hadn't seen a single ghostly archer, let alone an angel. I believed in evolution, in *acclimation*, in the responsibility of earthly Empire—and even that was an effort, sometimes.

* * * * * * *

I had no idea what to expect of the seeds, to begin with—whether they would begin to grow at all, or what kind of development they would produce if they did. One thing, however, was certain from day one, and that was the fact that they were material, and not the stuff of dreams. Perhaps they had been buried under the Antarctic ice for an unimaginable interval of time, perhaps they had somehow fallen into our familiar world from the mysterious "Other Antarctica," and perhaps they were from another world elsewhere on the cosmic battlefield, but they were made of the same elements as Earthly life, and probably from similar organic compounds, based on chains of carbon atoms. I wouldn't have been surprised to see them put forth shoots and roots, for the shoots to turn into stems, and for the stems to put forth branches.

Two of them *did* grow, but not like that. At first, in fact, they didn't grow up—or, for that matter, down. They grew sideways, putting out limbs of a sort, with a fundamental pentamerous symmetry that made then resemble starfish, at least a little. It was only when I changed the soil in the pots, or switched them to bigger containers, that I could see them clearly, but I did change the soil every couple of days, very carefully, because I was monitoring its content with respect to all the things that Oates had identified as necessary nutrients, and a few extra things besides—and the two that grew certainly seemed to be absorbing materials at a rapid rate.

I replanted the others too, of course, over and over, giving them every chance, but they weren't able to take advantage of the opportunities I gave them. If they weren't dead, they were very dormant indeed, and I couldn't find the magic kiss that would wake them up, no matter how hard I tried. All my analyses, and all my measurements, seemed to count for nothing. I couldn't claim any credit for the two that did develop; it was simply a matter of random luck. As to whether the luck was good or bad, time would presumably tell.

Within a week, I'd figured out that the two that had been resurrected had a prodigious appetite for blood, and that minced meat wasn't anywhere near as effective as the honest liquid. I had to come to a special arrangement with the local slaughterhouse for daily deliveries. Bovine blood seemed to be a little more effective than sheep's blood, but there wasn't much in it. They appreciated extra iron as well, as well as strong doses of magnesium and iodine, but I hadn't time enough or specimens enough to attempt fine discriminations with respect to other inorganic salts. Common salt, in fact, they didn't seem to mind at all, although they appreciated extra potassium as well, so I presumed that they had some kind of ion balance to maintain. They did *not* appreciate manure, or peat. Products of decay were definitely not their thing.

Their appetite for blood showed no sign of diminishing in week two; they were definitely going to grow up to be vampires of some sort—but I kept reminding myself that that didn't mean, necessarily, that they were going to develop apparatus for biting, or that they would suck victims dry with whatever apparatus they did develop for parasitizing live prey.

Prudent parasites don't kill their prey, I told myself; it's in their interests to keep them alive and healthy. If you live on blood, what's good for the organisms whose blood you drink is good for you: you want to keep them in the pink.

It did occur to me to wonder, though, how such organisms could every have found an environment of blood-soaked fields in which to evolve and thrive. Even the battlefields of Flanders wouldn't have sufficed. Ergo...but that was an uncomfortable thought, to begin with, and I shelved it for a while.

It was in week two that the two survivors began to peep above the surface—and it's possible that *peeping* was exactly what they were doing. They didn't have anything that looked like vertebrate eyes, or even insectile compound eyes, but the short stalks that began to protrude from the ground did have black shiny tips that were not entirely unlike the stalked eyes of lobsters. They did seem to be light-sensitive, and they seemed to appreciate the bright electric lighting with which I prolonged the shortening days of early November—though not as much, I presumed, as they appreciated the gas-powered underfloor heating and the humidifiers. The specimen that I briefly placed in cooler circumstances, by way of experiment, almost immediately fell behind its twin, so I soon stopped experiments of that sort and gave them both as much heat and humidity as I could without prejudicing the health of their Earthly neighbors.

Oates seemed to be a little disappointed with the Earthly neighbors. He didn't altogether disapprove of the pineapples, but the bananas seemed to him to be banal.

"Why bananas?" he asked, at one point. "I mean, there are bananas all over the world. They grow anywhere that's hot, with no difficulty at all"

"They do indeed," I told him. "There are Banana Republics in consequence, offering testimony to the awesome accomplishments of transplantation in the service of colonization. And it's all artifice. Bananas are dioecious: they have separate male and female trees—but only the female trees produce fruit, so they're the only ones of commercial interest. All the banana plantations outside of south-east Asia—and there are, as you say, an enormous number of them, scattered far and wide—consist entirely of female trees produced vegetatively, from cuttings of cuttings of cuttings; and none of their flowers is ever fertilized. There are only a handful of male banana trees left in the wild, and they're in danger of extinction, even while their female counterparts go on to ever-increasing triumphs of producing human fodder—but there's one over there in that corner: perhaps the only one in England, unless there's one at Kew. My harem of female bananas is the only population in the western world that ever gets any satisfaction"

He didn't seem particularly interested, any more than Helen had been when I had explained it to her. Mercy wasn't old enough yet to have that kind of intimate detail included in explanations—not in Helen's opinion, at any rate. Mercifully, she had never queried my bananas. The brat did, however, ask at dinner one night why Oates called me "Linny."

"It was his nickname at school," Oates explained.

"Yes," said Mercy, "but why? It's nothing like any of his names."

"I carried a key to British *Flora* around whenever I went out on the river," I explained. "I was learning to identify plants. The other boys called me Linny because it was short for Linnaeus, although his un-Latinized name was Linné, so it didn't really have to be a contraction. He produced the classification on which the key was based."

I refrained from adding that part of the joke was that Linnaeus' classification of plants was based on their sex organs, and that my Etonian comrades were trying to imply, in a tortured and silly way that only schoolboys can, that what I was doing was a kind of pornography. Oates knew better, of course.

Mercy wasn't frightened of Oates, as some of the maids still were, in spite of the manifest improvement in his condition. Even Hollis avoided him to the extent that he could, and if Helen didn't, it was mostly out of a sense of obligation, but Mercy seemed quite comfortable in his company, and would probably have sat on his lap if he'd let her.

He didn't. Oates seemed more uncomfortable in the brat's presence than she was in his, not because he didn't like her but because he was anxious that he was not fit company for a child. Helen hadn't tried to hide the sanitarium patients from Mercy while the house had been doing double duty, though, and the poor kid had not only grown accustomed to the proximity of the maimed and the shell-shocked but had joined in, to the extent that she could, with the work of their redemption.

Helen, of course, continued to help with the dressing on Oates' wounds, and took considerable relief from the fact that the old gunshot wound had stopped bleeding and begun to scar over again, and that his toes actually seemed to be getting better, impossible though that was.

"He's not so cold now," she reported to me, one night, after Oates had gone to bed. "He's actually coming back. I didn't think it was possible, but he is."

"That's good," I said, hoping that she wasn't going to make some remark about thawing me out in my turn.

"What about the *things*?" she asked. "Are *they* still cold to the touch?"

"Strangely enough, yes," I said. "Given the ambient temperature, I have no idea how they do it, but they do. It's as if they're negatively endothermic, needing a high external temperature but maintaining their internal temperature at a much lower level. It doesn't make sense metabolically; even though their metabolic cycles are obviously different from ours, they should still have the same optimum temperature—except, of course, that they're not mayflies."

"No," she said, "they're terrestrial starfish that live underground in baths of blood."

"That's not what I mean—Oates calls Earthly life-forms *mayflies* because they're short-lived. The creatures that used to live in Antarctica billions of years ago, according to him, live more slowly, and for much longer."

She ignored the correction. "At least," she said, modifying her own judgment, "that's what they are in their larval form."

"I'm not so sure," I said. "I think we might already have missed out on one form—but that doesn't mean that they only have two. They might have three—or thirty."

"Are the two you have the same sex, or different sexes?" she asked, obviously worried that they might start breeding, perhaps after some further metamorphosis.

"They seem to be identical," I said. "If they're different sexes, there don't appear to be any obvious external sexual characteristics. Being alien, of course, they might not have different sexes, or might have more than two. Even our kind of life only makes limited use of sex, although it's a pretty good shuffler of the Mendelian deck. If you're right about them being analogous to larvae, mind, they might not develop sex organs until the next phase."

"You don't sound as if you think I'm right," she observed, without too much injury in her tone.

"I don't know enough to know what to think. Extra phases increase an organism's ecological requirements, though, so I'm reluctant to make guesses based on the insect analogy."

"Is there any guess you do feel confident making?" she probed.

I took it as a challenge, although I'd been keeping the notion under wraps for a while. "I'm obviously supplying the two that are developing with makeshift incubators," I said. "Given their appetite for blood, their natural habitat must be inside some other organism—some quasi mammalian organism."

"Not dinosaurs then?" Helen concluded.

"Too recent," I said, "although it's possible that their blood would do in a pinch. Probably something we've never seen, even in fossil form. Fossils are mortal, and entire strata of the crust can be eroded away or pulverized, in the right catastrophic circumstances. If the Earth really is billions of years old, there might have been time for more than one evolutionary process, and if it really has been an object of colonization for more than one extraterrestrial species...."

"Do you still doubt what Oates says because you think he might be mad, or because you think he might be lying?" she asked, picking up on the covert implication of the "reallys." Her tone was a trifle sharp. If I really had thought that Oates was mad or lying, she thought that I ought to have warned her.

"Neither," I told her. "But I don't know how much faith one can place in tales told in dreams. Something saved him, or preserved him, in Antarctica—something with powers we can hardly imagine...but that doesn't mean that it's a reliable informant."

"How are *your* dreams?" she asked, not sharply at all. I was still suffering from night terrors. That was one of the reasons why we had separate bedrooms.

"No measurable change," I said. I hadn't been keeping a scrupulous log, so I wasn't absolutely sure that the frequency of the terrors wasn't decreasing, but they were still too frequent and too violent. I could almost have wished that Oates' mysterious manipulator, whatever it might be, had reached into my dreams and doused me in some kind of cosmic perspective: some kind of slow and monstrous consciousness of being. Anything but the front: the mud, the shells, the gas. Objectively speaking the latter might be the lesser of the evils now on the menu, and the lesser of the horrors too, but they were the ones that were still saturating my soul.

Mercy didn't say anything about having bad dreams, though, and nor did Helen. Whatever state Oates was in, it didn't seem to be contagious. Oates did admit that the Other Antarctica was still present in his head, in some mysterious fashion, while he was awake as well as in his sleep, but he didn't complain about it. He was glad not to be entirely dead, and he wasn't the kind of man who could be terrified by the mere thought of human insignificance in a vast and hostile universe.

I told him what Helen had hypothesized about the possibility of a further metamorphosis of the "starfish," and he nodded to concede the possibility, but I could tell that it wasn't what he was expecting—or maybe hoping for. I guessed that he was hoping for something, but I couldn't guess what it was, and it was something that he was keeping to himself.

By week three, the surviving creatures began to move bodily as well as wiggling their "eyestalks." They didn't move fast or far, but they did move. At the very least, they squirmed, as if testing their five limbs. They didn't seem to me to be at all threatening, even when I imagined them dragging themselves out of the soil and walking away like five-legged spiders balanced on the tips of their "feet." Indeed, they seem to me to be rather frail, unready to suffer any reduction in their daily bloodfest, let alone to suffer the English weather, which had grow markedly colder since the relatively mild day on which Oates had arrived.

If they showed any sign at all of becoming dangerous, I thought, all I had to do was turn off the gas and seal the padlock, and they'd probably be rendered helpless. I was being wildly optimistic. It seemed odd, though, given that—if any of what Oates had said was true—they must have been lying dormant beneath the Antarctic ice for a long time, but that they had had to come to me, and to very different conditions, in order to break out of their dormancy. It didn't seem paradoxical that they might be plunged back into it, even by something as simple as cold.

They were still cold to the touch themselves. Oates had warmed up to normality—I had taken his temperature and clocked it at ninety-eight point two—but that was natural for him. The "starfish" were presumably doing what was natural to them.

The more they moved, the longer their "legs" became. I'd already put them in bigger pots twice in weeks one and two, but at the end of week three I had to put the into much larger vessels, more like troughs—and had to move out some of the potted fruit-trees in consequence. If it went on, I thought, I might have to adopt an entire greenhouse for their exclusive use. As the "legs" got longer, the "feet" were physically modified, but not into something more like any kind of animal feet, or even cephalopod tentacles. The tips became soft, and covered in delicate hairs, like a cat's whiskers. Better than a scorpion's sting, I thought; the hairs looked to me like sensory organs—but what did I know?

"Nothing like your barrel-shaped entities, except for the pentamerous symmetry," I suggested to Oates. I wanted to know whether he had seen anything like them in his Other Antarctica, but didn't dare ask point-blank.

"No," he agreed, unhelpfully. "Nothing like them." He didn't bother to echo the qualifier.

"Perhaps you wouldn't have seen them," I mused, figuring that the cat was out of the bag now I'd mentioned out to Helen. "Their need to bathe in blood suggests that their natural habitat is inside a larger organism."

I hadn't asked him a direct question, but I knew I'd hit a dream-nerve by the way his face changed. His face would probably have gone pale, if it had remained capable of holding any color at all. I didn't feel guilty; I had only pointed out the obvious.

Maybe the barrel-boys' slave race had been their natural hosts, I suggested. They were plenty big enough, apparently, and, being domesticated, might have been adaptable as hosts to some other creature.

He wasn't even listening. He was looking up, at the glass roof. Dusk was only just falling, so I hadn't switched on the electric lights yet.

"Is that snow?" he asked.

I looked up, squinting at the glass. The reason why he was

uncertain was that the flakes were melting as soon as they hit the warm glass, and then fusing into streams of water. The glass was a very poor conductor of heat, though, so the outer surface wouldn't take long to cool down if snow or sleet fell upon it any volume.

"It's very light," I said. "Just flurries drifting in on an east wind, at a guess. We don't usually get serious snow until one of the Atlantic fronts comes barging in from the west and hits the colder air of a high-pressure area. *Then* you'll see a blizzard—not much by comparison with the Antarctic, mind. The worst of it usually arrives in January—that's when the roads inevitably get blocked and everything grinds to a standstill. Might have trouble with blood supplies from the abattoir then, although I dare say that I could lodge some sheep in the old stables, just in case."

"I doubt that I'll be here that long," Oates said, dully, still looking upwards. His face had settled again, to a near-human expression. Anxiety?

"Why do you doubt it?" I asked. "I've seen no sign that Tweedledum and Tweedledee are fully-grown yet, or that they're about to do anything spectacular that might justify their existence."

"I just have a feeling," he said. He didn't say it the way Helen might have said it, though. He said it like a man who *knows* that his feelings mean something.

"A *bad* feeling?"

"Just a feeling," he said—but he added: "Do you want to send Helen and Mercy away, just in case?"

"Do I need to?"

"I don't know—but I have a feeling. That *is* snow, you know—and not just a flurry."

I looked up. He was right. It was snowing quite hard. Judging by the slant of the flakes I could see through the side walls, the wind was actually blowing from the north now. The cold air was probably streaming all the way from the pole, picking up moisture over the ocean.

The Arctic, I knew, was just ice, sitting on top of water. Which didn't mean that there mightn't be Another Greenland, echoing ancient Hyperborea. The snow did seem somehow reassuring. It was unusual, but not wrong—not, at least, according to *my* vague feeling.

Oates had gone to the door and opened it. He was peering out into the snow, uncertainly.

"Shut the door," I said. "We don't want the starfish getting frostbite—or the bananas and pineapples, for that matter."

"I haven't seen snow for a long time," he said, perhaps a trifle bizarrely, considering that he'd fallen down a hole in the Antarctic seven years ago, and had only made brief trips to England since.

Perhaps, I thought, it didn't snow in the Other Antarctica. Perhaps the barrel-boys were too familiar with snow to bother to dream it. Oates certainly seemed puzzled by this particular snow, continually catching flakes in the palm of his hand and lifting them up to his eyes in order to inspect them.

"I'll mention the possibility to Helen of taking a little trip," I said. "Mind you, if it keeps on snowing like that for a few more hours, we might have difficulty getting out. Snow drifts in the wolds and the dales—we could get cut off, even in November. Mercy loves it, though. Children do, don't they?"

He didn't know. He seemed to have forgotten about Helen and Mercy already. Something was worrying him—or *them.*

"If the starfish do turn on us," I said, "you and I are the ones in the firing-line—and your blood seems to be in good condition, now that it's no longer leaking out. If the addicts get antsy because the slaughterhouse truck can't get through, it'll be you and me they turn on."

"If anything does happen," Oates promised, perhaps attempting to lighten the mood, or perhaps meaning exactly what he said, "I'll try to make sure that it happens to me first, so that you can watch and act as necessary."

"Thanks," I said. "I don't have a case of grenades hereabouts, but I do have my revolver close at hand—and the stopcock of the gas-supply. They're not exactly lightning-fast, are they?"

"No," he admitted. "Not fast." Whatever he was worrying about, it wasn't their speed over the ground.

"Come on," I said. "Let's go up to the house. Dinner will be ready soon enough, and I'll need to have a word with Hollis about contingency plans, if the snow does continue. If we do get cut off, we'll have to make accommodation for the girls, and the staff that don't live in. We should have plenty of supplies laid in, but it's not like before the war, when we still had half a dozen horses. We've only got one tractor, and if its engine won't start...."

I was talking myself into worry, but the snow really was coming down thick and fast. I locked the tropical house, after switching on the lights, and then ran to the other greenhouses to tell my assistants that they'd better stay for dinner...and maybe overnight.

By the time I got back to the house, though—ten minutes after Oates—Helen and Hollis were already in full swing, getting an action plan ready, just in case.

"Can I go out to play in the snow, Daddy?" Mercy asked. I knew that she must have already asked Helen, and was trying her luck.

"No, love," I said. "It's too dark. Tomorrow morning, it'll be better, if the snow hasn't melted overnight. You can build a snowman then. Anyway, it's nearly dinner time."

It wasn't a popular judgment, but the brat accepted it.

* * * * * * *

At dinner, it was obvious that something was the matter with Oates. I didn't understand it. He'd been to the South Pole. He'd probably seen and felt more snow than any human being alive, including Amundsen, who'd got there and back in a faster time.

"What's the matter, Titus?" I asked him. I thought that it might be something akin to my night terrors—which could explode by day if I happened to be taken by surprise by a loud bang or a motor-bike engine with a hole in its silencer. I thought perhaps the snowfall was taking him back, psychologically, to the terrible days before he'd sacrificed himself to give Scott, Bowers and Wilson a chance.

"They're not ready," he whispered.

I got the impression that he wasn't actually talking to me, but I was trying to help, and I didn't want to alarm Helen or Mercy—or the girls, who had stayed for dinner, and hadn't a clue what was going on, having hardly caught a glimpse of Oates since he'd arrived, and never having been formally introduced. "Come on, Titus," I said. "Cheer up. No shop talk at dinner, remember?"

He looked at me. I hoped to hell that nobody else could see what was in his eyes, as I could—but I, of course, had built up a sympathy with him. Sometimes, I feared that my face my start to blur as his did, and that I'd never get it back to normal again. When he shivered, I shivered.

I knew that his eyes didn't always see what my eyes saw, that they sometimes looked into another world that was more terrifying than he'd ever been able to communicate to me. Something was definitely wrong, I decided—but not something *here*: something *there*. Something was wrong in the dream of which he was somehow a part, the plan that he was following, in which I was a pawn.

Bu he was an officer, and a gentleman, not to mention a hero. He blinked—and I have never seen such a deliberate blink in my entire life. He blinked away the horror that was in his eyes, in order that no one but me should see it.

"Sorry, Lady Anderley," he said, deliberately addressing Helen instead of me. "I sometimes still get shooting pains. I should be grateful, I suppose—it reminds me how glad I ought to be that I'm alive...and getting better, thanks to you."

They say that it takes courage to go over the top, to charge the enemy, but it doesn't—not after the first time, anyhow. What it takes is something else entirely: resignation, desolation, an incapacity to care, a kind of madness. Sanity wouldn't allow you to do it a second time, but people can and do; they have to go mad, but they can and do. Courage is what it takes to sit at a dinner table in the presence of women and children, and keep a stuff upper lip, when you're absolutely sane, if not absolutely alive, and something has gone wrong, in a drama of which you're a part, and are trying with all your might not to be.

I'm not at all sure that I could have ever mustered that sort of courage—certainly not at Eton, or in Africa, and probably not now—but Titus could. He was cut from finer cloth than I was. He sat upright, and moved methodically, with hardly a tremor. He ate dinner—all four courses, because we hadn't started rationing yet—without turning a hair. He wasn't much of a conversationalist, mind, and he was careful not to look into my eyes again, but even in doing that he was thinking of others rather than himself.

I talked—babbled a bit, in fact—and my eyes must have been shifting back and forth like nobody's business, but I managed the far easier task of holding myself together. I had no idea what was wrong, of course, but I had a clue, on which my mind was working overtime.

They weren't ready.

Tweedledee and Tweedledum, obviously—but ready for what? And what might they, or what might *they* do, if they weren't ready, but had to act anyway, had to force the plan that was unfolding according to monad/human time rather than barrel-boy time, at pace to which *they* weren't accustomed, and with which they might not be able to cope, no matter how awesomely powerful and awesomely horribly *they* and their enemies were.

They and their enemies. Was that it?

Were we under attack?

From what? Snow?

Titus didn't want to stay for coffee. He looked at me again, sending shivers down my spine, and he said: "We have to get back, Linny."

I couldn't find it in my heart to thank him for that *we*,

although I could appreciate the necessity. We did have to get back. I hadn't a clue as to what kind of barrage was going to come down, but I knew that *we* had to face it. We were in it together, for better or for worse. We didn't have to understand it, but we did have to do it.

They weren't ready. But we had to do it anyway. Something wicked was coming our way. Oates didn't know what it was either, but I was willing to bet that his frostbitten thumbs were pricking like crazy.

While we'd been in the house—no more than two and a half hours—some four inches of snow had fallen. The wind was bitter, and furious. The clusters of flakes seemed to be coming at us horizontally, from the right. I was glad we didn't have to slog into the teeth of it to get to the palace of golden light that was beckoning to us in the Stygian gloom.

I no longer know who I was rooting for. Were Tweedledum and Tweedledee still the potential enemy, or was the other even worse? Was it one of those situations where the enemy of my enemy might be my friend, or one of those situations in which anyone in the crossfire was likely to be ripped apart no matter how the real contest worked out?

I staggered into the greenhouse about five yards ahead of Oates, who was struggling. I didn't hold the door, because my eyes had immediately gone to the troughs where the starfish were supposed to be, half-buried in bloody soil, peeping out at this world or another.

They weren't.

They didn't look much like starfish any more, either.

They were hanging from the branches of the poor male banana tree, like vast spiders' webs in an orchard, brought into temporary visibility by morning dew.

They had stretched...no, not stretched...they had *unraveled*— partially, at least. The tightly-wound fibers of which they were composed had loosened up and expanded, but without becoming in the least labyrinthine. They were more intricate now than anything I had ever seen or imagined, as if their folds extended into at least four dimensions, and perhaps many more.

The tree was visibly dying. It was perhaps the only male banana tree in England, and it was dying from contact with the aliens, or perhaps with the dimension into which they were reaching.

However absurd the sensation might have been, I felt angry on the tree's behalf. I could have taken it more easily if it had been one of the pineapples, or even one of the female bananas.

I looked back at Oates, intending to ask for an explanation— but I didn't say a word. He was trying to brush the snow off is clothing. At least, he was *trying* to try. He gave every indication of being a man in desperate conflict with himself, fighting for control of his own limbs—and his own face.

Something was trying to make his features blur again, but this time he was fighting back. Something was trying to make him do something else, too, but he was fighting that as well.

I wanted to help him, but I didn't know what to do, and he couldn't give me a hint. The snow was falling off his jacket, though, and the flakes that weren't falling were melting in the heat. I felt a chill run down my own spine. I was pretty sure that I hadn't been biologically contaminated by the starfish, and it was a long time since I had shaken Oates' hand, but I had developed a sympathy with him nevertheless, and for the first time, I felt that something was reaching out to me too, trying hard to get some sort of grip. I felt my toes and fingers going numb.

I had to do something. Even though I had no idea what to do, I had to react, because it was obvious that some kind of climax was developing, and I wanted to be able to take a hand in it.

I was still a soldier, in spite of everything. I reached for my gun.

Even as I did it, though, I realized how utterly absurd that reflex was. Was I going to *shoot* two monstrous cobwebs? How on Earth—or even in the Other Antarctica—could I expect to have any effect?

I had turned away from Oates, though, in order to pick up the gun, and I was looking at the poor dead banana tree again, still angry on behalf of my cherished specimen.

I raised the revolver, but I knew that it might just as well have been a crucifix: a symbol absurdly out of context, not very meaningful to me, and not at all meaningful to *them*.

I was helpless, and knew it.

And that was when things really started to go bad.

I turned my head again to look at Oates, perhaps hoping for some inspiration, some guidance, some spark of under-standing—but what I got was night terror, and then some.

Oates' face was tortured out of all recognition—not longer a face at all, but a shadow: a window to another world. I looked at where his eyes should have been, but all I could see was alien darkness, with the suggestion of cyclopean buildings in the distance. It seemed that I was looking into the heart of moun-tainous madness itself, made hideously incarnate.

Has still fighting, with every fiber of his flesh, but his arms were no longer flailing at the snow on his jacket. Indeed, he'd ripped the jacket open, popping the buttons, and he was clawing at the shirt underneath, ripping the cotton, and tearing at the skin underneath with his fingernails, drawing blood.

I felt sure that he was trying to stop, but that he couldn't. I didn't understand, but I knew that he'd never be able to dig a hole through his ribs with his fingernails.

He didn't have to. While he was working away from one side, impotently, something else was working from the other, more effectively, not cutting through the bone but somehow dissolving it. A hole appeared in Oates' bare and bloody chest, and expanded, like a dilating pupil, to reveal that same crazed darkness inside him, that same suggestion of distant architec-ture, lost in time and space.

Then something pulled itself out of the impossible void, through the gap in his ribs.

He didn't collapse. Prudent parasites, I reminded myself, don't kill their prey, even when the time comes to decamp.

Titus just stood there, as his face returned to what I still thought of as normal: his own face, as I remembered it from long ago. The craziness was leaving, and the void in his chest as no longer a void. I could see his beating heart through the hole. Oates could see it too, as he looked down at his ruined clothes, his spurting blood, and the thing that was crawling out of him, having been patiently incubated to a state of maturity not far short of its companions.

It looked something like a starfish, with long, long arms and hairy fists, and little eye-stalks peering curiously, perhaps into another world. It was wet with bright, rich blood and didn't know exactly where to go or how to get there, but it knew that it needed to go somewhere. It dangled, and let itself down on to the floor. There, it began to squirm.

Oates watched it go, standing very still, as if he dared not move while he had that gaping hole in his chest, in case his heart fell out.

The hole was closing again, though; the dissolved ribs were regenerating. He was holding his breath, waiting, perhaps knowing that he would have to wait for the pleural cavity to seal itself up before he could breathe again. His parasite was very prudent, it seemed—perhaps even generous. Or perhaps Oates was still needed, for further duties.

In the meantime, the third starfish—the only one that still looked like a starfish—was squirming on. It was definitely heading for its companions, but it had to get past me to get to the banana tree. I had the distinct impression—because rather than in spite of the chill within me that was trying to take control of my heart and limbs—that I ought to try to stop it. I had been nurturing the alien organisms for weeks, but I was convinced now that they were too dangerous to nurture any longer, no matter what the cost to poor Oates might be.

With my left hand, I reached out to twist the tap controlling the gas supply. The hand suddenly felt very cold indeed, but I completed the action. The fires under the floor went out. The door was still open, because Titus hadn't closed it, and I knew that the temperature would drop fairly swiftly, but the doorway was shielded from the wind, and I knew that "fairly swiftly" wouldn't be rapid enough.

I lowered the hand holding the gun, and took aim at the squirming thing. I couldn't help noticing that it wasn't identical to Tweeledum and Tweedledee. It was the same species, but a different morph. The aliens *did* have sex: just two of them... but two was enough. *They* had only had one suitable host available: Oates. To pair off the one they'd planted in him when he fell into their trap, they needed another way to grow it a counterpart. Titus had talked me up, without knowing what he was doing. He had given them a possible means. Now, there were male and female aliens abroad in *our* world, not the Other.

They weren't ready, apparently, but they were going for it anyway, perhaps in circumstances that were far from ideal, but allowing some chance of success. Maybe, from their point of view, it was one of those million-to-one shots so common in popular fiction, which just might work. I couldn't tell—but one thing I was sure of was that I was still in the way.

I fired the gun.

At least, I tried to fire it. I couldn't. It was as if the temperature of my hand had suddenly dropped two hundred degrees. It was incapable of movement, stuck hard to the butt of the gun, but incapable of pulling the trigger. The gun itself must have been locked solid, thanks to all the humidity in the atmosphere that had abruptly condensed into ice. It couldn't fire any longer. It was useless. So was I.

I raised my foot, intending to stamp on the squirming thing—which was by no means lightning fast, even though it had to be going as fast as it possibly could.

I couldn't do that, either. I was frozen to the spot, like a statue—probably not literally, or I'd have been dead, but psychologically.

The squirming thing began to climb up me—not because it was going to dig a hole in my chest and take up residence in the pleural cavity, next to my heart, but because it was going to use me as a ladder to get to its inamorata-to-be. I knew that when it got to my arm—the one that was clutching the useless gun, that I'd be unfrozen, at least partially. I'd be able to turn around, and pass the parasite that had crawled out of Oates' body on to its eager lovers...and that it probably wouldn't let me turn away again thereafter, for modesty's sake.

And what would happen *afterwards*....

They hadn't been able to reach any of us physically, as yet, apart from Oates. They hadn't been able to get *into* us, psychologically or physically, except to send a few secondary shivers down my spine, until that desperate burst of cold had chilled my hand and shocked me into stillness.

But afterwards—once the aliens were in *our* world, and capable of reproduction—who could tell what they might be able to do?

Mercy! I thought.

And suddenly, as if it were a word of power, there she was, in the doorway of the golden palace—with a snowball in her hand.

She threw it, without an instant's delay.

She threw it at me—or, to be strictly accurate, at the thing that was climbing me.

She was seven years old. She threw like a little girl—but a little girl who had played ball on the lawn with wounded soldiers: a little girl who had *done her best*.

It couldn't have hurt the monster, no matter how hot the monster liked its environment to be—not if it had really been a snowball, or just a snowball. But that, I realized, was what Oates' passenger had been worried about when he first looked up at the roof. It hadn't been worried about the snow being snow; it had been worried about the possibility that some of the snowflakes *weren't* snowflakes, that there was something else *riding* the snow.

There was.

Mercy must have found it by accident, when she'd slipped out to play regardless of parental orders, but once she'd had it in her hand it must have been able to guide her, or nudge her in the right direction. It hadn't been able to get inside her, but it must have helped her make up her mind what she was going to do with the snowball.

Perhaps she had always intended to throw it at me, and perhaps she thought that the thing on my body as just a target, conveniently placed by chance.

Either way, when the snowball hit the squirming thing that was squirming up my abdomen, fair and square, it suddenly found the capacity to squirm much more urgently than before.

It lost its grip. It fell—and it went on writhing. It wasn't dead—not by a long way. And the two that were hanging on the banana tree weren't injured at all.

My hand was unfrozen now, though, and my limbs too. I was fully myself again. I was a soldier. I was an officer. I had not merely to do but to know what I was doing—and I did. I had *presence of mind.*

I fired—not at the webs hanging on the banana tree but at the glass panes of the roof above them. In the two and a half hours that we'd been at dinner, the outer surface of the glass had cooled drastically, and the snow had begun to pile up there in spite of the wind, from which the relevant panes were sheltered by a flue-stack.

The panes shattered, and fell. I doubt that the shards of glass did much damage, but the snow that had piled up there wasn't just snow. It came down like avalanche, to begin with, followed by a gentle rain of clustered flakes.

The snow was melting even as it fell, even though the temperature was declining rapidly, and the unsnow seemed to be melting with it, perhaps becoming harmless as it did so—but while it was hiding among the snowflakes, it was deadly to the creatures from the Other Antarctica. It had to be a dedicated toxin: a weapon, or a pesticide. It had probably been in storage for billions of years, but it still worked.

I thought about Sir John Franklin, and all the Arctic explorers who had gone to search for him, and all of those bodies had never been found. Perhaps some of them had fallen into crevasses, and perhaps one of the crevasses had been a trap, and perhaps something billions of years old—far older than legendary

Hyperborea—was still lurking, underneath and in parallel with the ice of the various Arctic islands.

One thing that was certain was that the colonial war hadn't ended. Its warriors weren't mayflies. They took a much longer view than Earl Haig and Ludendorff.

The webs on the dead banana tree began to shrivel—not for want of blood or heat, but because they'd been blasted, gassed, shell-shocked...killed. The writhing thing was still writhing, but the hectic movements were its death-throes. It wasn't going anywhere

But the story wasn't over, even then.

I looked at Oates, who looked up from his lacerated but almost-intact torso and the blood that was no longer flowing in such profusion. I looked into his eyes, and I could see that he wasn't going to fall over, that the light of intelligence wasn't about to go out. He was still at least partly alive, still Captain Lawrence Oates, still a hero—but he was still connected to the Other World. He wasn't free. He was still a prisoner of war, but he was no puppet. Not any more. Perhaps he could have talked, if there had been time—but there wasn't.

"They weren't ready," he whispered—and this time he added: "Thank God."

He looked into my eyes, and all I could see was his eyes, looking into mine with a expression that combined affection, and longing, and apology....

We had been disconnected from the kind of chill that might freeze us at a moment's notice, but we had reconnected in a far more familiar and infinitely better way

"I'm just going to step outside, Linny," he said, with a quiet and heroic dignity, carefully deleting any expletives that might have sprung to mind. "I might be gone for some time."

I never saw him again, but I was infinitely glad that I had seen him that once, for a few brief weeks. It had been worth the price, and the risk.

I picked Mercy up just as Helen arrived in the doorway through which Oates had gone—chasing after her daughter, as usual, but way too late, as usual, to prevent her from going where she wanted to go.

I was weeping, but it wasn't conduct unbecoming, given the circumstances. Quite the opposite, in fact.

ABOUT THE AUTHOR

Brian Stableford was born in Yorkshire in 1948. He taught at the University of Reading for several years, but is now a full-time writer. He has written many science-fiction and fantasy novels, including *The Empire of Fear, The Werewolves of London, Year Zero, The Curse of the Coral Bride, The Stones of Camelot*, and *Prelude to Eternity*. Collections of his short stories include a long series of *Tales of the Biotech Revolution*, and such idiosyncratic items as *Sheena and Other Gothic Tales* and *The Innsmouth Heritage and Other Sequels*. He has written numerous nonfiction books, including *Scientific Romance in Britain, 1890-1950*; *Glorious Perversity: The Decline and Fall of Literary Decadence*; *Science Fact and Science Fiction: An Encyclopedia*; and *The Devil's Party: A Brief History of Satanic Abuse*. He has contributed hundreds of biographical and critical articles to reference books, and has also translated numerous novels from the French language, including books by Paul Féval, Albert Robida, Maurice Renard, and J. H. Rosny the Elder.

Printed in the USA
CPSIA information can be obtained
at www.ICGtesting.com
LVHW051323080124
768412LV00007B/202